FRACTURED SONATA

The second of the *Sonata* novels

Helen Weygang

The *Sonata* novels

Chance Sonata

Fractured Sonata

Beautiful Sonata

Pagan Sonata

For Paul - a beautiful, broken human being; a survivor.
Thanks for the mad conversations and the inspiration over the years.

Characters, names and events in this novel are purely fictional. Any coincidence of name or event is unintentional.

All tattoo designs Copyright © Weygang Designs 2020

Cover illustration Copyright © Paul Saunders 2023

César Franck – *Sonata in A major for violin and piano*

Anton Dvořák – *Piano trio No. 4 in E minor, Op. 90, B.166 (Dumky)*

Wolfgang Amadeus Mozart – *Piano trio in Bb major, K.502*

Claude Debussy – *Sonata for cello and piano*

Josef Suk – *Elegy for violin, cello and piano, Op.23*

Anton Dvořák – *Sonata for violin and piano in F major, Op. 67 (B.106)*

Johannes Brahms – *Quintet in F minor, Op. 34*

Sergei Rachmaninov – *Trio Elegiaque*

Franz Schubert – *An die Nachtingall, Op. 98/1, D497*

Johannes Brahms – *Trio in A minor for piano, viola and cello, Op, 114*

Sergei Rachmaninov – *Cello Sonata in G minor*

César Franck – *Sonata in A major for violin and piano*

Kathy knew the strange times were over when she played her first concert for what felt like months at the end of April in 1981. Although she had played in that festival back in February, it was almost as though she had been away from her working life for a year. She wondered how Piers had coped so well as his job meant he had to be kept up-to-date with so many things, and it made sense now that the airline had called him in for those couple of days so their pilot could pretty much go straight back to work when he was allowed to leave the farmhouse. Kathy had known she would love her life split between the sanctuary of Suffolk and the excitement of London but something nagged at her. Something her mother would have called the maggot in the apple. She felt almost guilty to be settling back into her music and her work while Jean-Guy stayed at home even though he now had his Leave to Remain. It was just that something wasn't quite right but she couldn't put her finger on it. Her new world should have been perfect, but something inside told her that the maggot was still in the apple even though it might not show itself for a long time.

May came in with a lot of sunshine and a very long letter from Emma grumbling about how much her ankles had swollen and she really wanted her baby to arrive as she was getting very fed up with waiting for it. Kathy was a bit concerned that they hadn't heard a word from Piers. He hadn't written or rung to say what he thought about all the furniture that had arrived in his house, he hadn't even let them know what he was doing in his professional life. And the few times Kathy had walked into the village to talk to Sarah she hadn't learned anything there either as Sarah, unusually, wasn't chatting that much these days.

It was the second Monday of the month, exactly four weeks since Sarah and Piers had got married when the usual quiet coffee time at the farmhouse was interrupted by Audrey racing out to the kitchen where the three people were gathered round the table and they had to whisk their drinks out of the way before she sent them flying. Audrey raced round and round the kitchen like a mad thing, yowling at the top of her voice and she had a very loud voice for such a small cat.

"Do you think she's in pain?" Kathy asked anxiously as she failed yet again to catch the fast-moving cat.

"No," Jean-Guy pointed out. "It is what she did when Piers came to pick her up from our flat. She must have heard his car."

"I think you're right," Kathy remembered. "But unless he's borrowed the Land Rover again he must have caught the bus from the station, which I can't believe he'd do, but I also can't believe he'd risk his car on that track out there."

The three listened but that was definitely the whining growl of a very cross Ferrari they could hear and they exchanged a wry smile to realise their pianist was still avoiding all forms of public transport.

The back door opened, Audrey gave one final yowl of unmistakeable delight and hurled herself at the man who had just come into the kitchen. He didn't seem at all surprised that an ecstatic tortoiseshell cat had landed on his shoulder and was now purring loudly in his ear.

Hi," said an uncertain Piers in greeting. "Is it OK if I stop for a couple of nights, please? Sarah rang me a few days ago and said she wants to speak to me."

The Prof got to his feet and made some coffee for the new arrival. "Of course it is. Jean-Guy has been hoping you'd drop by as he wants to talk to you about recitals now we have had Jane on the phone getting to work for him." He put the mug down in front of the man who had just sat at the table. "But there is one thing you must promise me first."

Piers paused with the mug halfway to his mouth. "I will if I can," was the best he was prepared to offer.

The Prof sat opposite him and looked at him solemnly. "That is a very sensible reply since you don't know what I am about to ask," he approved. "All I am asking of you is that you don't feel you have to ask or book yourself in. I want you to feel that this is your home too. We will keep your room ready for you, you can leave things here if you wish, and any time you want to come then you must. The only thing is if you are going to be late please let one of us know so you don't get locked out. Now, can you agree to that?"

"Well, yes, thank you. But for one thing, my car hates that drive of yours and for another aren't you going to want that room for your other guests who may be passing through?" He smiled at the other man over the rim of his mug. "You see, I know of your reputation too since I got introduced to your mates in Whitehall last month."

"I am giving up that side of my work," the Professor told the others without elaborating on what Piers had said. "I will still be involved in other ways which I'm not going to speak of but I have said I can't have any more house guests." He couldn't help smiling at his companions. "I have told them I can't risk getting fond of any more of them. You three are my new children now and I don't think I could cope with any more. So, Piers, what news on Chantal? Have you been in touch with her?"

"I tried. Her brother is still on the same number and he and I had a long talk. She's had her initial operation and the early signs are good, single mastectomy, now on the chemo. He said he'd tell her I'd called and they've now got the Earl's Court number so I won't be away too long but I don't hold out any great hope she'll want to see me again."

"Do you want to see her?" the Prof asked.

"Truthfully? Some days I do, other days I don't. Today is a 'don't' day. Yesterday I could have got on the Tube to Tooting and gone to find her. Well, I would have done but I spent most of yesterday in New York and only got back late last night."

"Ah-ha!" Kathy exclaimed. "So you're back on Concorde?"

"Oh, yes. Got back with my regular crew and you have no idea the remarks I got as officially I'd gone off long-term sick with an unspecified complaint and then I turn up a couple of months later, surprisingly healthy and with a ring on my finger. But I'm not putting Sarah on my personnel records until we've worked out if we're going to make a go of it." He finished his coffee. "Speaking of whom, I'd better go and see what she wants. And when I get back, Piglet, we need to talk cars."

"We do?"

"Yes. If I'm going to be coming back here more often than I'd thought, I'll need to borrow Matt's Land Rover each time as there's no way I'm risking Ferrari suspension on that track ever again. So, having had a good look at that wreck you've dumped outside here, I think it makes more sense if we sell both ours and get something practical, maybe even our own Land Rover if I can find one cheap enough, both go on the insurance for it and then fight over it as we need it. But that's for another time. I doubt if I'll be back for lunch but I'll ring you if I'm not back for supper."

The other three sat on at the table after Piers had gone and a disappointed Audrey wandered back into the sitting room to take up her position on top of the piano.

"Do you know what," Kathy offered in the silence. "For a bloke who looks like he does and has probably the wickedest sense of humour I have ever come across, he really is quite sensible."

Jean-Guy gave her a fond smile. "Somehow I don't think an irresponsible Concorde pilot would be a good idea, do you?"

"Not in the slightest," Kathy agreed. "But if he's getting back with Chantal, where does that leave Sarah?"

"I don't think..." Jean-Guy started but Kathy hadn't finished.

"And if he's going back to full flying and all the rest of it, where does that leave our trio?"

Jean-Guy had no answer to that but it felt to those in the kitchen that the Dodman Trio was falling apart before it had even properly begun.

Piers didn't ring the farmhouse and arrived in time for his supper as expected. He didn't say anything during the meal but had a quiet smile on his face so they were all aware that his mischievous sense of humour had kicked in and he was just waiting to see which one of them would ask first.

Kathy was almost bouncing with frustration by the time they were all eating up the leftover cake he had brought back from the café.

"Oh!" she exclaimed. "I give up. Just tell us. Please."

"I knew you'd crack," he told her delightedly. "It's a female thing. Yes, Sarah is expecting our first child. She's been to see the doctor and had it confirmed and they reckon she's between six and eight weeks gone but they'll confirm her due date after her first scan. Probably late December. So far only the two of us, her parents and Alison know and she's asked for it to stay that way until she's had her twelve-week check. Not sure I should have told you but I'm probably not going to be back again for a while now I'm working again, and I thought you'd rather hear it from me than from the village gossip network."

"Hang on," Kathy said before she thought about it. "How far along is she?" Piers didn't reply and as she had already started that train of thought, she decided to carry on. "Eight weeks maybe and you've only been married for four? Did her parents have a go at you about that?"

"No, actually, they didn't. I think her mother at least had an idea of what had been going on. Alison tried to bollock her but Sarah just told her to shut up and said that at least we were married and that was what mattered. No, her parents are being very supportive about it all."

He didn't sound at all pleased so the others didn't rush to offer congratulations. Kathy wondered if maybe he was thinking that this pregnancy could mean the end of his second marriage and he didn't want to have to separate from Sarah. But then she had another thought that made a lot more sense. "Are you going to tell Chantal?"

"No," he replied heavily. "It hit her very hard to learn that, if you want to put it this way, it was her fault we never had kids and I'm not going to pour petrol on the fire by letting her know I managed it with wife number two probably at our first attempt. If she and I ever become any sort of friend again then I guess she'll find out but that's it."

"And another five thousand pounds for you," Jean-Guy put in cynically.

Piers tilted his head back for a few moments, then looked at Jean-Guy and told him flatly. "I gave it back." Nobody said anything so he explained. "It never felt right even though the money would have been very handy with that bloody great mortgage I've got, to say nothing of the finance package on the car. But I couldn't do it. So I wrote out a cheque and gave it to Sarah today and told her…" He paused and shrugged, trying to pretend it was no big deal. "I told her I'd got too fond of her to take money to make her happy."

"Oh! You said those three little words to her, didn't you?" Kathy asked delightedly.

"Um, no, not quite. We've neither of us done that."

Jean-Guy realised he'd probably never get to grips with this English backchat. "What three little words?"

Kathy smiled at him fondly, took his face in her hands and kissed his nose. "'I love you'."

Petr Mihaly couldn't have expressed the relief he felt but he had to smile, and remarked kindly, "You're not quite the mercenary you have the reputation of being, are you?"

"Oh, I am," Piers said, all blue-eyed innocence. "Just not with people I like."

While Jane worked on building up an impressive round of engagements for the Czech cellist set to resume his phenomenal career with a concert at Snape Maltings in the autumn, she also carried on finding work for one of her most reliable violinists and Kathy was back in Earl's Court one blisteringly hot Friday in June with a rehearsal that afternoon and a concert on the Saturday evening. There was no sign of Piers so she reversed quite happily into the car port, smiling to remember his comments on her Vauxhall being such a wreck. So it had gone twice round the clock in its lifetime and the bodywork wasn't as good as it had been, but she hoped it would keep going a bit longer as she couldn't see how sharing a car with Piers, who commuted to Heathrow, could work. Kathy never bothered to lock her car in the hope somebody would steal it and she could claim the insurance but it was so old and dilapidated nobody even tried to break into it, but it somehow suited the faded grandeur of the house where it now lived. Reflecting that Piers was just being very sensible again when he said they would do best to sell both cars and get themselves a Land Rover, she went into the house to get ready to go out to her rehearsal while still trying to work out the logistics in her head.

The rehearsal room this particular group used was way out in Croydon but as parking round that way was as bad as it was in Earl's Court and she didn't have a permit to park there, she went down on the train. Timings of the rehearsal meant she travelled back to Earl's Court in the middle of the rush hour so she was hot and very grumpy when she got back to the house to find the Ferrari was back and parked neatly in front of her car. Somehow she felt her spirits lift as she let herself in through the side door.

"Good flight?" she asked the weary man in uniform who was standing with his back against the Aga and was sifting through his post. It was the first time she'd seen him properly in his uniform and she couldn't help thinking he really was even more remarkably stunning dressed like that. She thought of Jean-Guy in his jeans and sweatshirts and felt a bit of a traitor. Maybe her lovely Moly would look as good as that when he was in his tie and tails for a concert.

Piers seemed quite unaware of any feelings she may have been having. "Not bad. Just got back from a long-haul to Auckland."

"Oh? Not Concorde this time?"

"Yes, Concorde. Special charter. Your car made it here in one piece then?"

"Well, yes, why shouldn't it?" She felt oddly protective of her old car which had given her so much freedom when she had needed it. "We can't all afford Ferraris, you know."

He smiled then. "I'm not knocking it. You should have seen the heap of trash I drove before the Ferrari. Bloody thing. Taught me a hell of a lot about car mechanics the number of times it broke down. And I learned lots of new words from the drivers I held up on the M4 the time its windscreen shattered and I couldn't see where I was going. I just worry about you on your own in it, that's all."

Kathy sensed the same kind of fondness in his voice as she felt for her old car. "It'll do me for now. I can't think you'll want to give up your Ferrari so easily."

He gave her a wry smile of acknowledgement. "True. Good rehearsal?" was all he asked.

"Yes, pretty good. It's all pieces I've done before so bit of an easy ride for me. Concert tomorrow and it's down Covent Garden way so I can go on the Tube. Is it OK with you if I stop on until Monday? It's just that way I avoid the scheduled roadworks on the A12."

"Doesn't bother me in the slightest. I'm not working again now until Tuesday but I'll be out on Sunday morning so if you want your car before then we'll have to swap them round."

"Oh? Going somewhere nice?"

"Not really," was the unexpected reply. "I'm going to go to church."

"To see Chantal?"

"Yes. I've spoken to her brother a couple more times and also her pastor has rung here now and he suggested I just turn up and nobody will tell her I'm coming. She's talked to him a lot and even though it looks as though her cancer is under control she still isn't at peace in herself and he feels that maybe if I can join her in worship then that will help her."

"But you don't believe in her faith. Or even her God."

"No, I don't. But, unlike Sarah, she knew to respect my faith so in turn I respected hers. We had a civil wedding even though the station chaplain conducted it. So just sometimes I'd go along and sing her hymns and just sometimes she'd sit with me when I lit the Beltane fires or walked up to the veil on Samhain."

Kathy felt as though there was a large part of her education missing. "I've never heard of Beltane or Samhain," she admitted.

He gave her another tired smile. "Piglet, I have just come off a long flight. What I do now is have a bath and go to bed and sleep. Tomorrow if you like I will explain to you about the turn of the wheel but right now I'm finding it hard just to get my words in the right order."

"Oh, sorry. OK, goodnight then. See you tomorrow. I promise I'll be quiet and try not to disturb you."

"Thank you. And now, indeed, goodnight."

Kathy watched him go up the box staircase, shutting the door behind himself as he left the kitchen and she closed her eyes for a second. "He's just a friend," she muttered to herself. "He's my big brother and I really don't fancy him. He's married anyway and I've always sworn I'm not getting involved with a married man again."

"You alright down there?" came Piers' voice from half-way up the stairs.

She cursed his hearing and really hoped he hadn't been able to make out the words. "Yes, thanks. Sorry, just talking to myself. It's a habit of mine."

"First sign of madness, they say," he laughed. "Goodnight."

"'Night. Sweet dreams."

"Right, Piglet," was the greeting she got from her landlord when she came downstairs the next morning.

Kathy's immediate thought was that she was about to get a ticking-off for keeping him chatting yesterday and was about to apologise but Piers didn't seem to have noticed.

"We are going to need to sort out cars. It occurred to me in the bath last night that I'm pretty sure legally we can only park one car here as the car port is shared with the let half. I've tried over the years to find out who owns that mess next door or even the letting agent responsible for it but haven't had any luck. I think I've tried every estate agent within five miles of this place but nobody's admitting to knowing anything about it. Probably because they know I want to give them a bollocking over the state of it."

An idea came to Kathy while he was speaking. "But if we leave two cars here then that may make whoever owns it get in touch asking you to move one of them. What do you think?"

"Woman after my own heart," he laughed. "What are you smiling about?"

Kathy realised it wouldn't be too smart an idea to let him know she had been thinking things she shouldn't about him lying in the bath. "Oh, nothing really. What are your plans for today?"

He suddenly got rather vague. "Oh, none really. Bit of laundry. Should probably have a look at some of that music you've left on top of the piano for me. No doubt Jean-Guy gave it to you for me. You?"

Kathy could feel his mood changing and wasn't quite sure how to handle it. "Well, if I was still at Hogarth Road I'd be rushing about like a mad thing cleaning and shopping then dashing off to my concert. But this place is pretty clean and tidy anyway so I think I'll just get my room sorted out a bit more as I kind of threw all my stuff in there and at some point Jean-Guy's got to fit in there too."

He barely seemed to be listening now. "May see you for lunch tomorrow. Don't know. Did you want to do any music practice today while you've got an accompanist available?"

Kathy thought she knew what was occupying his mind. "I'm sure Chantal will be pleased to see you."

She wasn't expecting his mood to switch so suddenly.

"Are you?" he asked just a bit nastily. "Since when were you the bloody expert on what I, or Chantal, may be feeling?" He got up abruptly from the table and went up the staircase, slamming the door behind himself.

Kathy was too cross with him for speaking to her like that to go chasing after him with any kind of apology so she left him to have his sulk and went off to her own room to sort out some space for Jean-Guy and to decide what she was going to wear for the concert that evening. She realised that although Piers had just got snappy with her, she hadn't felt at all threatened as she would have done with her ex, but she now understood better why Sarah felt she couldn't live with him, no matter how delicious he looked.

Kathy didn't see Piers all the rest of Saturday and he had gone out by the time she got up on Sunday morning. She was getting her lunch ready when he came in through the side door looking unusually smart in his dark grey suit and tie, but she took one look at his face and totally forgave him for the way he had spoken to her yesterday.

"Sit," she told him. "I'll make you a coffee and throw a bit more in my lunch so we can eat together. What happened?"

He slackened his tie and undid a couple of shirt buttons as he sat despairingly at the table and sighed audibly. "Well, I've seen her."

Kathy parked a mug of coffee in front of him wondering why he didn't seem happier about it. "And?" she prompted gently, not thinking for one minute he was about to give her any bad news.

He looked at the drink as though he had forgotten what to do with it. "It was the first time she'd been to church since her operation and initial treatment so there were a lot of people there waiting to welcome her back. Bloody hell but I got some looks from them I can tell you but they wished me a very polite 'good morning' and at least three checked I had somewhere to go for lunch after the service. Then Chantal arrived with her brother and his family, and a load of people rushed forward to greet her and she looked so happy I nearly turned and walked away. She'd made her peace with her friends and with her God, she was starting to heal physically and who the hell was I to disturb that? Then she, I don't know, just looked across and saw me and she walked up to me and without saying a word put her arms round my neck and it was as though we'd never been apart." He took a thoughtful sip of the coffee. "I have no idea how long we just stood outside that church totally wrapped up in each other."

Kathy put her hand over his and he felt cold to her touch. "So did you go into the church and sing their hymns?"

"Yes."

To Kathy's distress, he closed his eyes and she was sure two tears splashed into his coffee. "What?" she asked softly. "Please, just tell me."

He took a deep breath and got control. "After the service we went back to her brother's house and she told me that the tumours have come back. At the moment they're very small and the doctors are hoping they can shrink them with chemo and radiotherapy but they have spread to her lungs and her spine. In just over an hour I went from seeing her looking so happy and believing she was getting better to learning the truth. I'm going to lose her again and this time it will be for ever."

Kathy went back to Suffolk alone on the Monday with a very heavy heart. It cheered her a little to see both the Prof and Jean-Guy were working on the Grieg Sonata when she joined them in the sitting room.

Jean-Guy was about to ask how her trip to London had gone but he saw the way she sat so heavily in one of the armchairs and didn't speak or smile even when Brno leaped up to join her. For a long, horrible moment he thought she was trying to find the words to tell him she was breaking up with him. But when she managed to tell the two men what she had to say it was in so many ways so much worse. She finished by saying Piers had refused her offer to stay with him, to invite Jean-Guy to stay with him or generally to accept any kind of support at this time when she felt he needed it the most. The Prof was sympathetic but pointed out that they couldn't force Piers to accept any help and the best they could do was to keep an eye on him and let him know they were there for him but always being careful not to appear to be interfering no matter how hard that was to do.

That evening, Kathy took out her violin and started doing some work on the Franck sonata as she liked to play that one when she wanted to think and she was aware that Jean-Guy was watching her from one of the armchairs by the fire with old Brno on his lap, a bit cross that a human had occupied his chair but willing to forgive in exchange for a cuddle.

"You OK?" Kathy asked as she made a complete mess of the end of the second movement and the renowned cellist didn't say anything.

"I was thinking," he admitted. "I miss my playing so much yet I stay here and practise for hours and hours and I have nothing before our concert in Snape in September. That is a long time before I can play. Yes, I know that Jane has to make all the bookings and I am lucky that she has managed to get me so many on such short notice, but to me, just being here day after day while you go to London and play, is making me sad for the music I don't have. That and I am now worried about Piers now on his own. We know he feels unwelcome at Sarah's house, I like to hope he feels welcome here, but it must be difficult for him."

Kathy thought that was just so adorably sweet and Molyish of him. Personally she didn't think luck had any part to play in so many venues wanting to book the celebrated cellist on short notice. "Well we can do two birds with one stone, as we say here. Just to get you back on a concert platform, why don't you do a couple of rank-and-file gigs? There are loads of groups crying out for cellists, and I bet if I have a word with some of the ones I'm booked with we could even go on stage together. And we'll also both be there to remind Piers we're not going to let him struggle with this on his own."

The excitement shot through Jean-Guy's veins. "Yes, I would like that. I think perhaps someone who isn't a musician wouldn't understand, but you do. And I will take a lot of music for Piers as I am sure his playing will do him good while he is so worried about Chantal."

Kathy put down her violin on top of the piano, picked up Brno and sat on Jean-Guy's lap with the old tabby cat purring in her arms. "You are so adorable," she told him and nuzzled her face into his neck.

Brno went out to the kitchen and left them to it.

Jane thought her most eminent client was being a bit odd to be asking for rank and file work and not at his usual fee either, but she could see his point. And even if the fee was very low for him it still got her a commission, so she conspired with Kathy to find a suitable concert booking. It didn't happen as soon as any of them would have liked as Piers hadn't been near Suffolk since that time Sarah had told him about her baby. In the end it was nearly the end of July when Kathy and Jean-Guy caught the London train giggling like a pair of children at the very thought of the internationally famous cellist being about to play as a rank and file member of a small chamber orchestra in a performance of some Haydn and Mozart symphonies.

London was warmer than the Suffolk coast and as Kathy opened the side door with her key she realised this was the first time Jean-Guy had set foot in what was going to be their London home.

He stopped and looked round the large kitchen. "Nice house," he said.

"Half a house," Kathy reminded him. "Be careful with your cello on the stairs as it's only got that soft case."

By the time Jean-Guy had explored the house and given it his approval, it was glaringly obvious their landlord wasn't in residence. So they pretended they lived there full time and got on with making up their bed and sorting through the kitchen to find some food for lunch. Jean-Guy was impressed by the well-stocked pantry and the fairly new fridge-freezer so there was no shortage of food in the house.

They were just clearing up after their lunch when Piers came in through the side door. "Anything left for me?" was all he said in greeting.

"Loads, and I'll pop up to Sainsbury's in a bit to restock," Kathy offered.

Piers knew what the other two wanted to hear. He didn't want to tell them but it saved them having to ask. "Been to the hospital with Chantal," he told them as he looked in the pantry and the fridge then just made himself some coffee.

Kathy hardly dared ask now, but she did. "And?"

"Not the best news. Not the worst but those blasted tumours aren't shrinking as fast as they'd hoped they would. So they're upping the chemo for a few weeks to see if that has any effect. Chantal's just wiped out so she's staying with her brother and his family for now. Anyway, glad you're here as I need to update you on things with Sarah." Before Kathy could even think about it, Piers smiled at her but his eyes told them how unhappy he was. "No, Piglet, we're not about to split up. I've had several long talks with her while Alison has been out of the way and I've explained that I'm not going back to my first wife but I'll be with an old friend while she goes through a difficult time in her life. Sarah is fine with that. But I know there will be some bloody vicious rumours about me going round that village just as soon as Alison gets wind of what's going on. I'd like you two to hear my truth before you hear her lies." He looked away from them towards the window. "So that's it. If you hear stories of me sleeping with a woman who is dying of cancer please remember it's not true."

The other two could see how upset he was getting and Kathy laid a hand on his arm. "It's OK, we understand. How is Sarah anyway?"

"She saw the midwife a couple of days ago and asked if she could have a home birth. It seems there's no chance of that happening as it turns out Sarah and I have managed to conceive triplets at our first attempt. Due date of twenty eighth of December so if anyone bothers to count up on their fingers they will maybe work out we were naughty children before we got married."

"I don't have enough fingers," Kathy told him lightly, a bit bothered he had told them his joyful news in the same flat tone he had used to tell them his sad. She consciously focussed on the happier event. "But, wow, triplets. Congratulations to both of you. Don't suppose there's any chance you could sneak out to a concert tonight to celebrate?"

Piers barely gave that invitation any consideration. "Not really. I need to get my rest in before I fly tomorrow." Then he obviously thought about it. "What time?"

"Seven. It's only in the Queen Elizabeth so we should be home not long after ten."

"What's so special about it?" Piers asked at last, his natural curiosity getting the better of him.

"Jean-Guy's playing in it."

Piers looked at the other man. "But I thought…"

"Yes, and you are right. But I am playing as inside player of the third desk of the cellos."

"Why the hell would you want to do that? You're a bloody soloist."

"True. But above all I am a musician and I had to get on a concert platform and play."

"Ah," Piers agreed, and seemed cheered by the idea. "The unreachable itch. Oh, go on then. Just this once. I'll curse you all when I've got to get up at six to be at the airport in time and if you hear the morning Concorde flight went all the way to San Francisco because the pilot was asleep then it'll be your faults."

"We'll risk it," Kathy told him, wondering for the first time if maybe he hadn't found it as easy to give up his music as he had always implied. "It's not every day you learn there are triplets on the way, is it?"

Emma and Derek stood side by side in the doorway of the living room of their flat in Southfields. Baby Peter was in his buggy, Emma's old green car was outside with all their worldly belongings in it and it was time to go.

"That's it then," Derek said quietly. "No more London living for us. Regrets?"

Emma tucked her arm round his waist and smiled. "Not yet. Ask me in a year or so when we're surrounded by rising damp and twenty five babies." She was going to say more but the phone rang just then.

Derek was good at guessing who was calling. "Bet that's Kathy just wanting to say goodbye to you. I'll get the stuff in the car. Tell her not to be long or we'll be in the middle of the rush hour."

He had been right but Emma wasn't consoled to hear the tone in her oldest friend's voice.

"You're off then?" was the rather abrupt greeting.

"Yes. Literally the car's packed and we're about to head off."

"Oh, sorry. I won't be long."

"Kath, what's the matter? Is everything OK with you and Jean-Guy?"

"I don't know," was the small reply.

"Quick, give me the run down before BT cut the line off as we've told them we're moving today."

She heard Kathy catch her breath. "Jean-Guy's started talking about babies."

"Oh. Well, can't say I was expecting that so soon. How do you feel about it?"

"I don't know."

Emma really didn't have the time for this. "Kath, the pair of you have only been together five minutes. Do you honestly think kids are a good idea right now?"

"Yes. I want to have his children. But after all that mess with Richard four years ago…"

What else Kathy was about to say, Emma never found out as British Telecom chose that exact moment to cut off the phone line and all was silent between Earl's Court and Southfields.

Kathy turned away from the phone in the sitting room and realised Piers had paused outside the room on the landing. He had that post-flight fatigued look about him and was still in his uniform.

"Sorry," he said and sounded as though he meant it. "Didn't mean to eavesdrop."

"How much did you hear?"

"Probably more than I should have done. Want to talk about it?"

"I don't know."

"Come and sit a minute," he invited and the two sat side by side on the sofa. "Right, Piglet, I'm going to put on my sensible big brother hat now. Did I glean from your side of things that Jean-Guy wants to be a father and sooner rather than later?"

"Yes."

"But you're not happy?"

Kathy didn't know what to do. This was something so intimate she wasn't sure she wanted to share. "I don't know," she repeated. And that's not me fobbing you off. I really don't know. Yes, I'd like to think we'll be together long enough to have kids but…"

"Are you not sure about your relationship?" he asked kindly but didn't touch her.

"Oh, no, I'm sure about the two of us. It's just that…" Kathy paused, took a deep breath and went for it. "I'm not sure I can have kids." She didn't know what she was expecting him to say to that and his silence didn't help. When he did speak, he still sounded perfectly calm but clearly not wanting to intrude on something that didn't concern him.

"Physically or mentally?" he asked. "If it's physical then you need to talk to a doctor. If it's mental, I don't know. I suppose you could talk to Sarah? She waited most of her life to have kids. But whichever it is, don't you think you need to discuss this with Jean-Guy?"

She huddled into his side like a child seeking reassurance and took some comfort from feeling his arm curl protectively round her. Like the wing of a raven mantling over her and shielding her from all the badness of the world. Tucked against him like this she was safe.

"What is it?" he asked softly. "Christ knows I have my own secrets to keep, some of them I still don't want to share. But if it would help you to tell me yours then I will keep it for you."

"I can't," she whispered. "You wouldn't understand."

"Try me? After some of the things I've done, I never judge other people."

Kathy pulled his jacket round herself, curled her fingers into his tie and wept hot tears all over his shirt as she told him the secret that only Emma knew.

"You have to tell Jean-Guy," he whispered to her when she had finished, and he brushed some of the sodden hair back off her face. "He'll understand."

"Will he?"

"I'm sure he'll try to."

Kathy pushed herself away from him a bit and tried to straighten out his mangled tie. "Are you? I'm not."

She could tell he didn't want to say what he said next. "Would you like me to tell him for you?"

It was very, very tempting. "No," she said quietly. "But thank you. It's probably not the kind of thing he wants to know I told you first." Her smile was wry as she patted the tie back into place.

"Can see that," he agreed. "OK, I'll keep out of this one. But if ever you want to talk about it, or if you change your mind, you'll let me know?"

Kathy nodded and gave the most enormous sniff before her nose made a mess of his jacket.

"Go and blow your nose and wash your face," he told her. "I'll take a shower and change and then I'll cook you something exotic and Chinese for your lunch."

Kathy started crying all over again. "But don't you want to go to bed for an hour or so?"

"Piglet, no, not the water works. Please. I'll cope. We had an overnight layover in Munich so it was only a quick hop this morning. Oh, for Christ's sake. Go and blow your bloody nose on something. No, don't wipe it on your sleeve, that's disgusting. Go on, hop it. Give me ten minutes and you can be my sous-chef."

Kathy had to smile as she got to her feet beside him. "I don't know anything about Chinese cooking."

"You will by lunch time," he promised her.

"And you really won't tell Jean-Guy anything?"

"Nobody will ever guess this conversation ever took place."

"Thank you."

He moved his head so she kissed his cheek and not his mouth. "Stop slobbering. Go and sort your nose out."

August was not a good month. The ugly rumours about Piers began circulating round the village and if his wife and his best friends stuck up for him, then nobody believed them but pitied their naivety. Piers stayed away from Suffolk even though they were all very aware the concert at Snape was getting ever closer as the venue was booked for September the eighth but he assured the other two he was working on his music at home.

Kathy had several bookings in August and she arrived in Earl's Court late in the evening of the day before her last one of the month as there had been a delay on the railway and by the time she arrived although the Ferrari was parked in front of her rather neglected car, it was obvious the car's owner had already gone to bed so she knew he would be flying the next day. Feeling oddly dissatisfied, she got herself ready for bed and totally forgot to ring Jean-Guy to tell him she had arrived.

Eventually he gave in to his worry and rang the house at just after midnight which woke up both the residents and although Kathy got to the phone first she still got a mild bollocking from her landlord who had grumpily come down from his room to the phone which was in the sitting room. He had gone to work by the time she got down in the morning but to her surprise was back in the kitchen by late afternoon.

"What happened to Concorde?" she asked.

"Nothing. I wasn't flying today. One-day training course."

She felt oddly relieved that he hadn't been flying after his disturbed night. "Oh? Anything interesting?"

"Hmm? Oh, kind of. I help out on these 'Fear of Flying' days sometimes. Can be quite rewarding."

Kathy privately thought that if any fearful passengers got an eyeful of the man in captain's uniform they'd be too busy fantasising about him to be scared of anything the plane might do. She watched as he shut the pantry door without taking any food out. "Aren't you eating?"

"Got fed on the course," he replied vaguely.

She wasn't quite sure she believed him but didn't like to say so. "Oh, OK. Anyway, my gig's in Guildford tonight so I'll be needing my car. Do you want to swap them round now or are you going to be awake for a while longer?"

"I'll be awake."

The day didn't get any better. Kathy didn't particularly enjoy the concert and was glad when it was time to set off for home. She had just got off the A3 and was working her way up through southwestern suburbs of London towards home when her car suddenly stopped and the engine died. It was nearly midnight; she didn't have a clue where she was and had never got round to organising any kind of breakdown cover. To her relief there was a phone box within sight and she knew she had some change so, not knowing what else to do, she rang Piers.

To her relief, Piers genuinely didn't seem to mind she had disturbed him and he was with her in less than half an hour having borrowed Matt's Land Rover. She just watched helplessly as he so calmly and efficiently got her car hitched to the back of the Land Rover and told her to get back in and hope the brakes and steering worked. They got back to Earl's Court at just after one o'clock in the morning and a remorselessly cheerful Matt was waiting on the pavement for them.

He took one look under the bonnet of the car and told Kathy, "Sorry, love, this old girl's had it. Let's face it, it's sixteen years old and just totally clapped out. Cost you more than it's worth to get it mended. You'd have done better to have abandoned it and declared it nicked."

"Except," Kathy said wryly, "knowing my luck they'd have found it and brought it back."

"And want to know the worse news?" Piers asked her. "This sod told me this evening he and the missis are moving out to Wales and taking the Land Rover with them."

Kathy looked at her old car and hated it for letting her down at the last minute, just thankful she had been able to call on someone to rescue her. "Guess that's it then," she said. "This one's for the scrap heap, the

Ferrari's for the finance company and we'll have to get ourselves a sensible car."

"But I like my Ferrari," Piers protested.

Matt laughed and replied in an excruciating accent based loosely on Hollywood's idea of a Native American in a bad Western. "Listen to your woman. She speak good sense."

"Oh, piss off," Piers told him. "Thanks for the loan of the bus."

"Any time. For the next few days at any rate. 'Night, you two. Don't get too noisy, the walls between us aren't that thick."

Kathy stayed on in London for a few more days so she and Piers could get things sorted out. Her insurance company didn't waste any time but wrote off her car and the money they said they would pay her would just be enough to buy a new case for Jean-Guy's cello if he wanted one. Piers, rather more reluctantly and a lot more easily, sold his beloved Ferrari and raised enough to clear the finance package on it.

With both cars gone and Matt's expertise available for just a few days, Piers took his neighbour with him to inspect a Land Rover being offered for sale in a local small ad. Matt knew the car when he saw it as he worked for a local dealership and he remembered doing the MoT on that one just a few months ago. On his strong recommendation, Piers haggled the price down as low as the seller would accept and the car moved to its new home in Earl's Court. It wasn't any smaller than Matt's vehicle but it was a bit younger and didn't smell of fish. Kathy thought Piers was being extraordinarily generous as he put her on his insurance for it and paid the annual premium over the phone.

Kathy was on her own in the house the evening the new car arrived as Piers was off to spend the night with Chantal who was no longer living with her brother as her care needs were so intensive at the moment. She had voluntarily put herself in a church-run nursing home so her ex-husband, her brother and his family wouldn't keep exhausting themselves trying to carry on with their lives and look after her at the same time. But they took it in turns to be with her when they could while the aggressive chemotherapy attacked the tumours that were in her body. Kathy sat in the sitting room of the house and cried, wishing she had gone home on the evening train rather than waiting for the morning one but she had chosen to stay here while she and Piers dealt with getting rid of their cars and getting the new one. He had even made her go out for a quick drive round the local streets only that afternoon. The car was so large, she felt as though she was driving a bus but it felt a lot more sturdy and reliable than her old one.

Jean-Guy rang her as he always did when she was away for the night in London and he offered to come and be with her when she told him where Piers had gone, which she thought was just too sweet for words as it was getting almost too late to catch the last train of the day, but she assured him Chantal had gone in for some respite care to give her family a bit of a break and it wasn't as bad as it sounded. Which she hoped was true. So they talked about cars, how she had got rid of her old one and driven the new one and Jean-Guy got madly excited at the idea of being able to buy his cello a new case. They talked about the concert at Snape Maltings, which was now just over a week away, they talked about the horrible gossip that would persist in the village, and by the time Jean-Guy had to hang up as it was getting so late, Kathy had stopped crying. She didn't want to go to bed that night. She wanted to stay next to the phone that was her link to her lovely Moly so many miles away, so she curled miserably round on the sofa for the night and was glad she was going home on the morning train.

Anton Dvořák - *Piano trio No. 4 in E minor, Op. 90, B.166 (Dumky)*

Three people waited backstage at Snape Maltings concert hall and listened to the sounds of the first of eight hundred and thirty two people filling it to capacity. The concert venue had put out publicity announcing the UK debut of the celebrated Czech cellist Jean-Guy Dechaume and tickets had sold out within twenty four hours of going on sale. So the venue had contacted the agent for the Dodman Trio who had spoken to all three members and they were booked to do a run of three concerts on the Tuesday, the Wednesday and the Friday of that week. One of them had grumbled a bit that he was now going to have to book a week's leave and would forget how to fly if he wasn't careful but the other two had just told him to shut up and be grateful he was still allowed to play with them.

Kathy stood quietly between the two men, holding her violin under her arm and thankful, in an irrelevant kind of way that Sarah's mother had made her three different dresses to wear. She was in the dark red that night as that was her favourite and this was, after all, the first night. She thought the men looked smart but not overdressed as Jean-Guy had had to accept that if this concert was going to go ahead the pianist, at least, was not going to be in the 'penguin suit' as he insisted on calling it. Kathy had managed to persuade Jean-Guy that it was quite acceptable to be a little less formal in 1980s England so he had finally agreed to compromise on full black with open-neck shirts. He had made sure, on several occasions, that the other man knew he wasn't happy about it but Piers just made sarky comments about how he didn't need to play the trios at all, until it got to the point where Kathy had told Jean-Guy to back off before they lost their pianist completely. Grudgingly he had seen her point but gave her the impression he wasn't going to give up trying once this first concert was over.

Kathy looked up at Piers and thought he looked exhausted and she was sure he had lost weight. "How's Chantal?" she asked for the sake of not standing there in silence.

"Going through a quiet patch at the moment."

She was going to ask what the latest prognosis was, but he turned his head away and she knew he wouldn't speak of Chantal any more that evening.

Jean-Guy had heard what was said and thought Piers looked very tired after his drive to Suffolk and there were shadows in his eyes that had suddenly aged him. Then he got totally distracted by that dress Kathy was wearing and he wished she would wear red more often.

Kathy was getting almost impatient to start now and wished she had at least brought a glass of water with her to drink. She looked again at the man standing quietly next to her and had a bad feeling that Piers had been right and he was slowly losing the only woman he had ever really loved. She had a sudden, awful sense that Piers was leaving them again. Slipping away to a life they couldn't share. It was a though he was closing a door between them and it frightened her. She laid a gentle hand on his arm. "You still OK for the spring tour of Europe?" she asked, hoping to remind him they had a future as a trio.

"Yes, fine. I've cleared the dates with the airline already." He looked across the stage which looked very large with just a piano, chairs and stands on it. "Are they all out there?"

"Oh, yes," Kathy told him. "Roisin with husband and three children, Sarah's not as she's five months gone with your triplets and reckons she wouldn't fit in the seat, but Alison's using her ticket. The Prof's here with Emma and Derek, Sarah's mum is looking after baby Peter for them."

He smiled vaguely. "Ah, yes, the firstborn. How long had they been married when he arrived?"

Kathy was glad he had found a happy thought. "Six months."

"And her a countess-in-training too," he remarked. "How can these people take so long to park their bums in seats?"

"All the mad excitement."

"Hmm. Speaking of which, I've bought myself a car."

"You've got a car."

"No, I've got a bus which I share with you."

"Silly. What did you buy?"

"Aston Martin V8. Maroon. Second hand. Should be able to pick it up in a couple of days which will leave the Land Rover pretty much for the pair of you which will make your lives easier."

"True," she admitted. "But isn't that a sports car?"

"Couldn't afford the top of the range models. Two doors but four seats so should take the three of us and the cello."

"Sounds posh enough for me," she laughed. "Can we go and yell at that lot to hurry up?"

"Wish they would. I could murder a drink of something."

"Me too. Must be first night nerves."

Just as Kathy was thinking she would go and find some water for them to drink, the stage manager arrived beside them. "All set to go? Everyone's in at last and it's already two minutes after start time. Took them ages to get settled in."

Jean-Guy looked at the other two. "Ready?"

They just nodded so the stage manager set off the applause that was taken up by an eager audience. Kathy, glad things were finally on the move, walked on stage next to Piers, both of them behind Jean-Guy who was the star of the show after all and the noise of the audience applause was deafening. She was between the two men as they took their bows to acknowledge the applause then she settled in her seat next to Piers so they could see each other with Jean-Guy a bit further along the piano, turned more towards the audience and artfully placed a little distant so the lights could pick him out just that little bit more. Kathy sorted out the music on her stand and put up the *Dumky* trio ready to start the concert. She was quite well aware that almost the entire audience was staring intently at the cellist who was tuning his instrument to the piano but a tiny movement caught her eye and she looked as best she could while tuning her violin. Just as she had suspected, the pianist had quietly eased his feet out of his shoes and discreetly shoved them under the piano stool.

She glanced across and he gave her one of his lovely smiles which Kathy returned with her best on-stage glare and, catching the amused smile of the cellist, turned her attention to her music as the audience noise died down, the house lights were dimmed and Jean-Guy gave the nod for the concert to start.

Jean-Guy couldn't believe how well they played. They had worked hard all three of them but he listened critically to the piano player, who still spent so much of his time doing his day job, and couldn't wait for the day, not far away now, when just the two of them would be on stage at the Festival Hall with a demanding programme of sonatas. But in the meantime he could look forward to living in Earl's Court again where he had been all too briefly before. As the three of them closed their first piece with total perfection, he oddly thought of the food in the Lebanese restaurant and started to feel quite hungry which was most unlike him when he was on stage. One thing he was certain of was that he wouldn't need to work there again as he and his cello were going to be busy for a long time ahead.

To Jean-Guy it seemed barely any time at all before he was sitting behind his cello in the hushed atmosphere of the Festival Hall and looking across at the man who had just tucked his shoes out of the way under the piano stool. One day he was going to find out why Piers did that but in the meantime, this was their first public recital. The last time he had been on a stage and it had been just him and a pianist he had been in Budapest and his father had been his accompanist and his chaperone.

Now he had the chance to play with the man who had grown up as the accompanist to Roisin Thompson and he had no idea when Piers had last played in a concert as the accompanist to a solo performer. He had never said. He didn't say much at all now but at least he seemed to have been eating and sleeping properly as he wasn't visiting Chantal for a few days while her mother and her sister Marguerite, known as Rita, had come to visit. Her grandmother had wanted to come too but the family had persuaded her that at her age a long-haul flight probably wasn't such a good idea and Piers had been quite sorry as he had always liked Chantal's grandmother. She had liked him too as he was the only person happy to sit with her for hours while she told stories of her childhood in Jamaica and filled his head with the myths and legends of her African heritage.

If there was one thing Jean-Guy had to admire about Piers it was his consummate skill as a musician. No matter what he was feeling inside, as soon as he stepped onto the stage, his ingrained professionalism cut in and his performance was nothing less than perfect. Jean-Guy listened as he played and knew he wanted this musical partnership to last. He had had so many accompanists in his career, some had tried to upstage him, some had been in awe of him, but none of them had played like this Concorde pilot did. Maybe that was it, Jean-Guy thought as the last notes of the Grieg Sonata brought the first half of the recital to an end. Maybe because this man flew planes for a living he really, genuinely, didn't give a damn about being the accompanist to such a well-known cellist and just got on with it.

Kathy had been on stage with the men as Piers' page-turner and wasn't surprised the concert was undoubtedly a success for the Czech cellist who had chosen to make his home in England. She was quite euphoric all the way home where she and Jean-Guy prepared themselves a light snack and sat at the kitchen table talking about the venue, the audience, the choice of repertoire and anything else they thought of while their minds still buzzed. They barely noticed that Piers hadn't even had a drink of anything but had just taken himself silently off to bed with only the briefest of goodnights.

"We're going to have to watch him," Kathy said to Jean-Guy, interrupting his analysis of his performance of the Grieg.

"What do you mean?"

"I don't like the way he's so quiet."

Jean-Guy looked at the closed door to the staircase. "I'm sure he's just tired. He is working full time for the airline as well as doing all that work for me as well as having Chantal to deal with. But I don't need him for a while now so he can take a break from his playing if that is what he wants to do. But he must be the best accompanist I have ever used. It's almost as though he doesn't care whether he plays with me or not."

Kathy too looked at the closed door of the box staircase and wondered what Piers was doing right now. Was he getting ready for bed, having a bath or a shower? Was he at peace within himself or churned up inside with losing Chantal and not being able to be with her for a few days. It was as though she could see him lying in his bed. Lying quietly, not reading, not thinking over the music he had just been playing. His broken mind refusing to shut down and give his exhausted body some rest. He knew he was staying away so Chantal's mother and sister could say goodbye to her. They weren't going to see her again in this life and, although they seemed to have accepted the ex-husband back into her life as she wished, Piers still felt like the outsider. The adulterous husband who had cheated on his wife. The one who regretted that brief affair more than he could ever tell anyone.

"Should I take him up a cup of tea?" Kathy asked Jean-Guy.

"I think if he wanted a drink he would have made one for himself," Jean-Guy pointed out, still not sure of the depth of Kathy's feelings for Piers.

"He worries me."

Jean-Guy went to her side and took her in a cuddle. "Kathy, you must be the loveliest person I know. We are all worried about him. But he won't let us help."

Kathy broke away and went to the kettle. "Can't help it. It's what we English do in a crisis. We make tea."

"Then you should make him some tea and we can both take it up to him and make sure he is OK."

Kathy realised Jean-Guy was a bit suspicious of her motives in going upstairs to take tea to the other man. "I'll be fine. I'm just going to take up the mug and if he's asleep I'll be straight back down again."

Jean-Guy knew he had to trust her on this one, even though he didn't like it. "Go on then."

Kathy almost slunk up two flights of stairs, feeling a bit guilty even though she genuinely only wanted to deliver the mug of tea. The door to Piers' room was open but the bathroom door was closed so she guessed maybe he was in the bath. She knocked gently on the bathroom door.

"Brought you some tea," she said. "Can I leave it in your room?"

The bathroom door clicked open and Piers came out wrapped in a towel and with his hair still wet from the shower. "Thanks," he said briefly and took the mug from her.

Seeing him stripped to the waist, Kathy could tell just how much weight he had lost. "Can I get you a sandwich or something to go with it?"

"No, really, thanks, this is fine. I'm not very hungry these days." He gave her an absent kiss on the cheek then went into his room, closing the door behind him.

Kathy went slowly back down the stairs but Jean-Guy had come up the first flight and they met on the landing. "He took the tea," she reported.

"Not asleep then?"

"No, been having a shower."

"There you are then, he is not neglecting himself. And I bet he was nicely shaved and smelled good too."

"True," she had to smile. "You can't look like him and not be a bit vain, can you? But I wish he'd eat a bit more. He's getting very thin."

Jean-Guy gave her a hug. "Double rations of bacon pudding next time he's in Suffolk," he suggested.

"Definitely. And now I think it's bed time for us too, don't you?"

"Definitely, as you just said."

Kathy tried so hard not to worry about Piers as the autumn cooled towards winter and she started having to wear her blue duffle coat when she went out and about to the village or on the streets of Earl's Court. She had enough work to keep her occupied but somehow she had an odd feeling of not quite restlessness, not quite anxiety, but something inside was going from whispering to shouting at her that all was far from well not just with Piers but with her and Jean-Guy too. The Prof kept a fatherly eye on her when she was in Suffolk and somehow wasn't surprised when she came up from London with a minor cold after a gig in early October and that cold turned into something more like flu which sent her to bed and kept her there for nearly a week.

Kathy honestly couldn't remember the last time she had felt so rough. Common sense, and the Prof, told her she hadn't been taking enough care of herself and in an odd way she was thankful that Jean-Guy was away for a fortnight, touring in the North of England with the Halle Orchestra at various venues round Leeds and Manchester. As she lightly dozed away the days and slowly recovered her appetite she was thankful he hadn't seen her looking so awful with her unbrushed hair and her face so pale.

"Kath, you look bloody awful!" declared an annoyingly cheerful voice and Kathy opened bleary eyes to see a grinning Emma standing beside the bed and holding a steaming mug of something. "Here, sit up and take this."

Kathy hauled herself into a sitting position and took the mug. "Ribena," she croaked delightedly. "You remembered."

Emma sat next to her on the bed and solemnly handed across a packet of biscuits. "Oh, I so well remember the go-to cold and flu remedy for you. Hot Ribena and Rich Tea biscuits. There you go. Stuff yourself silly."

Kathy scoffed three biscuits, gulped down half the mug of hot drink and immediately began to feel a lot better. "Why are you here?" she asked, suddenly remembering that Emma didn't live here any more.

"I was chatting with Dad the other evening and he told me you were quite poorly with the flu so I got a mad fit in my head and told Derek it was time we introduced baby Peter to his grandad properly and one night here after your Snape gig didn't count. So here we are." She thoughtfully watched her oldest friend get through a few more biscuits and the rest of the drink. "I gather your delicious landlord isn't too great at the moment either. We did think about stopping off in Earl's Court on our way here but it's quicker in so many ways just to tack north of London for the trip."

Kathy cradled the cooling mug in her hands. "What did your dad tell you?"

"Not that much really. I gather Piers' first wife is going through cancer treatment at the moment but Dad didn't seem to know what the prognosis is."

"No, we're not sure either. It seemed quite optimistic back in the spring when she started treatment but from the way he's been acting recently, I wouldn't like to guess." She tipped the last few dregs of the cold Ribena into her mouth. "Truthfully I feel as though we're losing him to her."

"But from the few things you've said and he hasn't said it wasn't the most pleasant of divorces they had. Hang it all, Kath. He cheated on her. And there's no nice way of putting that."

"I know. It's all so confusing. I get the impression that maybe he really regrets doing what he did and maybe she regrets how she treated him. I don't know. I don't understand it. I've never been through a divorce." She sighed. "I suppose if you want to look at it this way I was the 'other woman' with a married man but I knew he wasn't going to leave his wife for me even though he said he would."

"No you didn't. I remember telling you several times not to be such an idiot and he wasn't going to hang around once he'd done with you."

"True."

"And fortunately you saw sense and dumped the bastard before he did the dirty on you."

"Also true. And do you know what? He was having a fling with an oboe player probably about a week after I'd told him to get out of my life."

"No!"

"Oh, yes. At least Piers only cheated the once and he seems to have paid the price for it ever since."

"I bet he'd cheat on Sarah with you though."

Kathy humped down in the bed and pulled the covers over her ears. "Go away."

Emma just laughed and pulled the covers down again even as Kathy hung on to them. "Oh, my. Someone's blushing like a lobster in the sun. You know you want to."

"No I don't. Why don't you ask him? At least I tried a married man, you didn't."

"Ooh, bitchy Kath. Haven't seen you for a while. No, seriously, why don't you? He could easily have Sarah here and you in London and in a way you could do the same with him and Jean-Guy. Then everybody's happy."

Kathy churned the scenario over in her weary mind. "Because it's not the answer. I found that out when I had that fling with my driving teacher after the ex. Sure, the sex was off the scale but it didn't help. Well, yes, it did in a way as it was me in control of it and not him. But I don't want to control Piers."

For the first time, it occurred to Emma that her oldest friend had changed. She hadn't been the same since she had run from her ex but this was neither the teenage Kath who was always up for a laugh or a dare, nor was it the traumatised wreck of a woman who had cried in her arms when she had first run. This was a mature woman, admittedly one struggling with her feelings for two men, but certainly not one who would jump into bed with anyone any more. She looked at Kath who hadn't tried to sit up again in the bed but had closed her eyes and her mouth was set in almost a grimace of determination.

Emma rubbed her friend's shoulder. "I'm sorry, Kath. I see so little of you now I think we've lost what it was we had between us."

The blue eyes flicked open and the grimace turned into a smile. "Never. I need you as you're the one I run to when my life fractures into little pieces. I seem to remember crying on your shoulder a lot when it hadn't been my choice to end a relationship. You never cried on mine."

Emma almost wanted to laugh. "And that is because I used to dump the buggers usually after one night. Maybe the lucky ones were allowed to stay for two."

"And the good ones?"

"Oh, the really good ones had me for three."

Kathy flopped onto her back. "How many would Piers get?"

"I don't know. I'd have to give him a test drive first."

"Maybe you should be the one to offer him physical consolation."

Put so brutally, Emma backed down. "I think there are too many miles between us, don't you? Literal and figurative."

Kathy was so grateful yet again for the common sense of her oldest friend. "Will you teach me how to mend broken people?"

"What do you mean?"

Kathy wasn't going to cry in front of Emma this time. "I mean I have this image of Piers. He's standing in front of a mirror when there's this weird screaming noise which doesn't even sound like a person and the mirror breaks and I'm trying to catch all the pieces so I can put him back together again. But there are too many pieces and they're all so sharp they're cutting my hands. They're all fractured like rainbows and prisms and..."

Emma hated it when Kath got like this. "You've had flu, I think you've gone a bit doolally. You certainly don't smell too sweet. Now, go and have a bath, I'll change your bed for you then you can come downstairs and meet your godson."

The rainbows and prisms of Kathy's nightmare chased away again. "My who?"

"Your godson. Derek and I would really love it if you and Jean-Guy would stand as godparents to baby Peter."

"I, I don't know what to say. Thank you, I'd be delighted. But I can't answer for Jean-Guy, he's such an atheist he probably doesn't even know what a godfather is."

"Then he'll have to learn. I'm not taking no for an answer. From either of you. Go on, hop it, you stinker."

"Do I really stink?"

"Like a geriatric polecat."

Kathy was smiling as she dutifully went off to the bathroom to do as Emma had told her but she paused when she caught sight of herself in the mirror. She looked bad enough but she was convinced that behind her in the mirror she could see dark clouds gathering and those terrible splinters of fractured glass were falling like lightning.

"I can't hear the bath water running," came Emma's voice through the door.

Kathy had to smile and the dark clouds faded away again. "Bully."

"You need it. Just get a move on or Peter will be starting school before you've even got downstairs."

At the very end of October, much to Kathy's relief, Piers managed to snatch a long weekend away from his work and time with Chantal but the others knew this wasn't a happy visit as he had no sooner been greeted by his cat and given a mug of coffee by Kathy than he sat at the breakfast table with the other two and announced flatly: "I need to talk to you both about the trio."

Kathy didn't know what to say. She couldn't judge his mood from the tone of his voice but she knew instinctively that she wasn't going to let this one get away. "Just the trio?" she checked before her imagination ran away with her.

As always, he knew what she wasn't saying. "Just the trio. Nothing else will change between us. I hope."

Jean-Guy didn't like the sound of that. "What about the trio? Do you want to leave it?"

Piers put down his coffee mug with the drink untouched. "Not permanently. But I think it may be a good idea if you start considering a reserve pianist if you're planning on booking any more work for it in the near future."

The other two thought about that for a while and Kathy's first emotion was a thankfulness that Piers seemed to be being sensible about things again and wasn't going to run himself into the ground doing two jobs while looking after Chantal at the same time.

Before she could speak, Jean-Guy said quietly, "We don't need a trio. Kathy and I have plenty of work and I would rather have no trio at all than one without you in it."

"I agree," Kathy said, thankful Jean-Guy had said so well what she had been thinking. "I mean the Snape concert was fun but it's not something you'd ever consider doing as a full-time job anyway. And I'm quite sure you don't want to stop flying."

"It has been a good trio," Jean-Guy continued softly, "but I don't want it to be me and Kathy and some pianist or another Jane has managed to book for us."

Piers was silent for quite some time. "Do you know," he said almost sadly, "I think that's the best compliment I've ever been paid. So you two really don't mind? After you got that piano shipped in as well?"

"You're not giving up completely are you?" Kathy checked. "It'll still be nice for the three of us to play together when we have the time. And you spent so long working at it earlier this year it would be a shame just to let it all go again."

"I don't mind a bit of casual playing," he agreed. "But I right now I can't promise anything more than that."

"Please don't worry about the trio," Kathy reassured him. "Jean-Guy has a horrendous workload between now and Christmas and mine isn't much better." She looked at the exhausted man at the table. "Should we ask Jane to cancel our little tour in the spring?" she asked gently. "It'll be a shame to lose that but, honestly, your health is way more important than any concert bookings. You've got quite a few bookings with Jean-Guy to get through after our tour as well, but if you pull out now it'll give Jane time to get a sub in until you're available again."

"No," he said, barely above a hoarse whisper. "Let them stand."

It was at that point both Kathy and Jean-Guy knew Chantal had gone into the final stages of her care.

Want to talk about it?" Kathy asked sympathetically.

"No. Thank you. But this will be my last trip to Suffolk for a while."

"How long?" Kathy asked softly and laid a gentle hand on his arm.

There was no emotion in his voice. "She may make Christmas. She's off all treatment now except pain relief."

Kathy leaned briefly against his arm and thought how odd he felt. Not as solid somehow and the sense of calm reassurance had gone. "You don't have to do this on your own," she reminded him. "Don't cut us out when you need us the most."

He didn't reply, just touched her hand with his own for a second. To her surprise his touch was unusually hot; she looked up and realised his lashes were wet.

Petr Mihaly was appalled at the physical state of the pianist of the Dodman Trio who had avoided lunch by taking himself up to his room to rest but didn't eat more than half a dozen small mouthfuls of his supper. Not even tempted by the legendary bacon pudding.

"So," the Prof asked kindly as he watched the other man just push the food round his plate. "What pieces are you all working on for your tour in the spring?"

"Nothing new at the moment," Jean-Guy told him. "We have enough of a repertoire for that although it will mean playing the same pieces several times. But we are in four different countries so it will be different audiences."

"I'll have more time to learn new pieces in the new year," Piers said heavily.

The Professor's tone hardened. "And if modern medicine works its miracles and you still have Chantal in April? Will you be willing to leave her for a fortnight?"

Piers dropped his fork onto his plate. "Her current prognosis is less than two months. Back in May when they knew the treatment was failing they gave her six months to a year. But the tumours are spreading and she's said herself she's ready to go. She's made her Will, got her burial plot sorted and her funeral arranged."

"And what arrangements have you made?" the Prof asked. Piers just looked at him, genuinely puzzled. "Bereavement is one of the hardest things we ever have to face and this one is going to hit you very hard indeed. Please don't shut us out when you need us the most. We can't force you to let us help you but you know I don't go anywhere these days and I'd like your reassurance that you know you can come here any time it would help you. I will break my own rules and keep this house unlocked for you. I would have done the same for Kathy four years ago if I had known she needed it and you both know my door was open to Jean-Guy. I know you're more of the age of a brother to me but I see you three as the children I never managed to have and I see it as my duty to protect you. Can you understand?"

"Yes," he said and sounded a bit lost somehow." I wish I'd had a father like you when I needed one."

"I used to think that too," Kathy admitted. "I wish I'd told someone what was happening and run here sooner."

The Prof smiled at her. "But eventually you came here and I like to think Emma and I helped you." He looked at the uneaten food on Piers' plate and knew he had to speak out. "Starving yourself won't help you either," he said sternly. "Please try to eat just a little more."

"I'm fine," Piers said ungraciously and pushed his plate away. "Now if you'll excuse me, I'd just like a few minutes in your garden." He left the kitchen and Audrey went racing after him as she always did.

Kathy looked at the closed back door. "Funny, I remember going out into your garden when it all got to be too much."

"He's grieving," the Prof told her. "Even though she is still alive, he is in mourning for Chantal."

"He won't talk of it," Kathy admitted sadly. "I've tried to get him to open up and so has Jean-Guy, but it's as though he's put up a wall round himself and cut off all emotion."

"A large part of that is his training," the Prof advised her. "He is an airline captain and when he is flying he has to be in control the whole time. From a minor bit of turbulence to a hijacker holding a gun to his head, he has been trained never to lose control."

"True," she acknowledged. "We've never seen him 'at work' as it were. But he's negotiated to cut down on any long-haul charters and do more short-haul and regular JFK runs which means his bosses will love him as apparently nobody else wants to as it's no extra pay and plays merry hell with your body clock."

"Is there anywhere in the world he hasn't been?" Jean-Guy asked wistfully.

"Antarctica apparently. And a few war zones. Shall I take him a cup of tea or anything?"

"Truthfully I'd leave him for now," the Prof advised. "Sometimes we need time to sort out our thoughts."

"True," Kathy agreed. "Still, at least he's got Audrey to keep him company here."

"And you two must look after him when he hasn't got Audrey," the Prof told them. "He has such a strong control of his emotions it could be very damaging if he loses it."

"He'll survive," Jean-Guy offered thoughtfully. "But you are right. We none of us really know what we will do when we are pushed beyond our limits."

Kathy missed the nuance in his voice. It didn't occur to her then that maybe Jean-Guy had been pushed to his limits too and he hadn't been proud of the consequences. She didn't want to think of the circumstances under which she had been pushed as far as her mind and her body would go. "I'll take him some tea," she said and almost threw the drink together so she too could run out into the sanctuary of the garden. She found Piers sitting on the old stone bench near the back hedge and she sat silently next to him and passed across the mug.

"Thanks. You OK?" he asked and the warmth of his voice made her cry. "Hey, what's the matter?" he asked gently and it made her feel even worse as he was the one in mourning.

She sniffed rather inelegantly. "Sorry. They were getting a bit serious in there and I was starting to remember things I don't like to think about."

He put his arm across her shoulders and gave her a bit of a hug. "Sometimes we have to go to the dark places. Want to tell me about it? I don't mind."

"Drink your tea," she told him fondly. "You've got enough problems of your own."

He rested his cheek on top of her head and the simple gesture comforted her as she let her mind drift back to four years ago when, after he had finished with her, her ex had left her on the floor, naked and bleeding and had told her they were still getting married tomorrow. Then he had locked her in the flat and calmly gone out to work.

Numb with shock, Kathy had half-crawled into the bathroom and looked at herself in the mirror. All she had asked him was if she could spend the night before her wedding at her childhood home but he had told her she couldn't. She tried to plead with him saying it was traditional for a bride to do that, but he had hurled her against the wall like a rag doll, picked up the knife she had been using to cut up her breakfast fruit and had torn the nightdress off her. Winded but still struggling, she hadn't had the strength to fight him off and he had hurt her, inside and out. It was as if he had known that once she was out of his sight and his control she was going to run. Richard never hit her anywhere it would show but somehow Emma had known. She had told Kathy time and again to leave him and come and live with her, but Emma was still being Emma and seemed to have a different man in her bed most nights and Kathy didn't want to get in the way.

She had crawled into the shower and let the hot water pound on her face and body until she felt a little cleaner then she went to find some clothes to wear. Her body was too sore for her to bear clothes on it so she put on a loose dress and found her shabby espadrilles. She hauled herself into the living room and was startled by a large black bird suddenly landing on the balcony rail outside the window. She had never seen such a huge bird so close before and she was surprised it didn't frighten her as it was so big. The bird put its head on one side and looked at her quizzically as if wondering what she was up to on the other side of the glass. It made no attempt to fly away but watched as she made sure she had her passport and her diary in her bag.

She looked back at the bird. "He wanted to take my passport away," she explained to it as it perched there just watching her as if to make sure she was going to be alright. "But I said I'd left it in Wimbledon. I've hidden it from him for months. The other thing he doesn't know is Emma told me to get my keys copied and to keep the spares hidden from him as it was only a matter of time before he took my keys away and started locking me in. She told me to hide money from him too as he would be taking my cheque book away from me soon. Well, today he proved her right." Finding the presence of the bird somehow comforting, she walked up to the window but it still didn't fly away. High up in the sky beyond the bird on the balcony she noticed the morning Concorde flight which always left London that way heading west out towards the Atlantic. She had got quite used to seeing it most mornings since it had started its scheduled flights last year and there was something so beautiful and free about the black bird on her balcony rail and the white plane up in the sky.

Bird and aeroplane convinced her. She grabbed her handbag, her violin and her viola and literally ran from the block of flats to the railway station. She changed to the Tube when she got to Wembley and arrived at Maida Vale in the middle of the morning.

Emma Mihaly had only just got out of bed when the street door bell of her flat rang and she picked up the intercom. All she could hear was hysterical crying and she guessed who it was. A few moments later a violently sobbing Kathy arrived in her flat.

"I've left him!" Kathy almost screamed. "He's going to kill me this time."

Emma looked round at all the boxes in her flat as she was getting ready to move more into the centre of London and had just secured the lease on a flat in Earl's Court. But this was her oldest friend and Kath never got in states such as this. She picked up her car keys. "I'm taking you out to Dad's," was all she said.

Kathy hadn't realised she must have told her story out loud until the man sitting next to her on the bench softly kissed her cheek. "You are an incredible woman," he told her gently. "I wish I had half your courage."

She didn't speak, just quietly put her arm round his waist and the two sat in silence lost in their own thoughts and memories until the Prof came to fetch them in as it was far too cold to be sitting in the garden so late. He wasn't best pleased to see them looking so intimately cosy out there but he didn't say anything. Somehow he wasn't surprised when those two emotionally vulnerable people exchanged a soft kiss on the lips as they got up to come back into the house. Kathy tightened her arm round Piers' waist as he walked beside her and she was sure she felt some of the tension leave his body. Just outside the back door the two stopped and looked up at the stars and they both felt there was some kind of magic now in the love between them.

Wolfgang Amadeus Mozart – *Piano trio in Bb major, K 502*

Christmas was always a busy time for musicians and Kathy and Jean-Guy found themselves with so many bookings in London over the weeks of December, they didn't really have time to make sure their third was alright. Kathy met up with him briefly in the middle of the month when he dropped by the house to sort out his laundry but it was obvious he didn't want to talk to her. He started politely enough by telling her Sarah's due date was still December 28th but he couldn't attend the birth as he was rostered to work. Kathy wasn't sure she totally believed him but she could tell his rare temper was on a very short fuse. She got a rather curt admission that he was due to spend Christmas with Chantal's family and then he was back to work so they weren't to worry about him. He didn't like Christmas anyway as it was full of food he couldn't eat and why the hell should he celebrate the birth of a Saviour he didn't believe in? Kathy had never known him in such a mood but he looked tired and thin and she wasn't quite scared of him but she knew he was on the edge. He wouldn't let her get close to him physically and eventually his temper snapped and he told her, without sparing the expletives, to back off and leave him alone. It broke her heart but she couldn't get through to him and he left the house again not knowing she sat at the kitchen table after he had slammed the door behind himself and she had cried.

The Prof and Jean-Guy both reassured her that if Piers wouldn't let her help then there really was nothing else she could have done but she didn't feel any better when she and Jean-Guy arrived at the farmhouse late on Christmas Eve to find no signs of the Prof in the kitchen or sitting room so they guessed he was finishing off whatever work he had on deadline as it was Christmas and they thought nothing of it as they took their bags upstairs. Unusually there was no sign of Audrey downstairs but they found her sitting silently on Piers' bed, with her back to the east-facing window.

"At least she's quiet," Jean-Guy commented as he stood next to Kathy in the doorway to the back bedroom.

"She's gone," Kathy heard herself say very softly and she went into the room to sit next to the little cat who just continued looking west and made no attempt to climb on Kathy's lap for a cuddle.

Jean-Guy didn't understand what she meant but her tone of voice worried him. "Who has gone where?" he asked.

Kathy stayed on the bed where the man who believed in the old ways slept and she felt the spirits of the house. "Chantal. She's gone. Can't you feel it?"

Jean-Guy now knew what she meant but all he could feel was the howling draught that came in through the landing window which faced north and didn't fit very well. "Are you sure?" he checked. "I would hope Piers would ring us and tell us if that had happened. If we didn't reply on the London number he would ring here."

Kathy knew Jean-Guy was speaking sense. "True. Come on then, we'd better pop back down to the kitchen because I bet the Prof has emerged by now."

They went back to the kitchen leaving the little cat in Piers' room and they saw the sadness in the Prof's eyes.

"It's over isn't it?" Kathy hardly dared ask.

"Yes," he said quietly. "Piers rang earlier to say Chantal had, in his words, crossed the bridge this morning and he asked me to tell you when you arrived. I gave him our condolences, which seemed hopelessly inadequate and he's still with Chantal's brother as they're trying to get everything sorted before places close for Christmas."

Kathy didn't even try to pretend she wasn't crying. "Oh, how awful for him. On Christmas Eve too. Can I ring him back?" She let Jean-Guy take her into a lovely cuddle and knew both the men were upset too.

"He didn't give me the number," the Prof told her gently. "But I hope he will call us to let us know the date of the funeral, if nothing else."

"We're not going to lose him too, are we?"

"Kathy," the Prof tried to console her. "I think we have to be led by Piers on this one. I am sure he was being truthful about having to make all the arrangements, I am sure Chantal's brother will take care of him. And on an even more practical note, he is legally obliged to let you know if he is going to do anything that will affect your tenancy in his house."

For some reason Kathy felt oddly cheered. "Yes, I suppose he will. And he always was the sensible one. Isn't he?"

"Yes, he is," the Prof agreed and wished he could believe that too.

Kathy sniffed and wiped her nose on a ratty tissue she had found in her pocket. "I can write to him, can't I?" she almost pleaded.

"Of course you can," the Prof replied thinking that was a lovely idea. "If you look in the writing desk in the sitting room you should find some notelets you can use. Make sure you give him our condolences and love too."

"I will," Kathy promised and went to see what she could find to make what she had to say to the grieving man at least look nice even if the words didn't help.

Jean-Guy looked at the closed kitchen door. "Will she be alright too?" he asked quietly.

The Prof hadn't been expecting that. "Yes, I think so. We all only met Chantal once and I think we are all upset on his behalf rather than because we have lost a friend of our own. Why do you ask?"

Jean-Guy paused, then decided to admit to his fears. "Kathy and Piers are so close I find it hard to believe that they are simply the friends they claim to be. But I also don't think they are lovers. Is it possible to be so close to someone and not sleep with them?"

The Prof had long thought the same thing. "Yes, I think it is. She is close to Piers but not in the way she is close to you. Or to Emma. I don't think they are lovers either. He is a man who taps into things deeply spiritual and she seems to accept his faith and is becoming interested in it. I have done some reading on Celtic Paganism and in understanding his beliefs I can understand their relationship better. What is that phrase he uses? He walks the old ways?"

Jean-Guy felt oddly consoled by the older man's words. "Yes. And I think Kathy is starting to walk behind him. She was being very odd just now up in his room."

"And in what way is she being odd this time?"

"Audrey is sitting on the bed with her back to the sea. She didn't move, or meow or anything and for some reason that made Kathy decide that Chantal has died. As it turns out, she was right. How did she know?"

The Prof nodded sagely. "I can see that it would. Apparently the Celts believe that west is the direction of the dead so if Audrey was looking west then Piers would take it that someone has gone to join the dead."

The two men had the same thought but it was Jean-Guy who said it out loud. "But Audrey is Piers' cat. Why would she look west if..." he couldn't finish that line of thought. "No, I'm sure he is fine. Somebody would tell us something, wouldn't they?"

"How?" Petr Mihaly asked, not unthankful to have the excuse to express his own worst fears. "The main phone is unlisted and the two in the study don't even officially exist. We have no contact details for Chantal's brother and I have no doubt Piers hasn't given him our details either. It is as always, although I may be able to learn something unofficially through my contacts."

The two men watched as Audrey walked slowly into the kitchen and jumped onto the chair that Piers usually used but she still didn't speak, or purr.

The Professor gently rubbed the top of the cat's head. "There is nothing we can do except trust he will come back to us."

Kathy woke on Christmas morning and for a few moments had forgotten what day it was. She had never been at the farmhouse for Christmas before as she had always been with her family except for the two years her ex had insisted on taking her away and spoiling her with extravagances which she hadn't really wanted.

Over the years Petr Mihaly had come to understand the English concept of Christmas, mostly because of his daughter, but he didn't accept it as a religious festival and couldn't see the point of cooking an extravagant meal when it was just the two of them. But Father Christmas had diligently come to the farmhouse when Emma had been a child and father and daughter had exchanged gifts after a lunch that was usually just an English roast and more likely to be beef than chicken. For the first time in his life, Petr Mihaly got to grips with the idea of roasting a turkey for Christmas lunch but he had had to ask Kathy for advice and he had cheated and bought a pudding from the supermarket rather than attempt to make one.

Kathy wandered downstairs to find the Prof already in the kitchen with the turkey in its roasting tin and she could tell he was trying to calculate the cooking time.

"Four hours," he said to her vaguely. "I have never cooked a joint that needed so long to cook before. I hope that is right and we don't finish up with a tray of soot."

So the two recalculated the cooking time and Kathy had to agree with his maths, but she had never cooked a joint in an Aga so she didn't really have a clue either. "Oh well, if it smells as though it's cooked early we'll just have early lunch," she decided as she made herself some tea. "Don't forget the giblet gravy." It amused her to see the academically acclaimed Professor of Music look at her so helplessly. "Giblets? You make the gravy with them then feed them to the cats."

He handed her the bowl with the raw giblets in it. "Help?" he asked.

Somehow between the three of them they managed to cook a perfectly edible Christmas lunch and as they prepared to eat, the Prof raised his glass of red wine.

"Absent friends," he offered as the traditional toast.

"Absent friends," the other two agreed.

"Hope he's getting a decent Christmas dinner somewhere," Kathy added as she set to work on a rather daunting plateful of food. "And we so nearly got him to join us for Christmas. Don't you remember he corrected us and told us he doesn't celebrate Christmas and for him it's Yule? But funnily enough his Pagan Yule seemed to include Christmas lunch and giving presents."

Jean-Guy smiled as he resumed his own meal. "Somehow I don't think he would have done much for the season these last few years. I certainly never have before. The last twenty fifth of December I was in Prague was just an ordinary day for me. There were those who still worshipped but my family was never one of them. I blame my mother, the perfect Russian communist."

Kathy paused for moment to give her stomach a chance to get used to the idea. "So how did your perfect communist mother take to the idea that you wanted to defect?"

"My parents were the ones who told me I should go."

"Not your choice then?"

Jean-Guy looked across at the other man at the table. "Not entirely. Should I tell her?"

Professor Mihaly thought about that. "Yes, I think maybe you should. As much as you feel you can anyway. It's not an easy story to tell or to listen to."

"True," Jean-Guy agreed and took a few moments before he spoke again. "As I travelled so much with my cello, and have an uncle high-ranking in the Communist Party, I had been contacted by the Russian secret service to ask if I would work for them. I said no. I was a musician and that was all I wanted to be. They tried to persuade me. I still said no. So then they accused me of spying for the opposition. I pointed out that I couldn't as they never let me out without a chaperone. That was when they arrested me and flogged me then sent me home with a warning."

Kathy could see this was stirring up some very bad memories so she moved her chair closer to his and gave him a hug. "It's OK. You don't have to talk about all this now."

Petr Mihaly interrupted the story. "I have been a friend of Jean-Guy's father for a very long time. When I left the country with Emma as a baby, Jean-Guy would have been about three or four and his father, Karel, asked me if I would take him too. It was his mother who couldn't bear to part with her child so it was just Emma and me who left the country. But I arranged with Karel that if ever he wanted to get Jean-Guy out then he would hand in a note at the British Embassy in Prague. Of course, the British would read the note and so would any Czech infiltrators who had got in there so the note would ask me if I could send him a copy of the parts for Mozart's K502 trio in B flat as he was finding it impossible to get the music in Czechoslovakia. A perfectly innocent note and not the first he had sent as over the years he and I had made a smokescreen as he had asked me if I could send others but the Mozart was the one that told me Jean-Guy wanted to run. We used the diplomatic bag via the British Embassy as we couldn't be sure the normal postal service would get through."

"Brilliant," Kathy approved and realised that was everything she was going to learn today even though she was sure that wasn't all Jean-Guy wanted and needed to tell her. She resumed her lunch. "Remind me if we're doing this again next year to get some crackers."

The Prof looked sharply at the other man at the table but he too had gone back to his meal and the bad memories had obviously gone away again. "I don't understand. Emma became so English she was the same. Always we had to have crackers. But, honestly, what is the point of them?"

"Honestly?" Kathy laughed. "None. But the fact there isn't a point surely is the whole point?"

"Too intellectual for me," the Prof smiled, glad to see her mood had lifted too. "Please pass me some more of your delicious giblet gravy before you feed it to the cats."

There were a lot of cats who all wanted some of this Christmas treat and in the end Kathy had to split what there was between the bowls and let them argue over it but by the time she was picking up the bowls to wash them that evening, they had all been licked clean and there were a lot of happy cats in the house.

She looked at the little tortoiseshell who had been hopefully sniffing round the empty bowls. "Sorry, Audrey. All gone. I hope you got some. You're such a little cat I can imagine the others pushed you out of the way." Feeling oddly foolish for doing so, Kathy looked round the kitchen to make sure there weren't going to be any feline witnesses and she sneaked Audrey a piece of turkey skin. "There. Just don't tell the others or they'll all want some too." Audrey bolted down the skin then started weaving round Kathy's legs but she didn't speak. "What's up, puss?" Kathy asked but still this chattiest of cats remained mute so she sat on the floor, picked the cat up and put her on her lap. "Just meow at me, Audrey. Tell me everything's going to be OK?"

"Who on earth are you talking to?" came Jean-Guy's voice from the doorway.

"Audrey. I thought maybe she didn't get any giblets as she's so little so I've just fed her some turkey skin. But she's still not talking to me."

"Maybe she has a sore throat?" was the sensible suggestion. "Have you looked?"

So Kathy looked and Jean-Guy admired the way she just hooked open a cat's mouth and peered into it, seemingly oblivious to all those very sharp teeth. "Looks OK. But you may be right. I'll keep an eye on her but I'd rather not have to take her to the vet as an emergency over Christmas. Please tell me you haven't come out here looking for food? I don't think I'll eat another crumb for a week."

Jean-Guy laughed. "Oh, I am sure you will be eating lots of crumbs by breakfast time. No, I have just come to get a cup of tea. One for you too?"

Kathy was still trying to persuade Audrey to talk to her. "No, I'm fine, thanks."

He knew her well enough to know when she was hiding the truth from him. "Did you write your letter?"

"Yes. I'll walk into the village tomorrow to post it. You can come too if you like?"

Jean-Guy was glad to hear the smile in her voice as she knew what he was going to say. "Not at this time of year. And I'm sure he will be grateful that you took the trouble to write."

Kathy looked at the silent cat in her arms. "I hope so."

On Boxing Day, Kathy walked into the village to post her letter and the Prof asked her to bring back a pint of milk. The coast path was in its winter sleep as was most of the village but she knew the shop would be open for a few hours in the middle of the day for the locals like her who had run out of essentials or who just needed an excuse to get out for a while. She hadn't seen Sarah in the shop for a few weeks and wasn't surprised it was Sarah's mother who was again behind the counter and looking through a magazine as the shop was empty of customers.

She looked up on hearing the ping of the bell above the door. "Hullo, love. Merry Christmas. Did you have a nice day yesterday?"

"Merry Christmas," Kathy responded automatically as she put a pint of milk on the counter. "Oh, you know, quiet. Yours?"

"Much the same."

There was a heavy pause between them and Kathy said it first. "Did he ring you?"

"Yes he did. Christmas Eve about lunchtime. Spoke with Sarah for quite a while. All she could tell us was that, yes, he was upset but it wasn't unexpected and he was still due to go back to work in the next few days. I think Sarah's worried about him but he didn't leave her a contact number for where he's staying. She's been ringing his London number in case she can catch him between flights."

"Yes, I'd thought of doing the same thing. No signs of the babies coming yet?"

"They're taking her into hospital soon if she doesn't show any signs of labour. But she's being stubborn about it all and I think she's going to hang on until Alison gets back. Between you and me I think she was hoping Piers would be with her but what with his bereavement and his work I can't see that happening."

"Alison not with you?" Kathy asked, surprised that Sarah's lover hadn't been with the family.

"No, she went back to her folks in Cambridge, just for the holidays."

"With Sarah due while she's away?"

"Yes, I was a bit surprised too but Sarah has been very bad tempered recently. I suppose she's worried about having triplets and she, well there's no other word for it, she shouted at Alison and told her that her family is in Cambridge and if she can't have the babies' father with her then she'll go without."

"Wow. Harsh considering Alison's been with her for so long."

"Yes I thought so too. But Alison is only away until the New Year so with any luck she'll get back before they take Sarah in. Just the milk?"

Kathy impetuously added a bar of fruit and nut. "That's it for today. I'll probably be back again tomorrow. Gives me the excuse to go for a walk."

"True. I wish that husband of hers could be with her."

"He's probably assuming she's got Alison with her. And I understand Alison has made it quite clear that he's not wanted."

Sarah's mother snorted. "Hm. Maybe by her. But he's Sarah's husband and the father of her children. So I don't think it's up to Alison to tell him to stay away, do you?"

Kathy held up her hands. "I'm staying well out of that one."

"Very sensible," the prospective grandmother agreed. "Well, if Sarah does manage to get hold of him I'll ring you at the farmhouse and let you know."

"Thank you. And I'll do the same for you," Kathy promised and made her escape feeling oddly as though she had got away lightly with something.

Nobody felt like sitting up to see in 1982 so they hadn't bothered and the second day of the year dawned bitterly cold. Kathy had slept badly and woken late after a night disturbed by Jean-Guy and one of his more violent nightmares. He was gone from the bed when she woke but she knew he seldom remembered those dreams that made him thrash about and whimper in the darkness of the night.

She looked towards the door as she heard someone coming up the stairs and had a flash of hope that it was Piers, even though she knew he was working over the new year.

Jean-Guy poked his head round the door, saw Kathy was awake and came into the room with a mug of tea for her.

Kathy sat up and took the mug from him as he sat on the bed and smiled at her. "I'm sorry, I was dreaming again last night, wasn't I?"

She took some welcome sips of tea. "Yes, I'm afraid you were. Do you ever think it would help you to remember them?"

He wouldn't look at her. "I remember them when I am awake. Or rather I see them all over again. Most of them. But I think perhaps when I sleep my memory goes to the parts I won't let myself remember."

Kathy hated to see her lovely Moly so tortured by the memories he couldn't share. "Do you want to tell me what you remember when you're awake?"

"No," he said shortly, "I don't. I wish I could. Perhaps one day." He paused and took her hand that wasn't holding the mug. "Kathy, are you quite well?"

The question surprised her. "Well, yes, why wouldn't I be?"

His thumb gently rubbed her hand. "You have not been yourself. I think maybe since Piers quarrelled with you when you last saw him."

"It wasn't a quarrel..." she began but Jean-Guy carried on as though she hadn't spoken.

"He was rude and angry to you from what you have said and it upset you."

"Well, yes..."

"Is it more than that with you?"

"No, I don't think so. Yes, he upset me and I maybe shouldn't have yelled back at him like I did but it's so frustrating the way he pushes us away. It's just like Chantal said he did to her with his migraines all those years ago. It's as though he doesn't trust us to help him and that's the worst thing of all."

Jean-Guy was momentarily distracted. "Yes, it is like the old trick of do you trust someone behind you to catch you when you let yourself fall. It is as though he feels we will step away." He paused. "Is that how you feel too? That if you fall I will step away and not catch you?"

"What? No, not at all. I trust you totally. Like I'd always catch you. I'm half your size so I'd probably drop you after all but I'd have a darned good go. What's all this about?"

Jean-Guy looked slightly embarrassed. "So if you found out, for instance, you were expecting our child, you would trust me not to run away from you and leave you?"

Kathy put her mug of tea on the bedside table as she realised the torments he had gone through to dare to ask her that question. "Of course I would, you silly goose. Is that what you've been thinking? I'm sorry. But I'm not expecting. Trust me, I'd know if I was and I'd tell you as soon as I suspected anything so we could get madly excited together. But it's not our time yet."

"I think perhaps it is better that it is not," he said softly and gave her a lovely kiss. "We have so many new things to get used to in our lives perhaps a child wouldn't be the best thing for us right now."

She hated to see the hope die in his eyes. "We will. But I think you're right about maybe not just yet."

"I know you agreed I could stop, but do you want me to go back to Sarah's shop for some more supplies as Piers calls them?"

"No," Kathy said before she thought about it. "We're in a steady relationship, if it happens we'll work our way round it and it's not like I'm going to pop out a baby without warning, is it? We'll have a good few months to get ready."

"True. So I don't need to tell the Prof he's going to be a grandfather again?"

The idea made Kathy smile. "Not yet." She gulped down her tea. "Right, it's new year and traditionally this is when I start my spring-cleaning."

"Ah," Jean-Guy remembered. "Like Mole?"

"Just like Moly. You want to join in?"

"With the cleaning?" he asked with an unmistakeable gleam in his eye.

Kathy got the message and had to laugh. She pulled back the covers on his side of the bed. "Maybe after breakfast, huh?"

The physical labour of the cleaning helped Kathy's general sense of unease that had been nagging at her for days. She started in the back scullery and had moved through the laundry room into the kitchen by the end of the day. Petr Mihaly had had no idea his house could look so spotless, but he couldn't persuade Kathy to slow down as her labours were borderline desperate by evening. He left her to it and went to bed early just before ten o'clock leaving her washing the kitchen floor while Jean-Guy was in the sitting room listening to a late night programme on the radio.

Kathy was so physically drained she wanted to let the mop fall to the floor. She wanted to sit under the newly-scrubbed table and weep. She wanted the back door to open and Piers to come back to them. She had finished the floor and knew she had to stop now she had physically and emotionally exhausted herself. So she paused, leaning on the mop, and watched as Audrey came out and sniffed at the food bowls, ate a couple of mouthfuls and then was sick in front of the Aga all over the beautifully clean floor.

Kathy was glad of the distraction and moved across with a piece of kitchen paper to clean up the mess. "Too much turkey skin," she told the cat severely. "I'm not giving you any more."

Audrey dashed under the table and was sick again.

"Oh! You annoying cat!" Kathy exclaimed, feeling disproportionately cross, and got to work cleaning up the stinking piles.

"Problems?" Jean-Guy asked as he had heard a raised voice and wondered what was going on. He had thought Kathy was mad enough to be doing housework at such an hour but the physical exercise had seemed to help her so he had let her get on with it.

"That sodding Audrey has just hurled all over my nice clean floor."

"Oh. Maybe she has eaten something bad. Can I help?"

"No, I'm fine, thanks, I'm used to cat sick."

"Sooner you than me."

Kathy knelt down and put her head under the table where Audrey was sitting next to her latest offering. "Well, cat? What have you got to say for yourself?"

Audrey opened her mouth but no sound came out.

"Can cats get laryngitis?" Kathy asked out loud but then the little tortoiseshell cat screamed. It was the first sound she had made for over a week and the people in the house had never heard anything like it.

The Prof heard the noise all the way upstairs and he came running down to the kitchen thinking someone was in pain. "What is that noise?" he asked anxiously, relieved to see the other two didn't appear to be hurt.

Kathy had backed out from under the table. "That's Audrey. Right, I can't take any more of this. I'm getting in touch with him if I have to get the bloody airline to page him, and telling him to come and sort out his cat. Or at least speak to her."

Audrey stopped as suddenly as she had started and Kathy had the oddest sensation that the silence was the mirror of her imagination that had fractured into a thousand prisms covered in her blood as she tried to catch them. She looked at the two men who seemed as affected by it as she was. There was something terrible about that silence after the cat's lament and they all physically jumped when the phone rang.

Jean-Guy was the nearest and he picked up the receiver. "Hullo?" he asked cautiously as though afraid of what he might hear. "Oh, yes, she's here." He held out the receiver to Kathy. "It's Sarah for you."

Kathy hadn't been expecting that at all. "At this hour?" she asked softly as she took the receiver. She wondered if Sarah had heard from Piers and wasn't ready for the breathless voice on the phone.

"Kathy, I'm sorry to ask and please feel free to say no, but is there any chance you could drive me to the hospital please? I have to go to Ipswich as it's triplets. My dad's still not sobered up after yesterday and Alison's mum said she's already left so she'll be driving back from Cambridge."

"Oh, yes, of course. Be right with you. Ten minutes?"

Sarah gave a kind of strangled gasp. "Thank you. I tried ringing for an ambulance but they said they'll be at least an hour just getting here."

"I'll be with you in eight." Kathy banged the phone down and grabbed the keys for the Land Rover off the hook by the back door. "Sounds like the triplets are on the way at last. About time too, they were going to induce her next week."

"Oh hell," Jean-Guy offered. "Want me to come with you?"

Kathy gave him a short kiss of gratitude. "I'm sure I'll be fine. No idea when I'll be back but it may be a good idea to see if you can get a phone number for a

Pascal Montgomery in SW17 just in case we can get hold of Piers to tell him."

The marsh road from the farmhouse to the village was deserted and it was just over six minutes before Kathy and the Land Rover arrived at the house next to the shop. She guessed someone had been watching from the front room window as she had barely stopped when the front door opened and Sarah walked out quite calmly, carrying a small holdall which she threw onto the back seat then got in the front next to Kathy.

"I'm so grateful," she began.

"That's fine. Glad to be able to help." Kathy looked at her passenger. "Um, any chance you can get the seat belt round you?"

"No chance," Sarah smiled. "I'll hang on tight. Ow!"

Kathy had never seen a woman in labour before and it scared her. "Right, let's be off. I can stay with you as long as you want."

"Thank you. I'm sure Alison's on her way and as soon as she gets home my mum will tell her what's happened and she'll come to the hospital. I've got her down as my birthing partner."

Kathy set off for the A12 wishing the old Land Rover had the speed of an Aston Martin but guessing it wouldn't be quite such a disaster if Sarah gave birth all over the seats. "I thought you said you wanted that to be Piers' job" she said lightly, "Or did he chicken out?"

"I did, but then he told me he was working over my due date. Which was strange as he'd originally said he would. But Alison has been the one to go with me to all my appointments when I didn't go on my own. Not on purpose, it's just the way it worked out with Piers being away so much. I really wanted him to be with me but Alison said that he couldn't as he wouldn't be bringing the children up. And I think she must have told him that too as he changed his mind so suddenly. So one appointment when Alison wasn't with me I asked to have Piers put down as primary birthing partner. I hoped the babies would come while she was away and that's why I made her go to her family for Christmas. I never told her."

Those last four words bothered Kathy more than she would admit. They sounded like the kind of thing she would have said about her relationship with Richard. The necessary deception. Hiding her passport, her keys and some money so she could run away. She was going to say something but guessed it wasn't the conversation you wanted to have with a woman who was clearly very close to giving birth to triplets.

"Got any names in mind?" she asked instead.

"Yes," Sarah told her. "Me and Piers got very silly over the whole idea. I think it must have been about the last time we managed to have sex without the babies getting in the way. It was so lovely. We were just lying in my bed and saying names out loud as we thought of them and the other one would say it was a terrible idea."

Kathy wasn't expecting Sarah to be so candid with the details of her private life, and she wondered if she and Jean-Guy would ever cuddle up in bed and talk about what to name their children. "So you never came to any decisions?"

"Eventually. We picked three girls' names and three boys' names so we're covered whatever we get. We settled on Melanie Joan, Catherine Ivy and Violet May for girls or Andrew John, James Ivor and Christopher Sean for boys."

"Nothing unspellable in Gaelic then?"

Sarah smiled more enigmatically than Kathy had ever thought possible. "Not this time. Ow! Sorry, do you mind if I swear?"

"Swear your head off if it helps," Kathy told her as they finally made it onto the A12 and she just floored the accelerator thinking she would deal with any speeding fines later.

So Sarah swore all the way to the hospital and Kathy never knew the fat, frumpy shop girl was capable of such language. She would have been hard put to string some of those lines of expletives together herself.

Not knowing where to go, she headed towards Casualty when they got to the hospital and she guessed Sarah's mother had had the sense to ring the hospital and tell them her daughter was on her way as the Land Rover was met by two midwives with a wheelchair for the expectant mother of triplets. As it was on her notes that she may be bringing a female birthing partner, the midwives' mistake was understandable and Kathy found herself where she didn't really want to be, in the delivery room while Sarah gave up the non-stop swearing for a lot of panting and screaming, with just the occasional swear word mixed in.

Kathy felt so sorry for Sarah but thought she was being a bit of an idiot in refusing all pain relief as she finally gave birth to non-identical girl triplets in the small hours of the third of January. Melanie Joan arrived first at about a quarter past one, Catherine Ivy rushed out straight after her but Violet May took twenty minutes to think about it and then decided to join the party and landed yelling and screaming to join her sisters.

"Well done," Kathy said to the sweating and exhausted Sarah and held her hand for a few moments as the midwives got the babies sorted out then passed them across to their mother.

"Thank you," Sarah said to the woman sitting next to her then she looked at the bundles she had been given. "Which one's which?"

The midwife standing next to the bed smiled and admired the courage of the mother who had birthed triplets naturally with no pain relief. "Melanie in the blue, Catherine in the yellow and Violet in the pink. You have got three lovely babies. Congratulations, Sarah. We'll get you some tea and toast then you can pop along and have a bath. Tea and toast for you too?" she asked the birthing partner.

"Um, just a cup of tea would be lovely, thank you. Then I suppose I'd better start phoning people."

Sarah tucked her legs up and arranged the triplets in a row on her thighs. "I wish he was here," she said softly.

"I know," Kathy sympathised. "We all miss him too. Jean-Guy's going to see if he can find Chantal's brother through Directory Enquiries, but other than that we're going to have to see if we can track him down through the airline as it's more likely the silly sod's out in New York as he's supposed to be working over the New Year."

To Kathy's alarm, Sarah started to cry. "No, he's not. He's following her across the bridge. His journey is ending just as his daughters are starting on theirs."

Kathy was determined she wasn't going to let Sarah spook her like that. "No, you're just being silly," she said sternly. "You're over-wrought, emotional and, frankly probably totally knackered. He's with Chantal's family or his airline one and I'm sure he's quite safe. Come to think of it, I'm sure he was due to fly back from

New York on the second so he may even be at home in Earl's Court so he can get a few hours' sleep and he'll be grumpy that Jean-Guy woke him up, then he'll hear your news and get madly excited and drive all the way out here at three o'clock in the morning. Sarah, stop it. You're crying all over your babies." She shoved a tissue into Sarah's hand and to her relief the crying stopped just as the midwife came back with mugs of tea and the toast.

They checked Sarah's temperature and her blood pressure then went into a bit of a huddle.

"How are you feeling?" the senior midwife asked.

Sarah sniffed and blew her nose again. "I'm fine. Sorry."

"Oh, don't apologise," came the professional consolation. "I've seen many in a worse state than you and they only had one baby to cry about." She ruthlessly plucked Violet out of the line-up and passed her across to Kathy, adjusting the baby in her arms to make her more comfortable. "Sarah, have your tea and toast and then we'll pop you along to have a bath and get you settled on a ward for what's left of the night."

With only two babies on her lap, Sarah managed to have her tea and toast and Kathy, terrified she would somehow hurt the tiny infant in her arms, drank one of the worst cups of tea she had ever had.

"Right," the midwife instructed. "Sarah, bath time and, um, Alison isn't it? I suggest you go and phone a couple of all the people you've got to phone by which time we'll have Sarah on the ward then you can say goodnight to her and get off home. Well done to you too, by the way. Not the easiest thing in the world to sit with someone having triplets."

"I didn't mind," Kathy replied and didn't correct the name. "I just wish the father could have been here instead."

The midwife flicked back through the notes and saw there was indeed a father listed. She knew better than to speculate. "Maybe," she offered lightly. "Sadly we don't tend to find attending a birth acts as any kind of a contraceptive where the men are concerned. Didn't he want to come?"

"He works away from home a lot," Kathy said quickly. "He would have been in New York yesterday and he's on my list of people to ring."

"Good. Phone box just down the hall, hope you've got the right change. And not sure you can ring New York from it."

Kathy knew when she had been dismissed and went off to the phone booth where she dutifully rang Sarah's mother first and then she spoke to Jean-Guy who was still up even though it was getting on for three o'clock in the morning as it hadn't occurred to him that Kathy would stay for the birth and he had been expecting her home hours ago. On the off-chance she rang the number in Earl's Court but nobody answered.

She said a very quiet goodbye to Sarah who was barely awake in the maternity ward then walked swiftly out to the car park where the faithful Land Rover was waiting for her. "Well," she said to the car as there was nobody around. "I didn't expect the year to start quite like that."

The car started first time and Kathy set off home finding it very strange to be out and about in the small hours of the morning when there was no other traffic on the A12. She got back to the farmhouse and had only seen one other car travelling on the roads. She wasn't surprised that Jean-Guy was still sitting up and waiting for her, fighting sleep as he sat on the sofa with Audrey curled round on his lap.

"Well, don't you two look cosy," Kathy said softly. "Come on, bed. I'm worn out and I wasn't even the one having the babies."

Jean-Guy got stiffly to his feet and gently put Audrey down on the sofa. He gave Kathy a cuddle and a kiss, thankful for her safe return. "How are mother and children?"

"Fast asleep by the time I left. Anything to report here?"

"No, sorry. I rang Earl's Court as I'm sure he should have flown in yesterday but no reply. I tried Directory Enquiries for you but they said there is nobody with the name of Montgomery listed in SW17. So either he doesn't live there or his number isn't listed."

Kathy remembered what Sarah had said and suddenly shivered. There was no way she was going to let that thought into her mind. "Well, I guess all we can do is keep trying Earl's Court. Or do as we said we would and get in touch with the airline. They must know where he is. Maybe we misremembered and he's not back until later today. Or I suppose his flight could have been delayed or something."

"Maybe that's it," he had to agree but could tell from her face she didn't believe it either.

Kathy looked over her shoulder as the two left the sitting room to go upstairs to bed but Audrey was still lying on the sofa, apparently staring into the dying embers of the fire. For the first time since she had been there, she didn't spend the night in Piers' room. She was still lying on the sofa in the morning. She hadn't moved.

Nobody was expecting Alison to call at the farmhouse in the early afternoon of the next day. She had a cake tin in her hands and the broadest smile on her face anyone had ever seen. As she hadn't been to the house before, she had gone to the front door and rung the bell but she followed the Prof into the sitting room where the other two had been practising their music and, to the surprise of the men, walked up to Kathy and gave her a hug and a kiss on the cheek.

"Thank you," she said softly. "I went up to see Sarah this morning and she told me how brilliant you were yesterday. Wish I'd got there in time but my stupid van broke down just north of Stowmarket and I had to wait for the AA to come and pick me up. Had to walk miles in the dark to find a phone too. Anyway, mother and babies are all doing incredibly well and the doctors said Sarah was very brave to go through a natural birth with no pain relief."

There was one question she didn't ask so Kathy asked it for her. "Any news on the father?"

"No. Sorry," was the short reply. "Sarah said he would have been flying yesterday and I tried his London number this morning but he wasn't answering."

The others were silently astonished that she would ever have done such a thing.

Alison sighed and handed Kathy the cake tin. "She's got this mad idea stuck in her head that he's in some kind of trouble so I had to promise her that I'd keep ringing his London number until he replies. I mean, she was in such a state I began to think I'd do better to ring round all the London hospitals to see if anyone of that name has been admitted but there are a heck of a lot of hospitals in London."

Such a thought hadn't occurred to Kathy. "I tried Earl's Court too and didn't get a reply so we're thinking maybe he's on a delayed turnaround and if he brings the morning flight in he won't land at Heathrow until about five this evening. Even later if he's bringing in the afternoon flight."

"Good point," Alison agreed. "Can I leave you to keep ringing as you'll have a better idea of the timings? I just knocked together a simple sponge to say thank you for yesterday. You will come and visit Sarah and the babies when she's home, won't you?"

"Yes, of course," Kathy replied, pleased to have been asked. "I can't wait to see the babies again."

Alison smiled her thanks and turned to go, but then noticed something odd. "Is that cat alright?"

The others instinctively looked at Audrey who had at least got off the sofa but was now stretched out on the hearthrug still looking into the flames of the fire.

"That's Piers' cat," Kathy offered by way of explanation. "She ate too much turkey and made herself sick."

"I'd take her to the vet if I were you," was the advice. "Anyway, must be off. Let me know when you get through to him so I can tell Sarah."

There was still no answer from Earl's Court by ten o'clock in the evening so the residents of the farmhouse had to assume that Piers had brought Concorde back and then gone straight out to Chantal's family. They all felt a bit lost and downhearted somehow but gathered at the kitchen table for some bedtime cocoa. Nobody had said anything but the Prof suddenly pointed out quite logically that it would have been unlikely they could have arranged a funeral for those few days between Christmas and New Year so the final arrangements were probably still being made.

Faced with such common sense, Kathy accepted that maybe she was getting over-anxious. "Yes, I'm sure you're right. But if Audrey doesn't eat anything before tomorrow then she's off to the vet whether she likes it or not."

"Good for you," the Prof approved. "And here is Audrey now."

The little tortoiseshell cat walked slowly across to the food bowls and gave each of them a good sniff, drank some water and had a couple of mouthfuls of food from one of the bowls.

"There you are," Jean-Guy consoled. "Audrey is eating."

Kathy found a smile from somewhere. "She even ate the turkey flavour. You'd think she'd have learned her lesson."

The three heard a phone ringing in the house but it wasn't the line in the hall and the kitchen. Kathy and Jean-Guy had never seen the Professor move as fast as he did to go and answer the phone in his study.

"They never call that line," Kathy said. "Wonder what it's all about?"

"I expect they are hoping he may take another house guest," Jean-Guy tried, but each knew the other was thinking that the people the Professor still worked for also kept up to date on the man they were still trying to recruit.

Petr Mihaly didn't want to go back into that kitchen when his phone call ended. He knew the other two would know where the call had come from, and he went slowly back to join them then sat heavily at the table. "I have news. I don't need to tell you who has called with it. I am not allowed to tell you much, just that he was admitted to Hillingdon Hospital after an accident at work on the second of January. The hospital won't give us any information as we are not family."

"Can we tell Sarah?" Kathy asked as her mind whirled.

"No."

"But..."

"Kathy, I have passed on all I am allowed to tell you at this stage. There is no official next of kin on any of his paperwork so Sarah has no official right to be told anything."

"Right, well, I'm going to get devious. I'm so worried about him I did what Alison suggested and started ringing hospitals, OK?"

The Prof admired the thought behind that. "And eventually as you rang the London hospitals, you came to Hillingdon on your list. Very well. But you may only tell Sarah what the hospital tell you. If they won't even tell you he is there, then you can tell her nothing. Understood?"

Kathy nodded silently, then got the number she needed from Directory Enquiries and rang Hillingdon Hospital. Her call was put through and a very pleasant lady asked if she was family. So she had to say she was just a friend. The lady was very sorry but although she could confirm a patient of that name had been admitted, she couldn't give any details. She took Kathy's name and number and said she would pass on the information that she had been in contact. Armed with at least that much, she rang Sarah's number and was glad in a way it was Alison who answered the phone.

"He's in Hillingdon Hospital," she reported. "But they can't tell us anything as we're not family."

Alison tutted. "And I know Sarah told me that the last time she asked he hadn't got round to updating his records at work so the odds are we won't learn anything either. Oh well, thanks for that. I'll get her to ring them in the morning and tell them she's his wife and see what they say. I mean, they can always ask him if he's got a wife, can't they? I presume he can still talk."

Kathy began to wish she had told an out-and-out lie and said she was his sister. "True. OK, let me know?"

"Of course."

Kathy hung up the phone. "Well, as you've gathered, they told me almost less than nothing. But at least we know where he is." She noticed something horribly familiar by the cat bowls. "Is that what I think it is?"

"Yes," Jean-Guy had to admit. "Audrey just threw up the little she had eaten."

"That's it. Tomorrow she goes to the vet. I can't go on like this."

The vet confirmed there was nothing physically wrong with the little tortoiseshell cat so far as he could tell but recommended putting her on a light diet for a few days and making sure she drank sufficient water. He sold Kathy some vitamin pills to help the cat with her nutritional needs and took some samples for testing just in case but he reassured her that he saw a lot of sick cats and dogs in the aftermath of Christmas and he was sure Audrey would be back to her usual self in a day or so.

Sarah rang the same day that Audrey had gone to the vet. She had rung Hillingdon but all they said was that there was nothing on the patient's records to say he had a wife and they weren't going to breach any codes of conduct by asking him. Too exhausted by new motherhood to argue as she would have done once, Sarah took consolation from the fact they hadn't actually told her he had died so she asked them to pass on the message that she had rung too, and there they had to leave it. Kathy was convinced the Prof knew more than he had told them and bravely went into his study to ask.

Petr Mihaly sighed and took off his reading glasses to see her better. His voice was heavy as he said to her, "If you believe in any kind of a God then speak of him in your prayers. If, like me, you have no God, then hold him in your heart and your mind. Has he ever talked to you of Samhain?"

"Yes," she said softly. "It sounded very poetic. He said there is a bridge and on the far side of the bridge is a veil. You have to be careful if you step onto the bridge at Samhain because the veil is very thin and you might not notice it so you'll step through it and join the dead." She looked into the Prof's eyes and saw the man she loved as a brother standing on that bridge. "No," she gasped. "What's happened to him? It can't have been a plane crash or it would have been on the News."

It was one of the hardest things the Prof had ever had to do in his life. "Kathy, I am so sorry. I know how much you love him but I am bound by laws that mean I can't tell you anything."

"But he's alive?"

"The last I heard, yes."

"And if, if…" she couldn't say the words.

"If the worst happens they have promised me I will be told."

"Thank you," Kathy whispered without knowing why. She walked back through the kitchen and into the cold garden without stopping to put on her coat and sat as she had done many times before on the old stone seat. The stone was cold through the fabric of her trousers but she barely noticed. She closed her eyes and caught an image of Piers lying very still in a bed with a blue blanket on it. He was pale and cold and there was a blue tinge to his lips which were lifted slightly as though he was smiling at something. But the oddest thing she noticed was that there was a large black cat curled up in the crook of his right arm with one paw extended across his chest. Kathy knew Jean-Guy and the Prof were in the house but somehow she had never felt more alone in her life. It was as though part of her soul was dying.

Francis Franceour – *Sonata for cello in E major*

January continued hard and cold with nothing more said about the one who was missing from their lives. In a way it was consoling to know what had happened to him, worrying that they had no further news and weren't going to get any, and infuriating that he hadn't updated his personnel records at work so at least someone would have known what was going on. Kathy went to visit Sarah and the triplets several times as it gave a focus to her walks and she had to admire the way the babies were blossoming during those short winter days. She noticed too that, at least during her visits, Alison didn't make any more snide remarks about the father.

The last day of the month was another bright, clear day and the anniversary wasn't lost on Kathy as she went downstairs for her breakfast leaving Jean-Guy fast asleep in their bed as she so often did.

"Emma's first anniversary today," Kathy remarked to the Prof as she made herself a cup of tea. "I may ring her later and ask her what extravagant gifts Derek has showered her with."

The father of last year's bride had to smile. "I think with all the money they are having to pour into that house there won't be any extravagances today."

"I think you're right," Kathy agreed. "Mind if I join you?"

"Not at all. Any plans for your anniversary day too?"

"Yes, I suppose it is. A whole year since Jean-Guy sneezed his way into my life. Been one of the strangest years I think I have ever known. Some of the highest highs and the lowest lows in my life. Speaking of which, how's Audrey today?"

"I am sure those vitamins are helping her. She has been in and eaten and wasn't sick afterwards."

"Good, progress at last. But it's odd the way she's not sleeping on Piers' bed these days."

"Maybe because he isn't there to warm it up for her."

"I think she probably warms it up for him. Don't suppose you've heard anything else? No, silly me. Shouldn't even ask."

"Correct. But I haven't anyway."

"Well, it's a cold old day again but I think I'll walk along to see the babies today. They seem to be asleep in the afternoon so I'll pop along later this morning. Want anything bringing back for lunch?"

"Not really unless you want to bring us back some cake? That is a very bad habit we are getting into."

Kathy smiled. "OK, just a very small cake then."

In the end, it was an odd sort of day. Kathy walked into the village to find the babies had kept their mother awake most of the night so Alison was looking after them for an hour or so while Sarah caught up on her sleep as best she could. The village lady hadn't made any cakes for sale in the shop as she was away on holiday so Kathy had to make do with a box of jam tarts and when she rang Somerset in the early afternoon she was told by the mother-in-law that Emma and Derek were out for the day to celebrate their anniversary.

Kathy stayed at the kitchen table after her conversation with Emma's mother-in-law and listlessly looked at the newspaper she had brought back from the shop that morning. It was only another couple of weeks and she and Jean-Guy were due to resume their working lives but somehow, even though she could hear the cellist was putting in some hard practice, she had no inclination to get her violin out of its case.

Jean-Guy had got hot and thirsty battling with the Francoeur with its tricky second movement, and he missed the accompanist to help keep him on track with it. He carefully put his cello on its side next to the piano and went out to the kitchen to get himself a drink of water and there Kathy was, still sitting where he had last seen her when they had finished lunch.

"Have you got stuck?" he asked as he filled a glass with water from the tap.

"Might just as well," she replied glumly. "Sarah was asleep, Emma's gone out, and, I never thought I'd say this, but I'm actually a bit bored."

Jean-Guy knew perfectly well that remark translated as she had been thinking about Piers again and didn't know what to do for the best. He sat at the table to keep her company for a while and for some reason he looked at the clock on the wall. It was barely three in the afternoon and already it was getting dark and gloomy and the east wind could be heard whipping through the rhododendrons all around the house.

"I hope we hear some news soon," he offered. "We really need to be working on our repertoire for our tour in April. If he isn't back with us soon then we will have to start cancelling and I don't want to do that."

"We wouldn't have a choice," Kathy said sadly.

Jean-Guy didn't like to say it but he had to be practical. "Only if we ask Jane if she can find us another pianist."

"But we can't," Kathy said, horrified. "We promised him."

"Yes we did. But we made that promise not knowing he was going to drop so completely out of our lives. The Prof said he had an accident at work. For all we know he may not be able to play a piano any more."

Kathy thought about that. "No, as a musician the Prof would have given us some kind of a clue somehow if that were the case. Don't know how, but he's not daft. He'd have found a way."

Jean-Guy liked her logic and could see her point. "Good. Then we must also assume that the fact he hasn't given us any messages to imply we have lost our pianist is also an indication that he will be back with us."

"In time for our tour?" Kathy asked, suddenly weary. "Because you're right. You and I have other engagements coming up and we're going to need the time to work as a trio, especially if we're going to run out some new pieces. Maybe I'll have just a gentle go at him at tea time. Appeal to the musician in him."

"I think he will see it coming."

"Yup," Kathy had to agree. "I think you're right."

A silence fell in the kitchen, suddenly broken by a loud yowl from the sitting room and the small tortoiseshell cat who only a minute ago had been motionless before the fire came pelting into the room and started circling the table.

Kathy realised she was starting to feel some hope inside after all the weeks of not knowing. "Reckon she knows something we don't?"

"She's a cat. But always when she does this it means Piers will be with us in a few minutes."

Kathy felt the hope and relief surge through her and she hoped Audrey's instincts weren't going to let her down this time. "She's a witch, especially where Piers is concerned."

They both watched, but neither dared say what they were thinking, as Audrey raced across the table, bounced off the dresser then hurled herself at the back door just as it opened letting in a blast of cold evening air.

The two at the table couldn't quite believe it when a man with raven-black hair, and a tatty waxed cotton coat that came nearly to his ankles came into the kitchen and dropped a canvas holdall on the floor before closing the door and slumping rather than sitting at the table while his cat clung to his front and purred as though she would never stop.

Kathy and Jean-Guy both thought he looked terrible. His face was hollowed and shadowed and his eyes were dull.

"Tea?" Kathy asked and didn't dare touch him as he looked as though he might break.

"Just a glass of water. Thanks."

"You look bloody crap," Jean-Guy told him bluntly. "But we have all missed you so much. The Prof said you had had an accident at work. Was it very bad?"

Piers didn't say anything but after a couple of mouthfuls of water he took out a packet of cigarettes and lit one. Something told the other two it would be better not to make any comments just yet. Kathy silently put a saucer in front of him and they waited patiently. Half a glass of water and several long drags on the cigarette and Piers finally told them. "As I told you, Chantal died on Christmas Eve. She died in my arms with her brother and her pastor with us and there was a bloody gospel choir singing *Silent Night* in the room next door. We had the chance to have the funeral on the thirty first of December and we took it but it did mean there wasn't time to let people know. But she'd said she didn't want any fuss so it was just family, few close friends, that kind of thing. So she'd gone, I had no reason not to work and took the afternoon Concorde flight out to New York on New Year's Day as I'd been rostered to do. Flew back the next day with a crew I'd never worked with before and made almost the worst landing, certainly the worst civilian one, I have ever done in my life." He stopped as though even that explanation had been too much effort and went back to his cigarette and water.

"When did you last eat?" Kathy asked feeling so sorry for him but not wanting to question him too much. She moved her chair next to his and gave him a very gentle hug, but he didn't feel right. There was no solidity to him now and she almost felt as though she was touching a ghost.

Piers shrugged and stubbed out the cigarette in the saucer. "Don't know. Maybe yesterday, maybe the day before. Can't tell the days apart any more. But I know it was this morning they gave me the medical review to see if I was fit for discharge. They said I could go provided I came out here." He paused. "You know I've been in hospital because you rang them. So did Sarah. But the bastards didn't tell me until yesterday. Christ, but I gave them a bollocking. Probably the main reason they decided to let me go. You must have thought I'd abandoned you all. And don't lie to me, Piglet. You would have been the most faithful of all of them but I bet even you were starting to crumble after all this time." He looked in the packet of cigarettes but decided against smoking another one. "I've now been signed off on sick leave with no chance of even being assessed for work for three months, maybe even longer depending on how the medical checks go." He took a bottle of tablets out of his coat pocket, put it on the table next to the cigarettes and continued quite emotionlessly. "I've lost five stone in weight which makes me clinically malnourished, borderline starvation complications and they've put me on antidepressants." He added a packet of tablets. "And sleeping pills." Two more packets were added. "These are to wake me up when the sleeping pills have knocked me out, and some industrial strength painkillers."

"Any more?" Jean-Guy asked and looked at what was starting to resemble a chemist's shop.

Kathy was silent, wondering why a man whose symptoms seemed to be those of starvation would want painkillers. Or antidepressants come to that, but then he was still newly bereaved so she hoped the pills would help. She supposed the sleeping pills were all part of getting over his loss and resting enough to put some weight back on. He hadn't been fat in the first place so she had no idea where five stone could possibly have gone from.

"These. Stomach acid neutraliser and some multivitamins. Piglet, you have that brain overload look on your face. I'm on the mend, really. May not look like it right now but a month ago I was a hell of a lot worse."

Kathy was consoled that although he may have stood on the bridge something had made him turn back and return to them rather than lift the veil and pass to the other side. But that still didn't explain the black cat. She picked up the first bottle and saw the seal was intact. "Have you taken any of these yet?"

"No. They told me I'm not allowed to drive while I'm mixing that cocktail and someone else has to sign off a record sheet of what I've taken."

The Professor came into the kitchen. "Good, you're here. I thought I heard you. What are those tablets they've given you? I will ring them to confirm you are here." He picked up the bottles and packets and put all but one in his pockets. He glanced quickly at the printed card Piers had put with the medications, then that went in his pocket too. "These you may take, they are just vitamins. The painkillers and antacids I will look after, tell me when you need them. These other poisons I will keep locked away and we will see if you still need them in a couple of days. And that includes the tobacco." The Professor snatched up cigarettes and matches and went to investigate the contents of the saucepan on the Aga. "There is a little of our soup left from lunch time, you can eat that now. Kathy, please go and make up the bed in Piers' room and make sure he has extra blankets against the cold. Jean-Guy I would like you to cut me a slice of bread please. Not too thick. I have seen the effects of starvation too often before."

"What are you talking about?" came the hostile demand from the man who defensively pulled the cuffs of his sweater down to hide how thin his hands had become.

"You. I can tell from your eyes and your skin just how bad it is and now you are trying to hide it under loose clothes. It is a miracle you haven't lost your wedding ring it is so loose on your finger. I told you this bereavement would hit you hard but you didn't listen to me, didn't do as you were advised and could barely bring yourself to tell us when she passed away. I assume you've had the letter I suggested to Sarah that she wrote to you once we finally found out where you were?"

"Yes." Piers just pushed the spoon round in the soup and made no attempt to eat it. "Melanie, Catherine and Violet, I believe." He let go of the spoon with a bit of a clatter. "You don't understand," he suddenly snapped. "They wouldn't let me write to anyone, or phone anyone."

The Professor phrased his reply very carefully. "They were watching you. I think maybe you underestimate just how sick you were."

"I know just how bloody sick I was, thank you. And how come you found out so much about it? No, don't tell me. So I'm still being watched. All I've had is a change of guard."

"Please don't think of it like that. There are many people out there who are concerned about you, apart from us."

"Yeah, right. The only person who has ever given a shit about me is dead."

For some reason she could never have explained that annoyed Kathy. "Well, excuse us for caring too," she said more sharply than she had intended. "I'll have you know that the three of us, and Sarah, have been going out of our minds with worry. We didn't know whether you'd buggered off to Jamaica to be with her family or thrown yourself under the 93 bus because you couldn't cope. You didn't phone us or write to us. The bloody hospital wouldn't tell us anything because you, like an idiot, haven't put a next of kin on your paperwork. What the hell did you think we were doing during this last month? Having a bloody party? Just don't you ever, ever accuse us of not giving a shit about you. Alright?"

Not so long ago, she realised in the awful silence after her outburst, Piers would have pointed out that the 93 bus didn't go anywhere near where he had been, and then he would have smiled and given her a bit of a hug. But all he did was bow his head and remain mute and she thought for one horrible moment she had made him cry.

Before she could offer an apology the Professor interrupted. He laid a gentle hand on Piers' shoulder. "Eat the soup," he said kindly. "You know she has spoken for all of us, just not in her most diplomatic way. Kathy, I asked you to go and get the bed made up."

"Sorry," she mumbled, not quite sure who she was speaking to and went off to do as she had been told. By the time she returned, Piers was eating the soup very slowly and seemed to be having problems swallowing. He had eaten most of it but hadn't touched the bread when he gave up. "Had a letter from Kerryanne while I was in hospital too," he offered and sounded a little brighter. "Seems she's left the Air Force and taken up writing thrillers. Got a publishing deal agreed and first book due out in the States in March. Now how the hell do you suppose she found out where I was?"

"Not from me," the Professor assured him. "She has never been in contact with me and I've never met her. But you know her reputation. Finding people is what she does."

"True," he admitted and he looked at the piece of bread on his plate but didn't eat it.

"Well, that was nice of her," Kathy offered hoping to make amends for her earlier outburst. "I'm sorry, Ratty. I didn't mean to upset you. But you really have no idea how worried we all were about you. So please don't say we don't care about you. You know we do. All of us. And your cat."

It was a relief to see Piers was slowly remembering how to smile. "It's OK," he said. "I wasn't upset. Just didn't expect it from you."

"It was good of Kerryanne to write to you," she commented, still trying to be nice. "I didn't realise you'd stayed in touch."

"It's been sporadic, but if she was in New York the same time as me we'd sometimes meet up for a quick coffee, maybe lunch. Couple of dinners. Nothing more. I'm guessing she started looking for me when I didn't turn up for our breakfast meet a couple of weeks ago. Can I have my cigarettes back now?"

"No," the Professor told him severely. "Now you go and take a bath and then go to bed. One of us will bring you something light to eat later this evening but I need you to have complete and total rest."

Piers knew when he was being told off and obediently left the kitchen. They heard him go upstairs and nobody was surprised when Audrey went chasing after him, finally returning to the sleeping place she had abandoned.

There was a long silence in the kitchen after he had gone.

"He's not at all well, is he?" Kathy said half to herself. "You know what it is, don't you?" she challenged the Professor. "What on earth kind of accident was it? Was he hurt in the bad landing?"

"All I have heard are the official facts, they are unpleasant enough. And there are laws in place that mean I can't tell you so don't ask me to."

The Prof took a light snack up later but brought it back down again. "He is fast asleep. Best thing for him. We will leave him for now but I'll look in on him from time to time through the night."

"Do you do that for all your refugees?" Jean-Guy asked curiously, thinking that a year ago he had been one of them.

"All of them," the Prof confirmed. "Even you when you first arrived but you were so happy to be free and so falling in love with Kathy from the moment you first saw her, you slept through the nights with no problems." He smiled at the clearly embarrassed Jean-Guy, then put the tray down on the table and the other two thought they had never seen him look so upset. He shook his head and spoke almost to himself. "I just wish he had let us help. We might have stopped him going so far down."

Kathy and the Prof were breakfasting together the next morning when Piers wandered into the kitchen with Audrey still trotting behind him.

"Morning," he greeted them. "Is it porridge for breakfast?"

"At this time of year?" Kathy asked. "Of course. How hungry are you?"

"Not at all really but I've been told I must eat or I'll be readmitted to hospital. So I'll eat."

Petr Mihaly had to smile at the other man's lightly grudging tone. "Porridge will do you no harm. I always make it with water anyway and it was made a while ago now so it will be a bearable temperature for you."

A small quantity of porridge, two vitamin pills and a mug of cooled black tea later, Piers filled up his mug with water from the tap and drank that too. "Any chance of getting my cigarettes back now?"

"None whatsoever. Do you need the painkillers or the antacids? They will help you more than the nicotine will."

"I'll take a couple of the pain relief."

The Professor silently handed across two of the tablets from the bottle and made an entry on the printed card then he put the bottle and the card back in his pocket. "Good. Now, I suggest you go into the sitting room and find yourself some easy piano music to play. I think it will do you good in your mind and your fingers could also do with the work."

A second mug of water followed the first. "True. Coming, Piglet? You know you want to. But I'm not discussing my medical history with you or anyone."

"OK," she agreed and went into the sitting room with him. Her burning curiosity was eating her up inside but she knew he wouldn't tell her anything so she went off on another tack. "Want to do a bit of accompanying or would you rather play on your own?"

"I don't think I'm up to accompanying anything at the moment, but you're welcome to stay."

It consoled Kathy to see he still instinctively took his shoes off to play. "And you're really not going to tell us anything?"

"Nothing. And don't give me that wounded Bambi look. Maybe one day. I have too many adjustments to make right now and need to do things in my own time. And I apologise if that sounds harsh as you're a good friend and I don't want to cut you out."

Kathy took a steadying breath and hoped she wasn't about to make a big mistake. "You stood on the Samhain bridge, didn't you? I don't know what it was but something made you turn back rather than pass through the veil." She was not expecting him to get to his feet and take her in a gentle, silent hug.

"Yes I did. I could see Chantal through the veil but then I looked behind me and I saw all of you waiting for me and it was Sarah who led me off the bridge."

Kathy hated to hear the sadness in his voice. She slid tentative arms round him as he felt so fragile. "So where did the black cat fit in?"

"What black cat?" he asked, somehow curious but not surprised.

"I sat in the garden the day the Prof told us you'd had an accident at work and I saw you quite clearly in a hospital bed and you had a big black cat curled round in your elbow and it had a paw on your chest."

He was silent as though he didn't know whether to say anything or not. "The black cat is my spirit guide," he offered eventually and then he softly, briefly kissed her lips. "And I'm not making a pass at you. I'm just saying thank you for understanding the path I walk." He let go of her and sat back at the piano just as his cat leaped up to join him. "How's Audrey been?"

Kathy knew the moment of intimacy was over, but that had been a hell of a kiss and she just about managed to resist the urge to grab hold of him and kiss him straight back. Something in her perspective had shifted and she needed to make sure she didn't fall in love with this man in the same way she had with Jean-Guy or the consequences would wreck too many lives. "She's been just fine," she lied as it was easier to do that than to get all emotional again as she knew that wasn't going to help him get better.

Piers looked at Audrey purring again now she was back on the piano with her human sitting in front of her. "Audrey, you disappoint me. I was convinced you'd be moping around and missing me. You heartless cat." He looked at the keyboard for a few moments then, without saying a word, ran through the Canteloube *Baïlero* Kathy had always adored. He played it so beautifully from memory it gave her goose pimples and made her want to cry to think how that musical talent seemed so nearly to have been lost to them for ever. Before she could say anything to him, he closed the lid of the piano. "Sorry," he said shortly. "Just too much effort right now. I'll play for you another day."

"No, that's fine. I wasn't expecting any accompanying for a while." Kathy watched as Piers slowly left the room and she heard him go back upstairs. Audrey remained sitting on the piano, looked from Kathy to the door and back again, then she gave a quiet chirrup and went dashing off after her human. Feeling oddly angry and somehow frustrated she didn't know the truth, Kathy went out to the kitchen where the Prof was reading the newspaper. "Just how sick is he?" she demanded abruptly.

Petr Mihaly had guessed this would happen and he calmly folded up his paper. "Against my advice, he has instructed me not to say as he would rather tell you himself when he is ready. I rang Sarah yesterday to tell her as much as I can without breaching any confidences. She was very upset about it all and I have no idea what she will say to Alison. Will you go with him when he meets his children for the first time?"

Kathy was faintly surprised. "Do you think I should?"

"Yes. You and Sarah have got to know each other much better since you took her to the hospital and I think they will both need your support."

"Oh, OK. I'll ask Jean-Guy if he wants to come too, but I can't imagine it somehow. Can you?"

The Prof allowed himself a little smile. "Not at this time of year," he had to agree.

As Kathy had suspected he would, Jean-Guy declined a walk in the bitter east wind so it was only she and Piers who took the coast path, deserted again now for winter. Kathy wasn't surprised her companion walked a lot more slowly than he had last time they had done this walk together and they were barely half way to the village when she tucked her hand through his arm as she had done so many times before.

"If you're tired we can go home and get the car. I'm sorry, it never occurred to me you wouldn't want to walk and you didn't say anything."

He stopped for a moment to get his breath back. "I'll be OK. I'm not an invalid."

"Well excuse me," she teased him lightly. "But right now I think I'd disagree. You're so thin I'm surprised your clothes haven't fallen off you and you make me look as though I'm an Olympic runner next to you and my legs are half the length of yours."

"Short-arse," he said fondly and resumed their walk. "Yes, I've lost weight. Didn't even notice until people started making comments. Took me a while but the medics told me I was pretty much in the third stage of starvation."

"You bloody idiot," was her instinctive reaction. "Why? There was no fat on you in the first place."

"I just kept forgetting to eat. That was one very odd conversation with one of the medics and we went through this great long rigmarole that it probably goes all the way back to my childhood when I was starved by my parents and that began a mindset that meant I told myself food was a reward for good behaviour and I'd obviously decided I needed to be punished for something so I deprived myself of food. Silly cow. I told her I just hadn't had time to eat but she wouldn't believe me."

For a brief, treacherous moment, Kathy was inclined to side with the medic as she remembered the times she had seen Piers look in the various cupboards then not take out any food to eat. She made a mental note to talk to the Prof about this, but right now Piers needed all the support she could give him and agreeing with the medic did not seem at all the right thing to do. "Does sound a bit far-fetched," she had to agree. "But I suppose that was her opinion and she was allowed to voice it. She obviously didn't know that all you needed was a box of custard creams and a ton of fruit and nut chocolate."

"True," he agreed. "Funnily enough they didn't turn up on the hospital menu. But I got sick of bloody fish."

"At least you didn't get sick of turkey like the rest of us."

"Never been a huge fan of turkey," was all he offered then lapsed into a silence again as though even chatting was too much effort.

The main street was deserted as it often was at that time of year and Sarah's mother was in the shop without any customers. She looked startled by the appearance of her son-in-law and didn't immediately rush round from behind the counter as she would have done once.

She walked up to him quite slowly, almost as though she was approaching a stranger but then gave him a gentle hug and a kiss on the cheek. "So sorry to hear your news," she said awkwardly. "How are you feeling now?"

"I'm a lot better than I was," he told her and she looked much happier.

"Are you going next door to meet your daughters at last? Sarah will be so pleased to see you. I think Violet looks the most like you, definitely got your eyes, but Catherine is the very spit of my late mother-in-law. Melanie is a bit of a mix really but she's going to have terrible red hair. Any redheads in your family?" She paused for breath and smiled. "No, go. Go and meet your children. You don't want to be stuck with me babbling on all day. But it really is lovely to see you."

He gave her an impetuous kiss on the cheek just as some paying customers arrived. "Good to see you too," he assured her.

Kathy and Piers went next door where, as usual, the front door was unlocked and, as she always did, Kathy called down the hall when she stepped into the house. Sarah came out of the back room, saw Kathy wasn't on her own this time and fairly ran the length of the hall to hurl herself on her husband where she just stood with her arms round him as though she was terrified he would disappear again.

To his bafflement she put her chin on his left shoulder and blew quite hard past his ear. "Be gone," she said but so quietly even he, with his hearing, barely heard her. Then she turned her face into his neck and cried a little while he put his arms round her and felt her soft, comforting warmth and knew she would help him to heal.

"I was so sorry to hear about Chantal," she whispered. "It must have been so sad for you and after you'd all hoped she was going to get better. Do you want to talk about it?"

"Not right now." He sighed almost inaudibly and wished people didn't want him to talk about something he wasn't willing to share. "How have you been keeping?" he asked and held her close again, cradling her head against his shoulder.

Sarah raised her head and took a slow, gentle kiss from his lips. "Absolutely shattered," she smiled. "Alison's over at the café at the moment as she's thinking about opening a few hours at the weekends during the winter, mostly for locals and birdwatchers. But come on in. Come and say hello." She took him by the hand and led him to the back room.

Kathy had to smile to watch them and wondered to herself just when those two were going to wake up and realise they had fallen in love with each other.

The triplets were all fast asleep on a quilt in a play pen and looked deceptively angelic.

"Violet has your eyes exactly, right down to the speckle in the left one, but it's not such a gold speckle as yours, more of a hazel one. She's the one on the left. Melanie's in the middle with the red hair and Catherine is I think, although you mustn't ever tell her, going to be the most beautiful of them all."

Piers stood next to his wife, who was still holding on to his hand, and thought he had had forgotten human life started with something that small. It had been a long time since he had been that close to a baby. And he had never again expected to look at any baby, let alone three of them, and realise those lives had come into existence because of him. "And you and I really managed those between us?" was the first coherent sentence that formed in his brain.

"We did. But don't worry, I'm quite happy with three. I don't want any more. You're on the birth certificates as I promised. Kathy told me you were born in Drumahoe, County Londonderry, is that right? They needed to know for the certificates."

"Yes, that's right," he agreed vaguely, still looking at his daughters as though he couldn't quite believe they were real. Part of him wanted to pick one of them up to find out what she felt like and another part of him was terrified that such a tiny, fragile thing might break if he got his hands on it. "Although I'd have said Derry with no 'London' in it."

"Oh, sorry. The Registrar asked me where you were born and I felt a bit of an idiot as I didn't know but I had Kathy with me and fortunately she did."

Kathy could just tell what was going through the mind of the father of those adorable triplets and she thought it was too sweet for words. "And I was very careful to say 'not far from Derry' as you did," she pointed out. "But I got corrected by the Registrar."

"Bloody English bureaucrats," he commented sounding more like his old self.

Violet started stirring so her mother picked her up and gently put her in her father's arms, trying very hard to forget Alison's comment that men weren't to be trusted with babies. Violet opened her cornflower blue eyes and peered unseeing at her father then awarded him a very inelegant burp and a toothless smile.

Piers looked at this thing that had been dumped in his arms and didn't know what to do with it. He hadn't been expecting it to squirm and wriggle like that, but this was a very tiny human being with bones and muscles and fascinatingly perfect hands waving about at the ends of her sleeves.

Sarah realised her husband was clearly not used to handling babies. She adjusted their daughter to make her more comfortable and had to smile as some instinct made him lift the baby to his face so he could give her a soft kiss on the forehead which definitely met with Violet's approval. But then Catherine and Melanie sensed something was up and both started clamouring for attention.

"Welcome to the world of triplets," Sarah laughed. "Sit yourself on the sofa and just this once I'll do the nappies. But you can watch and learn and do the next lot."

"Will Alison let me?" was the surprisingly sharp question. "Or have I got to sneak in to see my children when my wife's lover is out of the way?"

Kathy began to understand why the Prof had told her to go with Piers. "I'm sure Alison won't get in your way," she put in quickly, hoping to avoid a spat between the couple.

He shot her a filthy look. "Uh-huh? And what has she been saying about me that makes you think that?"

"Oh, don't be so bloody paranoid," Kathy told him, trying to deflect his clearly rising temper on to herself. "If you must know, she's been very understanding and was actually quite worried about you."

"Just stop it," Sarah said a lot more kindly. "Alison has agreed that you as the father have full access to our children and I've told her she mustn't ever tell you you're anything less than welcome." She finished changing Melanie and handed him a clean baby.

He was learning how to hold a baby properly and his eldest daughter cooed at him adoringly, feeling safe as he cradled her against his chest and making him smile. "I understand from the Prof some people said I've broken our marriage vows, among other things. I haven't. I said months ago there'd be some nasty gossip about me and I was right, wasn't I?"

Sarah's face flushed and she was glad he hadn't mentioned Alison by name. "Yes, but I didn't believe any of it for one minute. People don't understand our marriage. I've always said you don't have to be faithful as I'm not. And now you've given me the children I asked for, you don't even have to stay if you don't want to. So if you want to divorce me because of my relationship with Alison I won't get in the way." The other two saw the tears that splashed onto a rather surprised Catherine who was half-dressed by this time.

Kathy thought of the glamorous honey blonde who had written to this man to tell him she was free of the military and presumably also any other official involvements and she wondered if the letter had also included any kind of invitation. She guessed Kerryanne knew he was married as he had been engaged when they worked together but she had a feeling that a wedding ring wouldn't put off a woman like that when she really wanted a man. In the meantime a beautiful scene was playing out in front of her as though she wasn't there and she wasn't going to interrupt it for anything in case they sent her out to the kitchen to make tea or something.

"Do you want me to go?" he asked softly.

Sarah couldn't speak but she shook her head and Catherine yelled as she got wet again.

Piers parked Melanie beside him and picked up his middle child so he could finish fastening her sleepsuit with her lying on his lap.

Kathy watched him carefully, ready to leap across and help but he seemed to have absorbed baby care as if by osmosis. She wondered if maybe he had handled babies before but she couldn't think how.

Sarah was wondering the same thing too. "Have you done that before?" she asked.

"No," he said sadly and Kathy wanted to give him a hug and tell him he'd be fine now but Sarah interrupted her.

"Did you and Chantal have children?" she asked him and her voice carried a warning that she wanted to know the truth this time.

Kathy heard her own breath catch in her throat as she saw the way Piers held his tiny daughters so protectively close.

"No, no we didn't," he admitted barely above a whisper.

Kathy didn't understand Sarah's reactions at all. She got up from the floor with a clean Violet in her arms and sat next to him somehow managing to cuddle him while making sure their babies were still safe. "I'm so sorry," she breathed. "Why did you never tell me?"

He blinked a bit and gave Melanie a soft kiss on the forehead. "It was a long time ago."

Something warned Kathy not to interrupt. She had a horrible feeling in the back of her mind now about the lack of children in Piers' first marriage.

"You could have told me," Sarah murmured to him. "And now I feel bad as I've made you unhappy all over again."

He gave her a gentle kiss. "You haven't. Really. You told me right from the start you wanted kids so I knew what I was letting myself in for."

"But I've made it worse."

"No you haven't," he replied and was starting to sound a bit tetchy now. "It was a long time ago. The baby was stillborn and the other pregnancies failed in their first few weeks."

Kathy felt herself instinctively put a hand over her mouth, so shocked at the quiet, calm way he had told his wife what had happened in his first marriage. It brought horrible waves of nausea washing over her and she couldn't speak as she watched to see what would happen next.

Sarah leaned against him with their daughters tucked close on their laps and sensed he didn't want to speak of it again. "I missed you so much. You've been so sick and you wouldn't let us help you. I don't understand why you did that."

"It's what I do," he said sadly. "I've had a lot of people talking with me and they've made me understand and accept that my way of coping is to retreat inside. Which is how I grew up. So we talked about you and Piglet and Jean-Guy and the Prof and I've got to learn that you four genuinely want to help me. It's not an easy lesson for me."

Sarah shuffled the babies around a bit so she could nestle properly against him on the sofa. "I don't care what Alison says, none of us is ever going to be horrible to you and I've told her she's got to be nice to you too because if she ever forced me to choose it wouldn't be her. That made her think."

Kathy couldn't have described how happy hearing that made her feel but she was starting to think that maybe she should go out to the kitchen. On the other hand, those two really didn't seem to mind her being there.

"And while we're on the subject of Alison," Sarah continued, "I can't say she didn't come back into my life these last few months. I've known her a long time and I've never tried to make you think she and I aren't lovers which is why I've always said you can get yourself someone for the times I can't be with you. I hate it when you're not here. I didn't think I would as much as I do, but you are the only man I have ever slept with and I still don't know how you managed it." Sarah wasn't one for deep conversations when there were hungry babies starting to grizzle in the background and she tapped him smartly on the thigh. "Now we have to go out to the kitchen to make up some bottles and you can have lesson number two. It's called how to feed three babies at once."

Kathy had helped quite a few times now and she felt like an old hand as she and Sarah got the feeding time organised. It certainly was a lot easier with one person per baby. She gave Violet her bottle, Piers was put in charge of Melanie's bottle and Sarah sat back next to him on the sofa and put Catherine to her breast. Kathy thought it was rather sweet the way Sarah was quite openly feeding her child in front of the baby's father but he seemed fascinated by the whole process, trying to watch one daughter while feeding another.

Piers was intrigued by the breastfeeding. He had never seen a woman feed a baby before and began to think he had led quite a sheltered life. He looked down at the tiny baby in the crook of his arm, eyes closed as she drank so greedily from the bottle she was nearly tugging it out of his hand and he smiled at her. Just briefly there was a regret for the children he had lost with Chantal but it passed like a dream.

Sarah caught his eye above Catherine's head. "Bet you never thought you'd be doing that a year ago," she said to him.

"A year ago," he mused. "Don't think I'd even met you, had I?" He watched as his wife sorted out her bra now Catherine had finished her feed. "So tell me," he said with almost a hint of a smile on his lips. "As the only bloke who's ever been allowed into your bed, would you let me sleep with you again?"

Sarah looked straight at him and couldn't find the words to say how happy he had just made her. "Ask me again when I haven't got month-old triplets and you never know what I might say. But, right now, I'm still sore and from the look of you, you haven't got the energy."

He tilted her face up by the chin and they exchanged a tender kiss. "But just twins next time, huh?" he checked.

"Go and get your supplies from Mum's shop. I'm not risking quads," she told him fondly.

The front door opened and closed with a bit of a bang and they heard Alison's voice in the hall. "Sarah? You down there?"

Both women noticed the tension shoot through Piers' body but he didn't say anything as he held his tiny daughter close against his chest.

"In the back room," she called back. "I've got Kathy and Piers here."

Forewarned, Alison came into the room with her best smile on her face but that faded as soon as she saw the father of the babies. "Bloody hell. How much bloody weight have you lost?"

Piers got to his feet and tenderly put his eldest child back in the play pen. "Too much," he said in reply to Alison's question. "Better be going, I suppose. The Prof still doesn't like us going along that path in the dark and it's even further to walk by the road."

To Kathy's admiration, Alison stood in front of the man she had been openly rude about and said bluntly, "Look, we got off to a bad start. I saw you as a threat to me and Sarah and if I've been less than polite to you then I apologise."

He gave her a tired smile. "I don't give a shit if you're rude to me. Just don't be rude about me, especially behind my back, spouting crap you couldn't possibly know anything about."

Alison took a sharp breath then coldly offered her hand. "Fresh start? For Sarah's sake?"

He took the hand and both Kathy and Sarah felt they could breathe again. "Fresh start," he agreed but his voice was as cold as hers. "Right, come on, Piglet. Hand over that baby. You'll have to tell Jean-Guy you want one of your own rather than stealing Sarah's."

Kathy gave Violet back to her mother and Sarah put the other two in with their sister then went with the visitors back into the hall, leaving Alison in the back room with the triplets. Sarah gave Piers a gentle cuddle. "Don't let Alison put you off. Please? I'd like them to grow up knowing you're their father. We are still married with all that means."

"When we've both stopped hurting so much," he agreed softly. "But, you never know, I may even have a go at nappy changing next time."

Sarah was about to slide her arms up his back but then she paused. "Have you still got that dreadful tattoo?"

"'Fraid so. They don't wash off."

Sarah shuddered and let him go with a loving smile. "Just don't leave it so long next time, huh?"

Kathy and Piers set off back along the coast path and to Kathy's profound relief, he was content to amble along at about half the speed he had walked at last summer which meant she could chat as they walked although she still felt she was taking three paces to his one.

"Glad you went?" she asked as they cleared the village and the only sound was the hissing of the sea on the shingle. There was something about the hunch of his shoulders that said certain topics weren't up for discussion and she knew she had to respect that. Perhaps it was something he would talk about with her one day but while he was still crawling away from the recent mess of his life this certainly wasn't the time.

He gave her a look and a quiet smile of gratitude, realising she knew to respect the memories he didn't want disturbed. "Yes. Can't get my head round the idea of being a father. I'm forty six years old and just become a dad for the first time."

"Oh," she said without thinking. "I thought you were forty five."

"I've had a birthday since then."

"True," she had to agree. "Birthdays do have a habit of sneaking up on you. I mean I'm now the grand old age of twenty seven."

"Bloody child," he said fondly. "Wait till you're my age."

"Geriatric," she told him and tucked her hand through his arm, determined to help him focus on more pleasant things rather than the unbearable sadness of his past. "Well, we now know Sarah hasn't changed her opinion on tattoos, but what did Kerryanne think of it?" she asked lightly.

Suddenly, unexpectedly, he went on the defensive. "I never said she's even seen it."

Kathy wasn't going to be put off, and her senses told her there was some juicy gossip here. She wasn't used to him being snappy but she could understand it. "You told us the pair of you were sharing a hotel suite last year," she persisted laughingly. "Do you expect me to believe you two spent the whole time getting changed in the bathroom? That wouldn't have convinced the people bugging your room for one minute."

"Piglet, you are asking me to trust you with secrets I have signed agreements not to tell. If anyone ever finds out I told you the brief Kerryanne and I had for that trip, never mind whether we shared a bed or not, I can be sent to prison. For a very long time."

She saw a way round it and guessed even he wouldn't come up with a counter-argument. "Oh! I knew it! Oh well, at least you weren't married to Sarah at the time. Anyway I saw she was wearing a ring that matched yours and you had to travel with her as a married man."

Piers didn't comment but stopped walking and looked at her.

Convinced she had sussed the truth, Kathy concluded triumphantly, "So you didn't tell me anything, I worked it out. Which means you haven't breached any secrets. Spill."

There was a faint smile just lifting his lips. "Got me there, you crafty little witch. OK, if it keeps the peace I'll tell you what I can. Just so long as you're willing to swear in a court of law that I haven't breached any secrecy agreements."

His tone was lighter than she would have expected and Kathy was consoled. "Hey, if it means I get all the goss, I'll swear it anywhere you like."

His smile widened as he looked down at her. "Kerryanne has a thing about tattoos."

"Oh dear," she sympathised. "Another one who can't stand them?"

"And when I say 'a thing' I mean she can't keep her hands off them." He gave her a look that reminded her just how wicked a sense of humour he had once had. "You want all the goss as you call it?"

Kathy could not have said how happy she was to see those lights in his eyes. "Not sure," she said truthfully. "You may have appointed yourself my big brother but I really don't think I want any sex education lessons from you."

Piers could not have said how happy he was just to be walking the path with this woman who had become perhaps his closest friend. "OK, I'll miss out all the sweaty love scenes. But I'm pretty sure it's not covered by the agreements if I tell you Kerryanne has body piercings in places I didn't know they could do them."

Kathy tried to rid herself of the image of Piers and Kerryanne in a sweaty love scene. She had not been expecting that and almost gawped at him. "Can USAF pilots do that? I mean, where? Sorry, no, not my business. But I'm guessing you've gone below the waist here."

It was as though a storm cloud was passing and there was sunshine in the distance. The darkness of his past was like a nightmare finally fading with the light of a new day. "Let's say below the belly button but above the knees."

"That must have hurt."

"Probably. She didn't say and I didn't ask. Want any more details?"

"Not sure I do now, thank you."

He leaned close and murmured in her ear. "She wanted me to get done as a pair."

"Oh!" Kathy shrieked and physically leaped away from him. She turned huge blue eyes on him not quite sure whether she was unexpectedly shocked, or very, very curious. "Oh, my God." Curiosity won. "And did you?"

He almost laughed which surprised her. "Thought you didn't want any more details. Come on, or it'll be getting dark."

Kathy thought about that all the rest of the way home and became ever more consumed with curiosity.

"Tell me?" she asked as they went in through the back door.

"Oh, no," was his light reply. "You said no more details."

"But…"

"No, Piglet."

"You can't do this to me," she protested.

"So now you do want details?"

"What the hell are you two going on about now?" Jean-Guy interrupted, thankful to hear the backchat and even more thankful that twenty four hours in the farmhouse seemed to have made one heck of an improvement in their pianist's health.

"Body piercings," Piers told him without a smile on his face.

"Oh? Have you got another one?"

"Now that's for me to know and Piglet to think about."

The Prof looked at the man who had slumped at that table barely twenty four hours ago with no hope left in him and those terrible shadows in his eyes. Now he was smiling, not the roguish smile he had shown them months ago but a gentler smile. One that said this was a man slowly learning to make his own kind of peace with his world.

"Tea?" he asked them. "Or did Sarah give you some?"

"Love some, thanks," Kathy said. "And he'll have some too, along with at least six custard creams."

"I'll be sick," Piers told her and there was a ring of truth in his reply. "But it's custard creams so I'm sure I can manage one."

"One is a good idea," the Prof approved. "I've spoken to your nutritionist this afternoon and she has given me a diet list for you so I will prepare a supper that shouldn't upset you. I'll also get a set of scales as I've never needed them before. Will you tell me truthfully what they say or do I have to stand next to you when you weigh yourself?"

Piers was still in a good mood after the afternoon with his children and the badinage with Kathy. "I'll tell you. Maybe."

The Prof hadn't expected such a spirited reply and didn't want to dampen the other man's mood by pointing out custard creams probably weren't the best biscuits for him, so he changed the topic. "What did you think of your children?"

Piers thoughtfully nibbled a bit off a biscuit that not so long ago he would have eaten in one mouthful. "Smelly, noisy, all over the place at once...."

"And totally adorable?" Kathy checked.

He smiled then. "Yeah, pretty much."

After tea the Dodman Trio got down to some serious work and by the time the Prof came to fetch them to come and eat their supper, they were storming through Mozart's B flat trio as though they had been playing it every day for a year. He thought to himself again that these three, not quite thrown together by chance but fortuitously helped by a small tortoiseshell cat, really did have a remarkable talent. It was just such a pity that the health of the pianist had had to collapse almost completely but if there was any kind of an upside it was that he now had time to work on his playing. But his afternoon had clearly put him in a much better place than he had been recently as he seemed more like his old self; ate without protest everything he was given to eat and didn't ask for his cigarettes.

The Prof was glad when Kathy offered to help with the washing up, leaving the other two men to go and do some work on the Prokofiev. He had watched Kathy and Piers together this last year, the intuition they shared, the oddly deep emotional attachment that neither would allow to become physical. At least he didn't think it had become physical but they spent quite a lot of time in London now and he couldn't advise those who asked to be told. There were eyes watching them that they didn't know about. If he had one wish it was that those eyes would look away now Piers' health was so bad.

"Piers seems so much better today," Kathy started the conversation. "And he was surprisingly good with the triplets. Mind you, they are adorable. And when I saw him with them I could see the likenesses so there's no doubting who the father is." She carefully dried a plate, wondering how to steer the conversation round to where she wanted it to go. Nobody had ever said what the 'accident at work' had been and as it was nearly a month before she had seen Piers again it was quite likely any physical injuries had healed. She didn't know, but thought it most likely he had been so malnourished by the end he had either fainted or fallen and hurt himself as he went down. "He's not coping well with losing her, is he? I can't help feeling today was a good day, tomorrow may not go so well."

The Prof was touched to hear the genuine concern in her voice and tried to work out how he could move the conversation on to the musical future of the Dodman Trio rather than follow her lead. "Not at all well and we all have to accept he will never get over it completely." The last plate was added to the draining rack. "We don't see the serious side of him often, but he is responsible for many lives when he flies that plane and that bad landing shook him up far more than he was expecting."

There was a silence in the kitchen as Kathy wondered why he would say such a thing. "Are you trying to tell me it's broken his nerve and he may never go back to flying?"

"I don't know. He and I talked a little last night. At the moment he is living one day to the next. And you were right. Today, as you said, he has had a good day. But until he is cleared to fly again, I think perhaps he should be encouraged to go back to his music. Do you have any trio gigs booked in the immediate future?"

Kathy couldn't have expressed the relief she felt to learn there was a chance Piers would get back to flying. But she realised his health wasn't up for discussion any more. "Not that immediate; nothing until we go to Europe in April. Do you think maybe he won't be OK on stage? I mean I saw this afternoon that just walking into the village exhausted him and he really is so thin now. It scares me to think how he so obviously nearly died. You don't lose five stone in weight and get put on all those pills, to say nothing of being signed off sick for three months unless it's something serious, do you? Can you at least tell me if he's got something terminal and he's just lied about what the pills are for?"

The Prof had to smile to see her worried little face as she tried to cope with yet another fear for her best friend. "Kathy, I'm sure I am breaching no confidences if I tell you the pills are exactly what he told you they are. Please don't think that about him. Just concentrate on the good days he can have as they will help him to get through the bad."

The shadows that had been gathering in her mind were fading now and Kathy felt herself smile. "Yes, he was chatty and smiley a bit today which is lovely to see but we have to get him physically better too, don't we?"

The Prof couldn't believe how well she understood. "Yes, we do. But I think he will be sensible about that and in a way I am less worried about his physical health. But I will encourage him to stay here until April so I can keep an eye while you and Jean-Guy carry on with your professional lives."

"Hmm. Can't imagine that'll go down too well."

"Oh, you'd be surprised. I managed Emma as a teenager so I am sure I am more than a match for a wilful Concorde pilot."

Kathy had to agree. "Yes, I think you probably are. So what do you suggest we do with him musically?"

"I don't know, and that's the truth. What are your immediate bookings?"

"Well, Jean-Guy has that run of three concerts in the Festival Hall with the Royal Philharmonic and I'm out pretty regularly with various groups for February and March. Nothing like as manic as Jean-Guy but enough to earn me a decent living."

"And nothing for the Dodman until April?"

"Nope, then we go round Europe and after that Jean-Guy and I are busy anyway. He does have some piano and cello recitals scheduled but they're a long way ahead in the autumn and into the winter season."

"So Jean-Guy has no small recitals coming up? Nothing too daunting for the accompanist to see how he copes?"

"Not really. He's too high profile for small gigs these days. Jane did say there was a festival somewhere, Yorkshire I think, that had had a cellist pull out of a recital and had asked if there was even the remotest chance he may be available. But I don't think he'll be tempted as the fee is very low for him. Although if we explain our reasons to him I know he'd do it just to help Piers." She half-shrugged. "Quite a good booking for someone like me though."

"When's that one?"

"May or June, I think. So after our visit to Europe anyway."

"Well, having heard Piers play with the two of you just now, I think he will cope with the trio work. Physically he is more hidden behind you and also I know you will pick up on his moods and if you aren't sure you will suggest you change the programme to something less demanding for him so he can cope. But Jean-Guy doesn't have your sensitivity and if the programme says they are to play the three most difficult cello sonatas ever written then he will expect his accompanist to be up to his standards. Maybe Yorkshire would be a good one for Piers to do just to get back into things. I'll speak to Jean-Guy and get him to select the more familiar works. Would you or he like to ring Jane and see if the festival is still looking to fill the slot?"

"They'll bite our hands off to get Jean-Guy on such a short-notice booking. But then that does run him right up to the gigs he's got in the Festival Hall and up in Manchester."

The Prof had another idea. "Well, why don't you do it? You and Piers. Take the slot in Yorkshire. I'm sure they won't mind if they switch from a cello recital to a violin one and they won't get two musicians of your calibre at such short notice otherwise. And if I am honest, I stick by what I said and I think you will be a better partner for him at his first recital."

"Me? Do a solo recital with just a piano?"

"Think about it. What the hell are those two up to now? What are they doing to Francoeur? I admire their courage but that can't be allowed to go on. It's like two express trains heading for the buffers. Excuse me."

The Prof wasn't surprised that the one of his 'children' who remained at home with him went from dark depressions to foul moods to a listlessness that scared even him, and then, just occasionally, got back some of his old energy and would spend hours at the piano going over the same passages time and again as though the very repetition brought him some kind of comfort.

He didn't like going into the village with its gossips and over-priced shop but he also knew that it wouldn't be a good idea just yet to let Piers out on his own so took him out and about to get away from the house for a while. They went to the supermarket, to Ipswich and to Woodbridge a couple of times and as Piers was still on full pay, he was persuaded to buy a few more clothes and books. He didn't need to buy any piano music, even if he had wanted to, as the Prof had an impressive collection of his own but Piers chose to stick to the parts for the trios and the sonatas he was going to need for his recitals with Jean-Guy, and showed no inclination to push himself to play anything other than the repertoire he needed to know. He let the Prof offer him some tutorials and then chose to ignore most of what he had been taught. But for the most part he honed what he needed to perfection and the Prof still thought, but didn't say, that this was one of the laziest pianists he had ever come across and probably one who would never realise his full potential.

Sarah had had a long phone conversation with the Prof one evening after Piers had gone to bed early as he was so tired and she had managed to find some time away from Alison who was working on a business plan for her beach café. Sarah learned that her husband wasn't yet trusted to be out on his own as he had so little energy so, to the Prof's unspoken admiration, she told Alison that she had to be the chauffeur as Piers wasn't driving yet, and she was to fetch him to come and visit his children just as often as he liked. The Prof didn't like to imagine what Alison must have said to that but if Piers rang the house and asked for a lift then she would turn up, always perfectly polite but not even trying to be friendly, and a couple of hours later she would bring him back again. If the Prof offered her tea or coffee she always declined and he didn't try too hard to persuade her. Secretly he was relieved to learn that Sarah seemed to be prepared to fight harder for her husband than she was for her lover. But he didn't say anything to Piers who continued to complain at the least opportunity that he was still being watched, sometimes he got angry and demanded to know why he was being kept as a prisoner but he didn't expect a reply. He knew.

The Prof could not have expressed his relief when Kathy and Jean-Guy came back to the farmhouse towards the end of February and he hugged them both in greeting.

"Good gigs?" he asked.

"Very good," Jean-Guy agreed. "And now we have a little while here to get our pianist back on track and then we are off again. Well, I am for a week."

The Prof looked at Kathy. "Nothing for you?"

"Not for a couple of weeks," she agreed. "Jean-Guy thinks I'm being picky with my bookings but honestly, there just doesn't seem to be much work at the moment. How's he been?"

"As expected. Good days and bad ones. Hard work."

"What? Our Ratty?" Kathy asked. "Don't believe you. Where is he?"

"Last seen reading in the sitting room. It's a bit cold to go out."

Kathy went off into the sitting room and there she found Piers draped sideways in an armchair and sound asleep again. He spent a lot of time sleeping these days, but whether that was because he was tired or because he was bored she didn't like to think. She looked at him for a moment, thinking that those awful hollows in his cheeks were starting to fill out a little but he still had that gorgeous bone structure to his face, and his skin definitely looked a better colour. His hair was all messy as it hadn't been cut for a while and had grown so long on top it almost had a curl in it, but she noticed he had shaved that morning and he seemed to have bought himself some new clothes as she didn't remember that rather nice dark blue sweater or those grey trousers that weren't hanging off him since he had lost so much weight.

As if aware of someone watching him, he snuffled a bit in his sleep and opened his eyes. "Hey," he said sleepily. "How was London?"

"Oh, still there. Missing you. Come on, time for some coffee and then we'll get more food down you. How's the fattening up programme coming on?"

He got out of the chair with that annoying suppleness he had but his shoulders cracked and clicked as he got them into place.

"Looking good," she approved. "Couple of stone gone back on?"

"Does it look like it?" he asked scathingly.

"This is the Prof's cooking we're talking about."

"True. Half a stone."

Kathy reached up and gave him a kiss on the cheek. "Well, it's obviously going on in all the right places."

"Flatterer," he smiled and returned the kiss. "Anyway, glad you're here. I need you to persuade the Prof I'm safe to be allowed out on my own."

"Why wouldn't you be?" she asked, thinking she might finally learn something.

There was a slight pause. "I think he's afraid I might fall down in a heap somewhere. But, honestly, I think I need the exercise more. I need to go back to my walking. Helps me to sort my head out when I can't fly."

"I'll have a word but I don't have that much faith in my powers of persuasion against the Prof."

Piers followed her out to the kitchen. "He was telling me you've signed us up for a recital in Yorkshire in June."

Kathy felt the first stab of mild panic and tried to keep her tone light. "Oh, yes. Sorry, wasn't going to mention it just yet."

"Any reason?" he asked, oddly cold as though he had guessed the truth.

Kathy realised Jean-Guy and the Prof were looking at her to see how she would get out of that one. "I, um, well, thought it might be good for me. I mean…"

"No you didn't," Piers interrupted irritably. "You think I'm in such a mess I can't be trusted to be an accompanist so you've set yourself up as the fall guy to make sure I don't disgrace the esteemed Jean-Guy when it's his turn. Just as the Prof doesn't trust me to walk into the village in case I do a left turn and wade out into the sea."

Kathy had to admit to herself that he may have been ill, but his mind had lost none of its sharpness. She owed him nothing less than the absolute truth, so she looked straight into those speckled cornflower blue eyes and told him, "Got it in one. What are you going to do to convince us otherwise?"

Piers hadn't been expecting such brutal honesty and judging from the silence that followed, nor had the other two. He barely glanced at the mug of coffee waiting for him on the table. "I'm going to walk into the village to see my wife and children. As soon as I go out of that door you can ring Sarah and tell her I'm on my way and I'll be probably nearer to half an hour these days as I don't walk too fast. So if I don't arrive at her house in forty five minutes she can send up the maroon for the Lifeboat. And as for your recital in Yorkshire, I am going to show you up as the third rate violinist you try to kid us you are. Which you're not. You're one of the best bloody violinists I've come across so don't you ever sell yourself short again. As it's the first time you've let me out on my own, I'll be back for lunch. If you're good and don't try to follow me along the path I'll bring back a cake." He went into the hall, came back through the kitchen and went out of the back door pulling on his coat as he left.

"And he's back," Kathy said.

"Thank Christ for that," Jean-Guy replied.

Petr Mihaly smiled quietly and shook his head. Just sometimes he thought Kathy had chosen the wrong one. "He's getting there," he had to agree.

Josef Suk – *Elegy for violin, cello and piano Op. 23*

April 1982 blessed them with mild weather and Kathy kept an eye on Piers as best she could with him being in Suffolk and she having a lot of London-based work but although he was quieter and more introverted than he had been last year she could tell that he was starting to look round him again and to realise he had been given another chance. She knew how much Sarah was helping and she learned from a very grudging Alison that Piers' baby-handling skills were getting pretty good now and Kathy was happy for him. Jean-Guy was away in Italy for a week shortly before the Dodman Trio was due to go on its short European tour but Kathy had a break during that week and was glad to be able to go out to Suffolk.

She found Piers in one of the best moods she had seen him in for weeks and was delighted when he offered to be her accompanist one morning. They started on the Franck but had moved on to the Bruch by coffee time when the Prof called them out to the kitchen.

"Are you seeing Sarah at some time today?" the Prof asked Piers as they settled at the table.

"Probably should," he agreed. "But I know that bloody Alison won't be too happy to see me."

"She seldom is," the Prof pointed out kindly. "But I think maybe today you should ignore her wants and be with your wife and children, don't you?"

Kathy had just realised that it was Tuesday, the first anniversary of Piers' wedding which made the Prof's comments make sense, but before she could say anything a shrill beeping noise seemed to be coming out of Piers' shirt pocket. He jumped as though one of the other two had hit him, then took a tiny box out of his pocket and looked at it.

"What the hell...?" he said then got to his feet. He excused himself to the other two and went out into the hall.

Kathy looked enquiringly at the Prof.

"Pager," he said briefly.

"What does that mean?"

"It means he has to ring the airline as they want to talk to him. Once it would have meant he has to go in on-call but they told him to bring it with him out here."

"So does that mean he's going back to flying?"

"They have phoned him a few times," the Prof admitted cautiously. "And I have been with him to the club in Ipswich a couple of times as his private licences are still valid. But they haven't paged him before so let us hope maybe this is the beginning of the new start for him."

Kathy felt as though she had caught a glimpse into some kind of alternate universe. "Hang on. I didn't know he's been flying again. When did this happen?"

"Last month. I'm sorry, Kathy, but he didn't want you to know."

"Oh. I suppose he thought I'd get too madly excited and think he was all better when he's still got quite a long way to go."

"Exactly," the Prof agreed with a fond smile. "You can be, um, quite enthusiastic at times. He was happy to be flying again but he had to have someone from the club in the plane with him and he had to send in photocopies of his log book and a letter from whoever had been with him. But I think it was very sensible of the airline to ask him to do that." He stopped as Piers came back to join them. "What news?"

Piers sat back at the table and took a couple of mouthfuls of his coffee. "Well, it's all a bit of a bloody mess as we're off to France next week but they've agreed to bring things forward so I have to report to Cranebank day after tomorrow and see where we go from there. Truthfully I don't think I'll get my licences back that quickly and I think probably all they want to do is see how I handle a commercial plane rather than those piddly little things at the club. But the club said I behaved myself and didn't go off the end of the runway or anything so the airline are happy to give me a go."

"You're going back to London?" the Prof checked, thinking how he was going to miss the other man's company after these last long weeks.

"Yes. I'll drive back tomorrow."

Kathy interrupted before the Prof even said anything. "I'm coming with you. And don't you argue with me. We're not leaving you to do this on your own."

He gave her a lovely smile, but his eyes were sad. "No, I don't suppose for one minute that you will."

"So what's at Cranebank?"

"Airline training centre."

"I've never seen an airline training centre."

"And nor will you this time."

"Oh, yes I will. If I have to hide in the boot of your car and get smuggled in. Just think of me as the barnacle glued to your hull."

To the unspoken delight of the other two, Piers so nearly laughed at that idea. "I'd better make sure I don't sit on you."

Kathy hadn't expected to be allowed into the training centre but they hadn't turned her away. She was glad she had taken her knitting and a book to read though as she spent a lot of the day hanging about waiting for Piers while various airline officials took him away and brought him back a few times. He didn't tell her much but she learned he had passed the medical checks in spite of his weight loss and he did well enough in the flight simulator for them to finish their day out at Heathrow. But it had been a long day and Piers was tired by this time. He didn't say anything at all on their way back to Earl's Court that evening and Kathy guessed from the silence that he hadn't got his licences back yet.

It was only three days after Piers' visit to the airline training centre that the Dodman Trio set off on the first leg of their trip round Europe. Kathy was glad to see he was in a surprisingly good mood when they left Earl's Court at some ridiculous hour to catch the early morning ferry at Dover which meant they should get to Paris in time for their evening meal. From Paris they were moving north and east across France into West Germany. Then they were doubling back to Brussels and finally north to Amsterdam before catching the overnight ferry at the Hook of Holland to bring them back to Harwich at the end of the fortnight.

Jean-Guy was asleep on the back seat by the time they were stuck in the queue for temporary traffic lights at roadworks on the A20.

"Will we still make Dover on time?" Kathy asked, starting to feel anxious.

"Easily," Piers assured her. "We've allowed ourselves a good hour to get stuck in traffic and we may even make an earlier ferry as we made good time this far."

Kathy felt this could be an opportunity to find out some details as he seemed in a calm mood, and not in the least bit grumpy today. "Was it funny being back at work after so long away? I know I found it mad enough after being shut in the farmhouse for three months last year."

"Was a bit," he admitted reluctantly.

"So what happens next? Are you alright? Or did you flunk the tests on purpose as you love playing trios so much?"

He gave her one of his lovely smiles. "Truthfully, I'm a lot better now. And one day I'll thank you for being such a bloody persistent barnacle. But there's a reason I'm not allowed back just yet although I do like your theory."

Kathy looked back at Jean-Guy but he was fast asleep in his adorable Moly way. "Is it because you're still underweight and they're afraid you might faint again?"

He looked at her a bit oddly. "No, nothing like that."

She had been so convinced that was what had happened, his reply threw her a little. "Did they not tell you the reason?"

"Didn't need to." Piers looked in the mirror and saw Jean-Guy was deeply asleep on the back seat. "Last thing they put me though was to send me up with a check pilot and he failed me on two minor points." The traffic crawled forward a few hundred yards. "Which wasn't what I wanted to hear. Common sense says I have to play their game and they really are being very good about it. I've got a good record, and they like me because I do the on-call work and cope with being type-rated on more than one kind of aeroplane. The shrink is very involved in my recovery plan now, and her strong recommendation was that I accept their offer of extra training to get me a type-rating on the Tristar or the DC-10 again, which is at least a start. My crew always said I could land a broken aeroplane in a blizzard, so it's kind of annoying that I'm not back to standard yet but they've said I can go out to Filton at some point in the next month or so after we're back."

Kathy was a bit bothered that he had mentioned in passing that a psychiatrist was part of his recovery. But then he had also mentioned the accusation that his nutritional self-neglect had been more psychosomatic than a simple case of forgetfulness. She looked across at him but he was apparently concentrating on his driving again now the traffic was on the move but she knew from his voice that he had done his thinking already.

"What's at Filton?"

"Concorde training."

"Well that sounds promising."

"Yes, it is. But first they want me to qualify on something that doesn't go quite so fast."

She had forgotten about his well-defined sense of irony. "So after you'd argued with them what was the final agreement?"

He smiled quietly. "You know me too well. Funnily enough, this time I agreed with them, which they weren't expecting. I had a type-rating on the Tristar which wasn't that lapsed so they're going to work me bloody hard to get rated on that again in the next few weeks. I'll be more of a first officer to begin with although they're letting me keep my rank and salary. So even when there are passengers in the cabin I won't be in overall charge of the flight for a while."

"And Concorde?" Kathy wanted to know. "I'm guessing that's still the ultimate aim."

"Yes. But once they're satisfied with me in the Tristar I know they're going to be cracking on with my update training for her. But once I've got my type-rating back and before I'm allowed to take her on a commercial flight they've said I'll have to turn into a teacher and get the new arrivals through the first flight sessions at Brize. A bit of a trade-off on their part. I don't mind. At least they didn't sling me out on my pension. But they've got to make bloody sure I'm safe before they turn me loose on the public again."

Kathy wondered if there was some reason he was being shown such favouritism but guessed the airline had its reasons. "Oh. Well that doesn't sound too bad. At least they're not taking your captaincy away from you. And I'm sure you'll have fun buzzing about in Concorde even if it's not going across the Atlantic."

He looked across at her with one of his lovely smiles and she couldn't have said how happy she was to see that smile again when not so long ago she had been afraid it had been lost to them for ever. "Not sure 'buzzing' is a word I'd apply to Concorde. But, no, give me another year or so and they'll be making me a senior captain which will mean a very welcome pay rise. So I'm going back after this tour and I've promised a lot of people, now including you, that I'm going to behave and work bloody hard to get back to where I was. As I said, they're being more than fair considering I nearly destroyed a very expensive aeroplane. The good thing is I didn't damage the plane or any people and they let me off the bollocking when they knew I was in hospital and, mercifully for me, no further action being taken over the incident."

Jean-Guy slept most of the way to Dover and woke up with a grumpy headache that wasn't made any better by the choppy crossing to Calais. The other two were quite worried about him as he spent most of the voyage in the gents' toilets being very sick indeed. He hadn't wanted Piers in there to keep an eye on him but preferred to suffer the indignity without witnesses and he looked pale and haggard when they got back in the car to continue their journey. Kathy thought it might help his general queasiness if he travelled in the passenger seat of the Land Rover but he had been sick twice more by the time they stopped in Amiens just for a bit of a break. They sat at a pavement table of a café with Jean-Guy drinking water and the other two, who hadn't been seasick, with coffees.

"I don't understand it," he grumbled to his fellow travellers. "I have never been so sick before in my life when I have been travelling. And I will tell you one thing," he finished resolutely, "there is no way I am going back on a ship as the crossing from Holland takes all night. I will get trains, buses, ride a donkey, whatever to get to the airport, but I am flying home from Holland."

"Your choice," Piers agreed. "I can bring the car back. So, Piglet, you get to choose who you'll travel home with from Amsterdam." He smiled at her. "Not that I need to guess which one of us you'll pick. Really missed my chance with you, didn't I?"

They played their two nights in Paris then set off across the country, their confidence boosted by the excellent reviews they had received in the Paris press. They couldn't help but notice that as they went from venue to venue so their audiences got bigger. They were just grateful that the first of the TV interviews was in France where Jean-Guy was near-fluent in the language and the other two knew enough not to appear rude by only speaking English. The interview had gone well but afterwards Jean-Guy told Kathy she spoke French like an English schoolgirl which she couldn't deny, and Piers that he spoke the weirdest French he had ever heard. Piers just laughed and didn't elaborate on the strange patois he knew and his odd pronunciation but he had been understandable and in turn had understood the more conventional French being spoken to him.

The West Germans adored the Dodman Trio and two concert venues had already booked them to return in two years' time before they left the country. Interviews were a bit harder in Germany as none of them spoke German but the reviews continued to be very favourable. Kathy and Piers knew that most of the critical acclaim was due to the undoubted talent of the cellist but they just basked in the reflected glory and let him take centre stage. It was a man from the audience of the Hamburg concert who saw the trio having lunch in a local café the day after and who approached them to ask in perfect English if the pianist was any sort of relation to Roisin Thompson because they looked remarkably similar.

To the admiration of the other two, Piers didn't falter but stuck to the storyline they had all worked out last year. "Yes, we are related, but it's too complicated to explain. Large family tree and all that."

"Have you ever performed together?" was the persistent question from the man who clearly knew his music.

"A few times in the past. She does have a lot of accompanists."

The man smiled then. "True. One other thing, if I may? If you were a violinist or a cellist, you take your instrument with you, but as the pianist you play a different instrument in each venue. How do you find that?"

Kathy couldn't help but notice that she and Jean-Guy were also waiting for the reply.

"I don't really think about it. I always get to have a warm-up on the piano before a concert, don't think I've ever gone into one completely cold as it were so you soon pick up the quirks and the sound of it. Some it's purely technical and you have to hit the keys a bit harder, or a pedal may be a bit sticky but they're all so finely tuned and adjusted these days, I've never had a problem with it."

The man considered that quite carefully then handed across a business card. "I think I may make enquiries about booking your trio for a recital when I get home. I found your Dvorak interpretation last night was one of the best I have ever known. Do you have a card for your agent?"

Kathy always had some of Jane's cards in her bag and she gave the man a smile as she handed one over.

He glanced at it quickly. "Thank you, I will give her a ring and see what she says. I hope it won't be a problem." He saw their slightly puzzled looks. "I am from Leipzig in East Germany. But I will make enquiries." He politely left them to their lunches.

"Well, would you?" Kathy asked Jean-Guy. "Go to Leipzig?"

He thoughtfully chewed an olive. "Not without an armed guard. Probably. But it would be very tempting. Who was he anyway?" He took the card from

Piers and read the name. "Oh, him. He used to be one of my father's associates. Not a close friend, but I know the name."

"Do you trust him?" came the rather sharp question from the man who had given up on his meal.

"I can't really trust anyone," Jean-Guy admitted. "But it may be a way to meet my family again just for a while if we can all make it to Leipzig at the same time. They are more likely to get travel permission if they stay their side of the iron curtain."

"Well, I don't suppose you'll listen to me for one minute, but I'd tell you not to risk it. You'd be way too close to the Russian border for my liking and I don't think your parents would be able to protect you."

"Maybe even though you are the one who flies crazy-fast planes, I am the risk-taker? For my family I would go."

"It's because I fly crazy-fast aeroplanes, as you put it so well, that I don't take risks. Let's wait and see what he offers Jane shall we? He may get back home to Leipzig and get told not to be such an idiot and it's never going to happen. Can't see it coming off somehow. So don't start getting excited about meeting up with Mum and Dad any time soon, huh?"

"Good idea," Kathy approved, glad to hear that one of the two was being sensible. "Aren't you going to eat your dinner?"

"Not really hungry today."

"You didn't eat breakfast either as you got up so late," Kathy chided him. "Go on, eat it. It's only a sandwich and Jean-Guy and I will then have time for cake too."

Piers rather grumpily finished off the sandwich, watched by Kathy to make sure he did, while Jean-Guy went and bought two cakes and coffees at the counter. He was grinning broadly when he came back to the table.

"What's so funny?" Kathy wanted to know, but pleased that at least one of them was smiling.

"I have just thought we are such a mixed trio. We have sensible Piers, irresponsible me and you who keeps mothering us. We have no, what was it you called Pippa? Divas. We always swap the order of names on the programmes so none of us is ever the headliner. We are three nationalities, our background lives could not be more different if we tried and yet when we come together to play music it is as though we all breathe as one."

Kathy thought that was a beautiful way of expressing it and knew just what he meant.

Piers didn't comment on what Jean-Guy had said but just swiped a chocolate curl off the top of Kathy's slice of cake and ate it. "Don't I get a coffee then?" He suddenly pulled a face and discreetly spat the chocolate back into a paper napkin. "You could have told me it's got cinnamon on it, you trying to make me ill?"

"Don't you look at me all accusing," she retorted fondly. "That's what you get for stealing chocolate."

"You shouldn't have put it within range. You know what I'm like with chocolate."

"Not so sensible now, huh?" She waved another curl at him. "Want to risk this one not having cinnamon on it?"

Jean-Guy got to his feet even though he quite liked to watch those two with their harmless banter. "I will buy you a coffee and a cake of your own. Do you want to come and choose it to make sure it is safe for you to eat?"

Piers smiled and shook his head. "I've just got through half a loaf of bread with a shoal of tuna in it, so no cake for me, thanks."

"You have a strange idea of loaves and shoals," Kathy told him and offered a chocolate curl that had definitely missed the cinnamon dusting. "Here, try this one."

Piers looked at it suspiciously. "Nah, you eat it. I'll find a proper chocolate shop and get myself something half decent. Might even get some for you if you'll just stop trying to shove cake up my nose."

Jean-Guy went to buy another coffee and left them to it.

From Germany they went non-stop across to Belgium which was a lot of driving and Jean-Guy was glad Kathy argued with Piers until he gave in and let her take on some of the hours behind the wheel. Their pianist may have been a hell of a lot better than he had been at the end of January but the other two could tell that by the time the Belgians were being enchanted by the Dodman Trio one of them had gone back to his habit of missing bits out so he could keep up as his stamina and concentration were failing. It always irritated Jean-Guy when Piers did that but he had had to accept over the last two weeks that even though they weren't playing anything very demanding and were repeating a lot of their repertoire, the piano player had started to struggle.

It didn't help to soothe Jean-Guy's frustration with the pianist that for the last two concerts of their tour they were playing in the concert hall where the Amsterdam Concertgebouw habitually performed and he just knew there were going to be several members of that renowned orchestra in the audience no doubt listening critically to the music. Not that it mattered too much to the other two who persisted in maintaining they didn't ever want to work as soloists, but Jean-Guy had been invited to play with the Dutch orchestra and he hoped they would be suitably impressed with his playing.

To his profound relief, it was as though the others knew how much these last concerts meant to him and he was so thankful that, even though they were all tiring now, Kathy and Piers drove themselves to a superbly high standard of playing and he couldn't have asked for their first tour to finish any better. He knew it had gone exceptionally well when the conductor of the Concertgebouw came backstage after the last concert and personally congratulated all three on their excellent playing.

Jean-Guy insisted on taking the other two out to a post-concert meal even though they had to be up fairly early to get to the airport as he and Kathy were flying home. He couldn't quite persuade Kathy to join him in a bottle of champagne to celebrate the end of what had really been a very successful first tour for the Dodman Trio but the two did share a bottle of wine. Piers had just laughed when offered some and reminded them both that he was driving tomorrow and if there was one thing he never did it was mix alcohol with flying or driving. He couldn't even be persuaded to toast the success of the tour with a glass of beer. But he did concede that it was a celebration so he accepted a bottle of sparkling water and consequently got the noisiest attack hiccups the other two had ever heard.

It was a cool and drizzly day in Holland when Piers drove them to Schiphol airport so Kathy and Jean-Guy could catch the flight back to Norwich. They felt a bit guilty that he was having to drive the Land Rover to the port and then up from Harwich all by himself but he assured them each time they asked that he would much rather do that than fly as a passenger. Besides which he had a perfectly good cabin booked on the overnight ferry and as seasickness had never bothered him in the past, he was looking forward to a good night's sleep.

Kathy hadn't done much flying before and was glad their luggage was staying in the Land Rover along with all the music they had bought on their travels. She was relieved Piers stayed with them and saw them through check in and passport control as it was all a bit confusing for her but he clearly knew his way round the airport and its systems. They arrived at the departure lounge and looked at the indicator board.

"There's you," he told her. "Air UK to Norwich. They'll call you when it's time to board."

"The planes look very small," she offered, looking out of the window.

"Best ones always are. You'll enjoy it once you get going." He had to smile to see the worried look on her face. "Piglet, you'll be fine. In fact, if you watch the runway for a while you'll see some much bigger planes coming in from all over the world. Look, there's a Pan Am 747 just coming in now. Just don't expect to see Concorde as she doesn't come here unless she's invited."

Jean-Guy looked at the huge plane making its arrival at Amsterdam and remembered the man standing with them used to fly those aircraft as well as the supersonic one. He was glad he was a cellist and not an airline pilot. He saw the critical way Piers was watching that landing. "You miss your flying so much, don't you?"

Piers was saved having to reply as a man in pilot's uniform walked swiftly up behind them, gave Piers a slap on the shoulders and said a bit too loudly for subtlety, "Please, please tell me you're not on my flight?" They all turned and saw a blond man with the three stripes of a first officer, who was grinning broadly. "Saw you at check-in. Where are you all off to?"

"These two are going to Norwich. I'm catching the overnight ferry."

"Thank Christ for that. I don't want you on my flight."

Kathy looked at Jean-Guy and knew she couldn't miss the opportunity. "Why not?"

The blond man laughed. "He has a reputation."

A couple of cabin crew wandered along to join them.

"Hi, Captain B," was the young man's greeting, which Kathy thought was rather informal. "Please tell me you're not on my flight?"

"He's catching the overnight ferry," the pilot replied.

"Thank Christ for that. I don't want you on my flight."

"My very words exactly."

The three uniformed air crew were suddenly all trying not to laugh too loudly in the middle of a public airport as it looked rather unprofessional. The cabin crew lady got her wits together first. "Which flight are you on?"

"Air UK to Norwich," Kathy replied, really wanting to know what the in-joke was.

"Oh, you'll be with Clare. Come along to the VIP lounge and we'll sneak you in there with the business class rather than have you waiting out here. She'll probably even find you some coffee and biscuits."

"Well, thank you," Kathy said politely and retuned the lady's smile which was a proper smile and not the professional one she would give the passengers when they were in her plane. "Why do you call him Captain B?"

"It's what he was known as in his Air France days. Seemed the French couldn't cope with his name. Forget how it came with him when he switched airlines but everyone's done it for years. Just laziness now probably. We have to be careful or we do it in front of the passengers."

"Makes him sound like the villain in a film," Kathy couldn't help thinking out loud and the three air crew had to mute their fresh howls of laughter.

"See you back home," was all Piers said and he left them with the three air crew calling remarks after him about he wouldn't be allowed to fly a car ferry even if he was an international villain. He just waved a rude gesture at them and didn't look back.

"Please tell me why you don't want him on your plane?" Kathy asked the blond pilot.

He just smiled vaguely. "He's damned good at his job and it really puts the pressure on the rest of his crew. I've been his first officer a few times and, not saying he's tough, well he is but he's always nice about it, but he doesn't let you get away with anything even if he's a passenger in the jump seat. Thank Christ they're putting him on Concorde training so I won't run across him. Bloody good move on their part though. You know he famously barrel-rolled that bus when he was helping test her in his France days, don't you?" He pulled a bit of a face. "Twice I've tried to pass the conversion course to fly her and didn't make it beyond the initial theory work. Bloody hard machine to fly and he handles her as well as two others. Bastard. I don't suppose he's told you the story of our landing a malfunctioning aircraft in a blizzard in that unpronounceable place in Greenland. That was the first time I'd flown with him and the weather conditions were so bad I have never, ever been so certain I was going to die in all my life. Hell really had frozen over that day and I don't know any other pilot who could have brought that aircraft in. And here's where I leave you as I've got to go to the briefing for my flight. Good to have met you." He went off along another corridor whistling something untuneful to himself, still without telling them his name and leaving the tantalising story untold.

Kathy remembered Piers' off-hand remark about landing a broken aeroplane in a blizzard but the pilot had obviously said all he was going to say on the subject. So she turned to the two cabin crew, who she had seen from their name badges were Linda and Edward.

"What blizzard?" she asked.

"Oh, that's one that's gone down in airline history," Linda told her.

Edward smiled too. "Certainly has. I've worked with a couple of the cabin crew who were on that flight. Just incredible. Anyway," he said to Linda "I must just powder my nose before the briefing. See you in there."

Linda escorted Kathy and Jean-Guy for a few more yards across the concourse then paused outside a door labelled VIP Lounge. "Is it true?" she asked suddenly.

"Is what true?" Kathy replied innocently.

Linda's next sentence blew apart all Kathy thought she had ever known about Piers but it suddenly made the comments and intrigue of the last few months make some kind of a horrible sense. "They're saying Captain B tried to commit suicide in the new year. Nearly caused a major incident with a runway excursion in Concorde but got it under control with less than a yard of runway to go and they found him a couple of hours later in the crew area full of sleeping pills and Scotch."

Kathy felt as though every drop of blood had left her body. She found herself unable to speak and too shocked even to cry as the pieces of the jigsaw began to fall into place. She didn't want to acknowledge it but it explained too much: the alleged 'accident', the medication, the constant watch by the hospital staff and then by the Professor, the doubts of the airline about his suitability to return to work, the quiet resumption of duties and not being in charge of a flight just yet. Jean-Guy put his arm across her shoulders and gave her a hug. He spoke very quietly but with a reassuring certainty and Kathy wasn't sure whether he didn't believe the rumour as she had or whether he was protecting a friend. "He has never said anything to us. I can't believe it, he's far too sensible. He was probably just tired and fell asleep. He does that sometimes."

Linda shrugged and tried to pretend it was no big deal. "I didn't like to think so either. It's just what some people said. I wasn't working that day but apparently he was taken away in an ambulance. And it's odd he's been off so long when they're desperately short of Concorde pilots." She hung on her professional smile. "Anyway, come and meet Clare, we used to work together until she switched airline, and she'll look after you for your flight."

Kathy couldn't wait to get back to the farmhouse. The taxi home from the airport was an extravagance but they were being well paid for their tour and didn't begrudge it. To Kathy's relief they arrived back just as the Prof had made a pot of tea and he was genuinely delighted to see them apparently arriving back a day early.

"I have been reading in the press that it all went very well. I expect you'll have a lot more interest in your trio now. But where is Piers? Have you left him in the flesh pots of Amsterdam? Kathy? What is the matter? Has there been an accident?"

So she told him, fighting back her tears and not comforted by the expression on his face.

"I'm sorry you had to hear it like that," the Prof said. "What you have been told is part true and part hearsay. I was given the facts by the people I work for so I knew exactly why he was in hospital, but he also gave me his version that first night here when he was at his worst. Now you have been told some inaccuracies by a third party I am happy to correct what you were told by giving you the true facts. His side of the story he asked me not to tell but I hope he will do that himself now you know the worst of it. The Scotch is true but he mixed it with industrial cleaning fluid not pills as that is what was to hand. He was physically burned inside from his mouth to his stomach, and nobody knows what the long-term damage will be. He is only with us because his co-pilot had forgotten something and returned to the crew area in time to get some fingers down his throat and make him sick as he thought Piers had swallowed pills. It made the burns worse but at least kept most of it out of the rest of his organs. Officially it was put out that he was most definitely off duty, had a bit too much to drink when he was tired and fell, hence the call for the ambulance. And that is why they wouldn't discharge him to go home by himself and I must admit I was surprised they trusted him to drive himself here and didn't bring him in an ambulance. And which is why someone else had to monitor his drugs in case he tried to take too many at once." He looked at the other two who were just sitting at the table and staring at him as though they didn't believe a word he was saying. "Which he has never tried to do," he offered in an attempt to reassure them.

"Will they ever let him fly again?" Kathy hardly dared ask. "I mean really fly? Supersonic to New York and not just hopping round Europe in a geriatric Tristar and teaching the young bloods on the plane he used to fly every week."

"As I have mentioned to you before, the security services need him to keep flying so there is a lot of pressure on the airline to do as they are told. The psychiatrist is satisfied it was a direct reaction to losing Chantal taken at a time when he was mentally exhausted and just not thinking straight. Her exact phrase was that 'the balance of his mind was disturbed' and I have to agree with that. She is certain it won't be repeated and on her recommendations, as well as those I work for, the airline are breaking him back in slowly. Fortunately attitudes are changing and companies such as his airline now realise actions like his mean he needs help and not the instant dismissal he would have had once. Personally, having had him to myself for that time, I know he is not sorry to have survived. We have had many conversations, he doesn't know it but I had to tape them or make notes and send them in to those I work for, and we also are satisfied it won't be repeated. Now, have your tea then go and relax after your travels. I'm guessing you left Piers to bring all the instruments back so that gives you an evening off?"

"Just one evening," Jean-Guy replied, still trying to believe what the Prof had told them. "I think we've earned that much."

"Where's Audrey?" Kathy thought to ask, looking round for the cat.

"On the piano waiting for you, last time I saw her." The Prof consoled. "Been a bit of a terror while you've been away and brought in her first mouse for me this morning. So she's fine. Which in your mind no doubt means Piers is fine too?"

Kathy smiled. "Of course. Do you think that's why she was so odd at new year? I actually managed to convince myself she'd eaten too much turkey."

The two men looked at her. "Don't you dare," Jean-Guy said. "Don't you dare speculate that that cat was throwing up turkey at exactly the time her human was having his stomach pumped."

"Wasn't going to," Kathy lied. "But I'm going to be optimistic and say the mouse is a present and she's saying 'thank you' on behalf of her human."

Kathy spent an anxious night now she knew the truth and she felt as though she was finally able to breathe again as Audrey set off her early warning signal while Kathy and Jean-Guy were breakfasting late the next morning.

Piers was a bit surprised when he walked in to the kitchen through the back door to be greeted first by Audrey throwing herself onto his chest then having Kathy give him a tight hug, nearly squashing the cat, and a kiss that was dangerously closer to his mouth than his cheek.

"Nice greeting," he told her as he put his cat on the floor then carefully returned the kiss on the cheek as her boyfriend was, after all, watching them.

She stood in front of him, with her hands on his arms, five foot two of incandescent rage and yelled at him, "Why the hell didn't you tell us?"

He looked over her head at Jean-Guy. "What have I done now?"

Jean-Guy wasn't smiling, but he thought an angry Kathy was a massive turn-on. "Tried to kill yourself," he said more brutally than he had intended but that wasn't where his mind was going.

To Kathy's great comfort, Piers put his arms round her and gave her a lovely cuddle. "Oh, Piglet. I didn't know how to tell you two, and now you've found out all the wrong way round, but I guess that's what happens when my worlds collide."

"Tell us what happened," she asked him softly and didn't let go.

She heard him sigh quietly above her head. Then he told them dispassionately and without apology. "Don't really remember much about it. Just odd images like a set of photos. Sitting in the crew area, really late, cursing myself for that landing and knowing I was going to get an official reprimand on my records. Feeling so tired I wanted to fall asleep and not wake up ever again. I have no memory of finding the Scotch, where the hell I got the bleach or of actually drinking the stuff. Dacre, my regular first officer, told me he'd forgotten the bottle he'd bought himself and came back to get it, found me on the floor, bottle in one hand and bleeding from the mouth and nose so at first he thought I'd fallen and smacked my face. He shouted at a nearby cleaner to call the ambulance. I didn't know until he told me later but he lost his younger daughter to an overdose several years ago so he soon worked out I hadn't just passed out pissed and stuffed his fingers down my throat assuming I'd taken pills. He stayed with me all the way to the hospital, he must have done but I don't remember that either. Vague memory of half waking up in the emergency room, think I may actually have been screaming with pain at that point, and soaked in blood and water as they were flushing me out. They said his actions had saved me even if it had made the burns worse. He and his wife Angela stayed with me for four whole days while I was in intensive care until the medics said my internal organs had survived and I was out of danger. He thought I lived alone and there's no next of kin on my paperwork so there wasn't anyone he could ring. Apparently I owe him a hefty dry cleaning bill and a bottle of single malt since I drank most of his. I think I owe him a hell of a lot more."

Kathy hugged him close not sure whether she was going to cry or be sick herself, and still mad at him for making her feel guilty as though she had somehow failed him. She was shocked by the hard physical facts of what he had done and could accept now that it wasn't something he was going to get over quickly. "I'm glad you've told us," she said gently. "It can't have been easy to talk about. But will you promise me one thing?"

"Depends what it is," he said cautiously but relieved the other two knew at last.

"If you ever feel like that again you will call me or Jean-Guy straight away? I don't care what time zones we're all in. I don't want you to feel you have to cope alone like that ever again. And get someone on your paperwork." She squeezed him a bit too hard. "Promise?"

"Ow! That's two promises. OK, OK, I promise. Twice. Just don't break my ribs. Shit but you're strong for such a little runt."

Kathy still hadn't quite got over her temper. "Have you told Sarah?"

"Not about the bleach, no. And I'm not going to. So I'd be grateful if you didn't either."

"I don't agree but I'll respect your decision. I'd guess she's officially your next of kin but if you don't want her listed for any reason, then put any or all of us three but for pity's sake put someone. Now eat some breakfast, because I bet you didn't eat on the ferry." She knew he was about to refuse. "Want any more broken ribs?"

"OK, you win. I'll eat quietly."

A thought suddenly occurred to her. "Are you on a special diet now?"

"No. They just told me they have no idea what will happen long term but if it hurts a lot or I bleed internally I have to go to hospital as an emergency. They even gave me some kind of alert tag to wear. I got the impression I was the first survivor they'd had to deal with so they're basically working on theories. Their advice is drink water, the colder the better, to keep the acids diluted. I can't take anything hot, temperature or spice, as it inflames the wounds and apparently I've been mildly dairy intolerant for years. Wondered why cheese always seemed to give me stomach ache. And I shouldn't sneeze too hard as I even managed to burn the membranes in my nose."

"And where is the tag?" Kathy asked, glad his suddenly peculiar diet had been explained.

She got the reply she wasn't expecting. "Round my neck on a chain. Want to see it?"

"Go on then."

Piers fished a silver disc out from under his shirt and showed it to her. On one side was the caduceus symbol of medical emergency and on the other a simple engraving of *Internal chemical burns*.

"I'm impressed," she admitted. "I was convinced you were going to say you'd left it in Earl's Court."

"Don't be impressed, I'm the sensible one, remember? I don't often take it off especially if I'm travelling alone."

Jean-Guy had listened to the whole story, thankful the other two knew not to speak too fast near him even now so he had understood every word. Understood the words, but couldn't understand the concept. The distress of hearing what Piers had done had even made him forget how erotic the angry Kathy had been. He sounded like a man waking from a nightmare. "How could you do that? How could you mix bleach and Scotch and then drink it? It must have burned like hell from the first taste. How? How could you go on swallowing it and burning up inside? I have been low in my time. At my worst before I defected, I had thought about cutting my wrists or even taking twenty pills in one go. Quick, spontaneous. But that, that was so…so… I have run out of words. I will never understand you icy English. Everything so cold and thought out."

The other two could tell from the tone of his voice just how upset he was. To Kathy's relief she heard Piers smile above her head.

"I guess I used what there was to hand. And please stop calling me English. I am no more English than you are Chinese."

They tried something different that morning and had a go at the Suk *Elegy* which none of them knew but they had bought it in a music shop in Brussels. The Prof listened from his study for a while then wandered in to find out what it was they were playing.

He sat, as he sometimes did during their practice sessions, on the piano stool with Piers, and quietly turned the pages of the piano score so he could see what should be happening as well as hear what was actually being played. It wasn't a piece commonly in the repertoire and he thought the three of them handled the simplicity of it very well without making it over sweet.

"Not really your style," he assessed and happened to glance down at the pianist's feet. "Shoes?" he asked.

"No chance."

"Kathy, Jean-Guy please tell me this man wore shoes when you were on tour?"

Kathy laughed. "I don't think you wore them for any concert did you?"

"Not a single one," Jean-Guy confirmed. "Still at least you don't wear noisy socks."

To the astonishment of the other three, their pianist suddenly snorted at great risk to the membranes in his nose and burst into his rare, infectious laugh until his eyes were streaming and they had all joined in.

"Sorry," he finally managed to say. "I shouldn't laugh as I can't speak a word of Czech but the idea of noisy socks is a good one. What sort of noise do they make?"

"They squeak," Kathy told him. "You know he meant loud patterns. And you're right, it's mean to laugh at Jean-Guy's English. Go on, make him say it in Czech."

Jean-Guy really didn't mind, he was pleased to see the other man so amused. "You must be joking. I've heard what he does to French."

No offence was taken by any party and the Prof was glad to see that the three could still be so comfortable with each other as only good friends could. "Seriously," he said to Piers. "You aren't safe sliding across stages in socks. Would you fly Concorde in socks?"

Piers and Kathy caught each other's eye and they were both weeping with laughter all over again.

"Bloody long socks," Piers wheezed.

"I'm not offering to knit them," Kathy put in and mopped her streaming eyes on the cuffs of her pink sweatshirt.

The Prof worked out what had amused them so much. "Go and make us all some coffee the pair of you and calm down a bit." He listened fondly to the shrieks and howls of laughter still coming from the kitchen. "I think your tour has done your pianist no end of good," he said quietly in Czech, just in case they were still in earshot of the legendary rabbit-ears.

"It has done us all good. I think we are a stronger trio for it all."

"Good. And unanimously excellent reviews too. But I mean it. You won't be such a good trio if your pianist has broken his neck. Why does he do it anyway?"

"He says it helps him feel the pedals. And you have to admit he does have a very subtle pedalling technique. I don't know any other pianist who can play like that."

"Interesting comment. I often wonder who taught him to play."

"I've never asked as he would have learned as a young child and he is not comfortable talking about those times. But his style is hardly conventional, is it? I'm not going to worry about it. So long as he plays like he does and there aren't any broken necks I'm not going to tell him to keep his shoes on."

Piers and Kathy came back with the coffees to have the Prof ask politely of the former, "Who taught you to play the piano?"

"My mother mostly," he replied, being less snappy than he would have been if either of the other two had asked the question.

"Was she a good pianist?"

As always when his childhood was mentioned, the shutters came crashing down. "No idea," was the cold reply.

Jean-Guy diplomatically changed the conversation. "I'm not sure the Suk is the right piece for us."

"It's OK," Kathy decided, picking up on his tactic. "But it's a bit boring." She raised her mug of coffee. "Here's to cracking the Mendelssohn."

Thinking about his childhood always made Piers either grumpy or withdrawn and nobody was surprised when he wandered out into the garden to sit on the old stone bench after coffee rather than go back to his music. Jean-Guy tried so hard to understand why Kathy felt the need to go out there to keep him company but he was learning to trust her and at least so long as they sat on the bench anyone looking out of the kitchen window could see them.

"Going to see Sarah tonight?" Kathy asked as an opening remark, hoping to steer Piers' mind back to the present from the past.

"Not tonight," he replied quietly and wouldn't look at her.

"Things OK between you two?"

"Yes," he replied and she heard him smile. "Funnily enough I think we're stronger now than we've ever been. Much to Alison's disgust. In fact, without going into too much detail, the last time we were in bed together Sarah got the shirt off me so she could see the tattoo. Not saying she likes it, but she's come to accept it's part of what I am. And then she told me the strangest thing." He stopped, clearly not sure how much more he should say. "Oh, what the hell. If anyone's going to understand, it's you. I'm sure you know she comes from a long line of women who have been called witches for generations. She has always tried to deny it, but she is a shadow-seer."

Kathy had no idea what he was talking about. "I don't understand," she offered diplomatically.

"In her own way, she walks the old ways too. We both felt it that day you introduced us and we shook hands. Someone in your past has walked the ways and that is what you and I have in common that Jean-Guy can't share and struggles so much to accept."

It all started to make sense now. Their deep friendship that existed on a level she had never known with anyone else. A shared understanding, if not a faith, that united their souls without them feeling the need to let their bodies follow. She glanced sideways at his perfect profile, half-shadowed by the old crabapple tree. "And what is a shadow-seer?"

"Sarah sees shadows, usually behind people, if they have something dark or bad in their life. She saw it growing in you about five years ago apparently but she never said anything as she didn't know you so well then, but she says your shadow is almost gone now. Mine, apparently has been getting darker and larger ever since our wedding and she thought at first it was because I was unhappy with her."

"And are you?"

"No. Not at all. And once she understood about Chantal she knew what the cause of the shadow is."

"Do you still have the shadow?"

"Apparently it's fading."

"I'm glad," Kathy said softly and felt her head lean on his shoulder. "I think you're right that we both tap into something the others can't share, but I've never learned anything about it. Just sometimes, I see things, all my life, I've... No, you'll be the one thinking I'm ridiculous."

"I'll never think you're ridiculous," he promised her but her body language told him she wished she hadn't said anything. It had been a little too personal to share. "But I can understand how it scares you. Tell me about what you see," he encouraged.

Kathy hesitated. "I don't like to call them visions, that sounds too religious. Like you and the black cat. It's not déjà vu. I don't what it is. I half-said something to Emma once when we were pretty drunk. Probably about fifteen or sixteen."

Piers hadn't moved his shoulder away. "How long did she laugh at you for?"

Kathy smiled to remember. "At least a month. Then I shocked her even more by... oh, never mind, it was a long time ago. Anyway, she's never mentioned it again once she'd established I couldn't visualise what was going to come up on the Pools."

"So your images aren't predictions or premonitions?" was the calmly sensible question.

"No. And there's only one I have more than once."

"Which is?"

"Oh, it sounds silly. But I'm standing in a doorway. It's either a tall door or I've shrunk to about three feet high, and I'm looking down a brick path with really big flowers either side of it. Then everything goes black and I start flying and I'm really scared. Struggling and screaming in a language I don't recognise but I just keep flying. I used to see it a lot. I can close my eyes and see it now."

"Then it isn't an image, it's a memory. Did you ever ask your parents?"

"Only once, but they didn't have a clue either. We all tried to think of where it could have been but our front path at home is crazy paving not bricks. My aunt lives in a flat. I've got other relations but we couldn't think of one single house with a brick path. Something I dreamt about I suppose. Funny how some dreams stick with you."

"True," Piers agreed. "I still remember one about being chased through the cottage by my granny's spinning wheel. I can't have been more than about three or four and we hadn't been living with her for long."

"I wish I'd known her," Kathy mused without thinking. "She could have spun me some lovely Irish wool."

The shoulder moved from under her head so abruptly Kathy nearly fell sideways.

"She spun flax to make linen," Piers said coldly but politely as though acknowledging he had started this conversation. "Roisin and I weren't allowed to touch the flax but she let us have a go with some wool when she was in a good mood."

Kathy sat upright and looked at him with new eyes. "So you can spin?"

There was a pause. "Yes, a long time ago, Quite liked the monotony of it. Taught Kerryanne one time as she was complaining she couldn't get the kind of wool mix she wanted so I, not knowing any better, asked her why she didn't spin her own. Next time I saw her she presented me with bags of fleece and silk and Christ knows what else and a wheel and demanded lessons. I wasn't happy about it but she traded the chance to formation fly a USAF Phantom so I taught her. Silly cow wanted to spin the thinnest stuff she could. Cobweb she called it."

Kathy had never even dared try knitting with cobweb wool let alone spinning it. She guessed it maybe wouldn't be a good idea to ask Piers if he could teach her to spin too. "And did she?"

"Eventually."

"But you had a lot more fun in the Phantom."

"Certainly did."

Kathy glanced towards the house and saw Jean-Guy looking out from the kitchen window. "Seems you got a good trade."

Piers saw where she was looking. "He's watching us, isn't he?"

"Yup."

"He could always come and join us. Bench is big enough for three."

Kathy smiled and gave Jean-Guy a wave. "He won't. Too cold for him. He doesn't do cold."

"I had noticed. Are you sure you're not from the cold, wet mists of Ireland like me?"

She caught the light fondness in his tone. "Nope. Dad's family have always been in south London if not specifically Wimbledon. In fact he told me once his grandad used to drive a Hansom cab round Waterloo station way. Mum's almost exotic by comparison as she was born as far south as Norbiton so she grew up kind of Kingston way."

"You surprise me. I could have sworn there's a lick of the foreigner in you." Piers got to his feet rather stiffly and his knees cracked as they so often did. "Right, time to go back indoors and as I'm seeing Sarah tomorrow and as she keeps hinting three kids may not be enough after all I'd better not let the cold do what the lack of food managed."

Kathy stood beside him and looked quizzically up at him. "What do you mean?" She was so happy to be given one of his most wicked smiles.

"One of the side effects of starvation. Reproductive systems pack up."

"Oh!" she exclaimed and had to laugh. "I'll say it again, I'm so pleased I didn't have you for a big brother when I was a teenager."

He paused in his walk back to the house. "Uh-huh? And that is another story you're going to tell me one day."

"No chance!" she told him delightedly as the two went into the warmth of the kitchen.

Jean-Guy didn't even pretend he hadn't been watching them. "Got frostbite?" he asked cheerfully and tried not to mind too much that they had obviously been sharing quite a deep conversation.

"Not quite," Piers admitted. "Right, back to the piano for me."

Kathy warmed her hands over the Aga once Piers had left the kitchen. "We do have some strange conversations, Piers and I."

"Oh?" he asked curiously, obviously trying not to show it bothered him.

She turned from the warmth of the Aga and put loving arms round him. "Just conversations. We got through about three aspects of Paganism, spinning flax, and formation flying a Phantom." She gave Jean-Guy one of her most reassuring smiles. "He was telling me more about the old ways and I didn't realise how much he and Sarah have got in common. A lot more than I'd ever realised. He's finally, genuinely happy with Sarah and it sounds as though she wants more babies out of him."

"Bloody hell. I'd have thought three in one go would be enough for anyone."

"Well, yes, so would I." She fondly tapped his nose with one cold finger. "Please don't worry about me and Piers. We'd never do anything to hurt you. Or Sarah."

He gave her a fond smile and wished he could believe her. "You'd better not. I want to keep him as my accompanist."

"And I want to keep him as my friend," she replied and he knew he had been warned.

Antonín Dvořák – *Sonata for violin and piano in F, Op. 67 (B.106)*

Less than a week after their return from Europe, all three were back in London to pick up their separate working lives. Kathy felt a lot more settled now Piers was back with the airline again even if he was unusually quiet and grumbled it was all short-haul in a Tristar these days. At first, because of the work he was doing, he tended to get home more often in the evenings and just sometimes all three would manage to share a meal and sit in the living room and either play music or watch TV for a while. It was Kathy who noticed first that Piers always found some reason or another to leave the room when the television News was on but it was Jean-Guy who made the connection between Piers suddenly deciding he needed to go and make coffee or have a bath and the News coverage of RAF pilots on active service in the Falkland Islands. They knew he was still in touch with some of his friends from his days in the military but somehow didn't like to ask if any of them were now flying off South America. They wondered if perhaps a small part of him regretted that the chance for such intensive combat flying hadn't come his way during his years in the military. But he never said anything. Then in mid-May his working hours changed and he eventually admitted he was now commuting out Brize Norton and the airline had put him back where he had always vowed he would never be and was a full-time trainer on Concorde. But under the grumbling he had to admit it was good to be back with his old aeroplane again, even if it was only as a teacher.

Piers came back to Suffolk with them towards the end of May, still a bit cross that he was stuck with training duties and after one night in the farmhouse set off to visit his wife and children telling the Prof he didn't know when he'd be back but not to cook any supper for him.

The residents of the farmhouse were a bit surprised when Piers wasn't back the next day but he had the manners to ring them to let them know he would be with Sarah for another couple of days yet. He made some sarky comment about the pair of them were seeing just how long they could put up with each other and somehow nobody disbelieved him.

Jean-Guy was quite aware how anxious Kathy was getting over her upcoming recital in Yorkshire in early June and he was a bit cross with their pianist for not being around to practise with her more.

"Do you suppose he's not happy flying Concorde again?" Kathy asked Jean-Guy as he sat with her in the sitting room while she went through the Franck Sonata for the umpteenth time and still wasn't happy with it. "I can't imagine that somehow."

"Last time he told me anything it was that, yes, he is finding it frustrating that all they're allowing him to do is training but a lot of this training is demonstrating take offs and landings to the students before they get to have a go. And we mustn't forget that maybe one of the events that pushed him too far was that he made such a bad landing in the plane. But now he is landing her lots of times a day which I am sure is all part of the plan for his full recovery. Please stop playing that now. Even I can tell you are sick of it."

She thankfully stopped. "Sorry. I just really want this recital to go well and he's not helping my general state of panic by not being here."

"Right, that's it," Jean-Guy said so firmly Kathy was a bit worried.

"What is?"

"I'm telling him that he needs to be here with you until this recital is over. He spends more and more time with Sarah these days and I know she's his wife so I can understand why he wants to be with her so much but he does need to spend time on his music too. But, you know what he is like. He is too lazy to go over it like you do and no doubt thinks he can play it well enough. It is because he is firstly a pilot and we can't make him understand that this is as important to us as flying is to him."

"It is a bit like herding cats, isn't it?" she agreed. "I wish I could be more like him but if there was one thing I'm guilty of it's over-rehearsing. I suppose it's a basic lack of confidence in my own playing."

"But you shouldn't lack confidence. You are an excellent violinist," Jean-Guy told her loyally.

Kathy loved him for his belief in her and made herself put her violin away so she could join him on the sofa and cuddle against him. "Well, I'm flattered you think so."

He kissed the top of her head. "Can the truth be called flattery? And now, please don't think I am making little of your Yorkshire gig but I have to tell you that Jane called me earlier today. She's agreed a booking for me in New York with their Philharmonic Orchestra. It's one she's been negotiating for months so it's a bit short notice now."

Kathy was impressed. "Wow. Puts Yorkshire into perspective. When?"

"March next year. They've asked for the Shostakovich one night, but the other two nights I can choose. I'm to let them know fairly soon though so they can work it into their rehearsal schedules."

For a moment, Kathy forgot about Yorkshire. "Can I have a ticket?"

"Of course," he smiled. "What do you think I should play?"

"Well, I'm always a sucker for the Elgar."

"Too cliché for me. But if you like it so much, I will play it for you. I haven't run through it for a long time so I will need to herd the cat that is our rehearsal pianist some time soon. What else?"

Her smile was pure mischief. "How about the Prokofiev *Sinfonia Concertante* you've been working on since last year? The gig's nearly a year away so you and they will have plenty of time to polish up the parts. Then you're doing three very different pieces so people can come to all three concerts and not feel they're being fobbed off with the same programme over again."

Audrey had been curled round on top of the piano but she stirred and lifted her head to listen.

"Always a good sign," Kathy remarked.

The two of them listened too and, sure enough, about three minutes later they heard someone come into the kitchen.

"I thought you'd emigrated!" the Prof greeted the arrival cheerfully. "Are you joining us for lunch today?"

"Yes please. And supper. But not too much, I'm getting way too fat."

"Who says?"

"Me. Either that or someone's been shrinking my clothes in the wash. So either way it's your fault."

Kathy and Jean-Guy shared a smile of relief. Piers came blasting into the sitting room like fresh air after a heatwave and Audrey leaped delightedly from the piano straight onto his shoulder and purred loudly in his ear. "OK, Sarah's had enough of me for a while, the airline don't want me until next Tuesday, so what do you want to do with me?"

"Hang you up by the toenails," Kathy laughed. "I was just saying to Jean-Guy that getting you to play the piano is like herding cats these days." She looked at him a bit critically in his jeans and, unusually for him, a polo shirt and could see what he had meant in his remark to the Prof. He was definitely putting on the inches round his waistline which looked a bit odd with the perfect bone structure of his face now it had lost those awful hollows and shadows. Rather than worry Jean-Guy any more by staring at the man who was clearly putting weight back on again, she went back to what she had been saying. "Anyway, he needs you as rehearsal pianist for the Elgar and the Shostakovich. Then the idea is, just when you think you're winning, you can perfect the Prokofiev too. So you two can get on with it as that's one heck of a programme to get through and that's before I start having a go at you for not soothing my nerves over this gig in Yorkshire."

Piers looked along the music on the shelves in the alcove to find the pieces for Jean-Guy. "What nerves, you dozy cow? You're going to bring the house down. Even if I play a wrong note in every bar nobody will care." He put two pieces to one side. "Can't find the Elgar."

"Don't have it," Jean-Guy said briefly. "I will buy a copy. You would not be so unprofessional that you would deliberately play wrong notes?"

Piers reminded them just what a lovely smile he had. "Won't need to if she wears her red dress. With her in that outfit I could play Schoenberg in the nude and nobody would notice."

"Now that I would pay a lot of money to see!" Kathy laughed and suddenly felt a whole lot better. "I hope you know where the music is for Yorkshire and you're not now going to spend all your time with Jean-Guy."

Piers tapped the pile of music Audrey was sitting on. "All lined up in programme order."

"Do you think I should have a run-through of it all now?" she asked with some of the nagging worry returning.

"No I bloody don't. You've over-rehearsed to the point where you sound bored with the whole lot and that won't go down too well with the fee-paying public."

Kathy looked at Jean-Guy who shrugged and smiled before telling her, "We mustn't forget that he knows what he's talking about when it comes to accompanying. And was I not saying the exact same thing to you just before he arrived to back up my opinion? So, may I borrow your pianist between now and lunch?"

"He's all yours," she assured him. "And don't let him get away with anything."

The Yorkshire festival sent a complimentary programme book to their last performer to be booked, thankful they weren't going to have an empty slot, and Kathy looked at it over breakfast the day before they were due to travel there on a beautiful day in June. They had made the listings just in time to make the printed programme book and she looked first at her entry. It made her pause to see it there in black and white: *Kathy Fairbanks, violin and Piers Buchanan, piano.* She missed seeing Jean-Guy's name listed as well and the butterflies came back to her stomach. Jane had sent the festival organisers one of the better studio portraits Kathy had had taken but it was a few years old and her hair was longer now and she didn't wear nearly as much make-up even on stage. She couldn't have been more than twenty three when that picture was taken and although that was only four years ago, she felt she had matured a heck of a lot in that time.

"You know what we need?" she said to the Prof. "Some decent, up-to-date publicity photos. Jane's sent them one of me which is one of my better portraits but shouldn't there be a photo of Piers as well? I mean, it's not like it was when he accompanied Roisin and his name wasn't even mentioned. I feel a bit mean now. He'll think I'm hogging all the limelight."

Petr Mihaly smiled indulgently. "I think he will be happier letting you take the centre stage. It is what he expects as that is how it used to be for him, but I agree that the days of the uncredited accompanist are gone and a good thing too. Did you ask him for a photo for the programme?"

"Um, no," Kathy said and felt rather guilty. "It's something Jean-Guy and I talked about when we were putting together material for the European tour but then Piers went wandering off so we never got round to organising anything with him in it. We've got photos of me and Jean-Guy but nothing of the three of us."

"And Jean-Guy didn't get anything sorted out for his recital with Piers back in the autumn?"

"No, he was spending so much time with Chantal we hardly saw him back then. Oh, I do hope he'll be alright."

The Prof sat at the table with her and knew exactly what she wasn't saying. "Kathy, stop worrying about him. He is trying to move on from his life with Chantal and the best way we can all help him is to look to his future with Sarah and the children and his music. When Yorkshire is over, get Jane to bully him into a photo session with you two and then she can hold them on her files."

Kathy sighed and cupped her chin in her hands. "Can you imagine it? A really good studio photo of him? He'll become the pin-up of all the female music college students in the country."

The Prof went back to the washing up. "Yes, I rather think he will. A few more broken hearts on his record?"

Kathy knew when she was being teased. "Probably. But mine won't be one of them. But I can still worry about him, can't I?" She turned a couple of pages then stopped abruptly. "Oh my goodness," was all she said but the tone of her voice got the Prof's attention.

"Something exciting?"

"Do you remember I've talked about Danny Tarling who taught me to drive? He's a nephew of David Tarling and in Yorkshire as part of the Stretto Quartet. I'd never have recognised him if it weren't for the name. He looks totally different. At least I assume it's him. There can't be two Danny Tarlings who play the viola."

"Unlikely," the Prof agreed. "Well, so the second nephew of David Tarling has taken to the stage with a viola now, has he? I wonder what his brother Donald will make of that. Is Danny the younger of the two?"

"Oh, he and Donald can't stand each other. Danny's about fourteen years older than Donald anyway and they had different mothers as Danny's mother died when he was about thirteen and then his father remarried and less than a year later he got a baby half-brother."

Petr Mihaly did some rapid calculations. "So how old is Danny now?"

"Don't really know. I think he could be well into his thirties. He's a bit like Piers and never did look his age."

"Ah. So he would have known his famous uncle David?"

"Yes. I only asked him once and, well, I don't like to use such language in front of you so let's just say his memories aren't pleasant ones. He wouldn't go into any great detail but he certainly had a different point of view from all the official biographers."

"I would be curious to meet your driving teacher one day. I edited a biography of David Tarling not that long ago and the only descendent ever mentioned was the now-celebrated Donald. I never even knew there was a half-brother."

"I don't know the full story. He was another one who ran off to join the military when he was a teenager but Danny went into the Army. That's all I know. Then he left the Army after not very long at all and took up driving for a career. He has a damaged hand so he never played the viola professionally although he did occasionally play in amateur orchestras. He was in one in Parsons Green when I knew him." She went back to the programme book before the questions involved just how well she 'knew' Danny Tarling. "They've got an Olga Danilova on first, Samuel Blumenthal on second and a Kristian Engström on cello. Sounds quite multinational. I wonder how they all got together?"

The Prof hadn't raised his daughter and not learned what that blush and sudden switch of topic meant, but he guessed it was in the past so he didn't say anything. "Hmm, so I'm guessing they have an Englishman, a Russian, an Israeli and possibly a Swede or Norwegian. Pity they can't join with you and you could throw a Czech and an Irishman into the mix. When are they playing?"

"Day before us. Oh, we're going up a day early anyway so we could possibly meet up."

"I'll be curious to know what you think of the playing. If they are selling records at their concert you must bring one back with you. Pity you and Piers never got round to going into the recording studio."

"Neither of us wants to," Kathy said and closed the book after a last look at the viola player of the Stretto Quartet. "I think he's going to have to with Jean-Guy but it's not something I want to do. Recording the trios, fine. But just me and a piano? No." She saw the Prof looked almost disappointed. "Tell you what, if I get the chance to talk to Danny I'll invite him to Suffolk for a weekend, shall I? Then you can interrogate him about his relationship with his famous uncle."

"I think 'interrogate' may be slightly too strong a word. But I would be curious to ask."

They arrived in the small North Yorkshire town the day before Kathy's recital. Roadworks and a diversion on the M1 had delayed them by about two hours so there was barely time to drop their bags off at their B and B and grab a quick cup of takeaway tea from a café close to where they were staying before they had to get to the church where the Stretto Quartet were playing. It wasn't a very large town and everything to do with the music festival was centrally located, but the accommodation they had been booked into was a little way out of the town centre as everything closer had already been filled. Kathy hated being late for a concert whether she was playing in it or attending it and even more she hated that there hadn't been time to do more than have a quick visit to the bathroom before they had to go so she arrived at the church with the other two feeling rather shabby and dishevelled in the trousers and polo shirt she had worn all day. Jean-Guy looked a bit crumpled too as he had fallen asleep in the car again but at least he hadn't been sick this time. Annoyingly Piers, who had done all the driving, was as handsome as ever and looked the most respectable of the three of them.

Because the festival had published a programme book, there wasn't a separate one for each concert, just a single sheet of paper giving the running order and the three dutifully picked up one each as they filed into a pew half way down the church, with Kathy in the middle and Jean-Guy next to the aisle. It wasn't particularly warm in the church and Kathy wished she'd thought to grab a cardigan before they had rushed out. Nor was it a large audience for the concert but the church was respectably over half full and Kathy knew she would be lucky to get such an audience for her recital tomorrow.

"So which is the one you know?" Piers checked with her as he briefly read through the piece of paper.

"Danny, the viola player. Taught me to drive." She saw the way he was looking at her and realised he had worked out just how well she knew the viola player.

He didn't say anything but his knowing smile said more than words ever could. "Behave yourself," she hissed at him.

"I always behave in church," he assured her perfectly seriously. "Are we playing in a place this size tomorrow?"

"Doubt it. Apparently we're in the WI Room."

"Uh-huh. Think they'll leave us out some pots of jam?"

"More likely to make you sing *Jerusalem* before we start playing."

"What are you two going on about now?" Jean-Guy asked. "Sometimes I think you two have your own language that nobody else can understand."

Kathy tucked one hand through his arm and gave him what she hoped was a consoling smile. "Oh, it's easy enough to learn. I'll teach you one day."

"Please do," he requested and didn't sound as light-hearted as she had expected.

Before she could reply the quartet walked on to good applause and Kathy could feel herself staring at the viola player. He had put weight on and wasn't the skinny, long-haired but incredibly desirable scruff she remembered. He had rather an attractive physique now and his straight brown hair was neatly cut. Not as short as Piers habitually wore his to comply with the airline dress code, but short enough at the sides to show he had a gold ring in his left ear. He also, Kathy noticed and felt slightly disappointed, had a silver ring on his wedding finger and she stared at him hard enough to think that maybe his hand wasn't quite as distorted as she remembered it.

She jumped as Piers dug her in the ribs with his elbow. "Stop dribbling," he whispered to her with a deliciously wicked smile on his face.

Kathy stuck her tongue out at him as she couldn't think of anything smart to say.

The four players at the front were on a slightly raised dais and as they stood in a row for a few seconds before taking their places they all bowed to the audience. There was a smile of acknowledgement from the viola player and Kathy realised her ex lover had seen what she had just done.

Fortunately for Kathy, Jean-Guy chose to ignore the mutterings and backchat she and Piers were exchanging. "That is never the Danny who came to your flat," he remarked to her and watched almost with disbelief as three out of the four players remained standing, there was no music in front of any of them and only the cellist was seated. He realised they were about to play string quartets from memory which was an impressive feat in itself.

"Well, I can't believe there's another one," she managed and nudged Piers back in the ribs before he could say anything else.

Kathy and Jean-Guy looked again at the viola player as the musicians checked their tuning. "What the hell happened to him?" Jean-Guy asked.

Piers had been skimming the programme notes again. "Humour me. What are you two talking about?"

"You won't remember him. That time you dashed in with Audrey we had a string quartet in the room. Danny was our viola player but he didn't look like that."

Piers looked up. "No it's not. That was some skinny bloke with long hair half way down his back."

"His hair wasn't that long. Wonder how old he is," Kathy mused. She caught Piers' eye and went suddenly mute before he could start teasing her again.

Jean-Guy missed the nuances and leaned across her to mutter to Piers. "You see, they are happy in their penguin suits."

"Well good for them," he replied. "But there's still no chance you'll ever get me to dress up like that again."

"Hush," Kathy chastised them and used both her elbows at once to shut her companions up as three of the Stretto Quartet looked to the first violin for their cue to start the music.

The audience were treated to a very good first half of Bruckner and Haydn at the end of which the first violin announced in accented English that light refreshments were available at the back of the church and the quartet left the stage.

Kathy, Jean-Guy and Piers were still deliberating whether to join the scrum round the table to get a cup of tea or wait until the first rush had died down and risk it being stewed, when the viola player they had just been watching came to join them. He had changed from the white tie and tails into a black denim shirt with the sleeves roughly torn out, slashed black jeans and biker boots complete with chains.

"Hi, Kathy. How are you?" he asked as though he had seen her only last week instead of almost eighteen months ago.

The two exchanged a kiss on the cheek and she felt herself going all hot and flustered knowing the other two were watching her. "I'm fine. You look so different I didn't recognise you."

"That's what happens when you give up teaching driving, marry a Russian, move to Stockholm and take up playing in a string quartet. We all met on that music course I went on back in February last year."

A lot was explained and Kathy stored the information away to pass on to the Prof. "How's the hand holding out?"

Danny extended his left hand and showed the other three an ingenious system of strapping had been put on and then hidden under a fingerless glove and they wondered why he hadn't worn it for the first half of the concert. "Just about hanging together. I've had four fairly major operations and hours of physio on it already so it's on a rest period at the moment. Only another ten operations to go. Anyway, can't stop right now, just wanted to ask if you can hang on at the end for a proper catch-up and you can meet the others."

"Love to. Have you seen it's my turn tomorrow?"

"You're doing a recital? You've always said you'd never do solo work."

Kathy was a bit disappointed that he clearly hadn't studied the programme book as she had. "I'm not really. It's just, oh, I don't know. Anyway, it's tomorrow evening in the WI room so nowhere near as grand as this."

"Grand? It's a poxy little two-hundred seat chapel."

She had forgotten just what good company Danny was and she suddenly missed him as a friend. "Well, it'll do me good to do something other than the ensemble work I'm used to and at least I won't disgrace myself in front of too many people. This is Piers my pianist and you remember Jean-Guy don't you?"

"Of course, glad to hear you got your Leave to Remain. Olga's still trying to get hers," Danny acknowledged and the men formally shook hands. "I think I remember you too," he said to Piers. "You brought a cat round to the flat and scared Kathy's ex away."

"Something like that," he admitted. "Flattered you remember."

Danny just smiled. "See you all later. And, just bear in mind, whatever you see us doing in the second half, it's only acting."

He disappeared back into the side aisle of the church and the other three went to get their tea and cake.

"Not surprised he remembers you," Jean-Guy teased the other man. "Pippa had just announced you'd arrived in a black Ferrari and then you turn up in uniform and were in and out like a tornado."

"Yes, that was a bit of a mad day," Piers remembered. "I thought I'd got away with that on-call but the buggers paged me at gone nine o'clock as they knew I could make it so the flight would get away on time as I was only heavy crew. One of the few times I wished I lived in Brighton or somewhere." He suddenly smiled. "You did look a disparate lot though. What was the sound like?"

"Surprisingly good," Jean-Guy told him. "Except Pippa would insist on playing first although Kathy is the much better player. What happened to Pippa anyway?"

"Oh, she had her baby and married its father in that order and the last I heard of her they'd moved out to Wiltshire or somewhere as he had a job in telecoms and his firm relocated. We kind of lost touch after that."

"Oh dear," Piers said sympathetically. "So Piglet lost her Winnie-the-Pooh?"

Finally, Jean-Guy got the joke as he had now read the books. "Ah. So that is why you call her Piglet. I have often wondered. Now it makes sense. So which one of us two is Eeyore? No," he said to Piers. "You will have to be Tigger."

"Really?" came the sarky reply.

Jean-Guy wasn't going to be put off. "Oh, yes. When you are in the right mood you are the bounciest person I know. We could run light bulbs off you as you put out so much energy."

Kathy wasn't quite sure how Piers would take that these days and she was profoundly relieved when he bowed his head for a few seconds but couldn't stop the snort of laughter escaping.

"What do you think I am?" he asked with the happiest smile on his face the other two had seen for months. "A bloody Christmas tree?"

People who had come to hear the Stretto Quartet were also recognising the well-known Czech cellist and they looked through their programme books but he wasn't mentioned in the list of artistes in the index and didn't appear to have his name listed for any of the ensemble concerts.

Piers had moved a few paces away from the other two while he got over his fit of laughter at being likened to Tigger but he was still smiling as he came back again. "They're talking about you," he said to Jean-Guy.

"Who are?"

"Oh, you know, just word on the street. But I've heard your name at least three times now. There's a group of what look like music students over there. Stop staring at Piglet for two seconds and look their way."

"What the hell are you talking about?"

"Go on, just try it."

So Jean-Guy looked across to the group of half a dozen young people. One of the women half smiled, made up her mind about something and came across to them.

"Sorry," she said very apologetically. "But you are Jean-Guy Dechaume aren't you? Would you sign my programme for me?"

Piers gave Kathy one of his lovely smiles. "Come on, let's leave him to the adoring fans."

The programme had just said that the entire second half was going to be the UK premiere of the *Lithuanian Quartet Op 1* by Dmitri Orlov. From the date next to the title, the audience could see it had been composed last year and from the brief notes that it had been written especially for the Stretto Quartet and was a contemporary blend of string quartet playing and music theatre. The programme notes described it as a complex work, offering an insight into the brutality behind beauty. Kathy wasn't quite sure what that was supposed to mean but even such an obscure description in no way prepared the audience for a phenomenal piece of musicianship which involved not only all four players having to memorise what were technically demanding parts, but also called for some choreography that was quite shocking in places. From the outset it was obvious that the 'character' being portrayed by Danny was the villain and protagonist and the piece hadn't been going more than five minutes before he had kissed the cellist and it wasn't a brotherly peck on the cheek. Kathy could sense her two male companions were a bit uncomfortable with that but they realised what Danny had meant when he said it was acting. By the time the piece was about half way through, Danny and Samuel had performed a bewildering few bars where they were both standing on a chair, each holding the other in place by having their legs locked close together and swapping bows just to make it even more complicated. Kathy was glad that Jean-Guy took her hand and gave it a gentle squeeze when it got to the moment where Danny dramatically tore Olga's top to expose her bra and then hurled her to the stage. She could only admire the Russian violinist who never stopped playing a ridiculously complicated duet with the viola player even when they were in such an intimate tangle on the floor and Olga was at extreme risk of baring her right breast to the audience.

Jean-Guy tried to distract himself from what may be about to happen and leaned across to whisper in the ear of the woman next to him. "Got to be bloody fit to play this one."

Kathy just shook her head and didn't trust herself to speak. She could never, ever imagine herself daring to do anything like that and she was profoundly relieved that breast and underwear managed not to part company even when Olga got to her feet after an overtly suggestive manoeuvre with the viola player.

The audience wasn't quite sure how to take the choreography, but the Dodman Trio players were getting the distinct feeling that the piece was getting to be a bit too shocking for the comfort of many of those watching. But it turned out that the Olga and Danny on the floor scene had been the worst of it and as the piece built up to its finale, all four were in one very close group round the cellist with Danny and Samuel on the floor at his feet and Olga standing behind. There were some dramatic discordant screaming noises played on the cello, Danny and Samuel fell together in a heap with Samuel on top, and Olga made an unseen violin switch. She put her right leg over Kristian's shoulder, smashed an instrument across her knee and the screaming stopped as the splinters of wood showered down on the four players.

There were a few seconds of stunned silence then the audience rose as one and voiced its appreciation of such musicianship even if it hadn't been what they were expecting.

Kathy heard Piers say some very ungentlemanly things under his breath but then he said to Jean-Guy, "Don't go getting any ideas. You want to dance around like that you can go and play with them."

"I couldn't do it," he admitted. "Not only are they incredible musicians but their memory skills are unbelievable. And don't get me started on the choreography."

There weren't many people left in the church when Danny came out to find them. He was dressed quite unremarkably in blue jeans and a brown tweed jacket over a grey T shirt this time. Kathy took a surreptitious extra hard look at that tweed jacket. It was nothing like the scruffy things Danny had worn when she had been going out with him and if she hadn't known better she would have said there was a touch of the designer label about it. But unless he had struck lucky in a charity shop that didn't seem at all possible.

Danny didn't even notice how his ex-girlfriend was analysing his jacket. "Come on, we're all hiding in the vestry. And don't worry, we're all changed and decent. I told Olga not to wear that old bra but she wouldn't listen. Silly cow. One day she's going to fall out of it and get us all arrested."

"I think you're more likely to get arrested for sticking your tongue down Kristian's throat," Kathy told him and her companions really wished she hadn't put that thought in their heads.

Kathy was a bit disappointed when she saw Olga close up and out of her stage clothes. The Russian woman was a green-eyed redhead who was not as slight as she looked, there was a hardness to her eyes which Kathy didn't like and she wondered why on earth Danny had ever married her. Samuel, when he wasn't playing a part, was a shy young man and the cellist was a blond, blue-eye Swede who turned out to be seventeen and not the slightest bit bothered by what the viola player did to him when they performed that piece. There was an easy familiarity between the four which Kathy guessed had come about largely due to the way they got so physical with each other on stage.

"I don't know how you can play like that," she complimented Olga. "I don't think I could even learn all those notes."

"Oh, it took us all some time," she admitted breezily. "But we had work written for us by one of Professors of music in Leningrad. It is political, of course, but most people just see sex and not what it represents. We had to classify it as music-theatre otherwise several countries would have banned us from performing it." She shrugged and sounded as though she couldn't care less. "It won't be same when Danny has left us, but he can't play much longer and we have replacement already."

"He's leaving the quartet?" Kathy asked, wondering if her old driving instructor was going back to his cars.

"Yes. He has many more operations to go on his hand and shouldn't have played today. We have new viola player but she had commitment already which meant she couldn't get here today. Then she is free for us and will be joining us permanently in Stockholm. Dmitri Ivanovich says he is working on quintet for us that will make this piece look like kindergarten playtime." She smiled at Danny and they exchanged a kiss that didn't seem to have much affection behind it. "How is your hand?"

He had taken off the glove and the others could see the strapping was stained with blood. "Not the best idea I've ever had. I've probably pulled the graft apart. Anyway I've taken some codeine and now I'm going outside for a smoke and then you lot can decide what you're all going to do. I think we've lost Kristian to Jean-Guy and they're now talking some technical cello stuff that only they understand. I'm afraid your pianist has been left with Samuel but they seem to be talking about aeroplanes. I never knew Samuel had done his national service in the Israeli Air Force. Funny the things you learn if you bother to listen," he concluded with a glare at his wife which she ignored.

"Is he good pianist?" Olga asked Kathy.

"Yes, but he could be a really good one if he tried. He's not a full-time musician."

"Yes, Danny told me he's pilot."

"Commercial airline so a lot of people to be responsible for."

"True, not job I would like to do. Danny says you are doing recital. When is it?"

"Tomorrow night in the WI Room. It's just me and Piers as Jean-Guy is playing three nights in Manchester from the day after. I haven't done a recital on my own since I left college so it's a bit daunting."

"I think we shall come and hear you play. And if Piers is any good we will make use of him occasionally."

Kathy really didn't like the Russian woman's attitude. "Well, good luck with that. He won't wear white tie and tails for any gig no matter how formal and he doesn't even wear shoes when he's playing. Anyway, please do come and listen. I'm not expecting a large audience but I'm sure it'll do my confidence good."

Olga sniffed. "Maybe. Maybe if you are any good we make use of you too."

"And Jean-Guy?" Kathy asked, feeling piqued that one of the three of them apparently wasn't in the picture.

Olga waved a dismissive hand. "He is celebrated soloist. He is too busy and couldn't learn our ways now."

When Kathy passed on to Jean-Guy what Olga had said he wasn't quite sure whether he was relieved or mildly insulted to have been scorned so lightly.

"Would you want to join the Strettos?" he asked her as he looked at the menu board above the counter in the fish and chip shop. It was getting late, none of them had eaten since lunch and the other two knew that Piers needed to eat to give his stomach acids something to work on rather than eating into the scarred and damaged lining.

"I don't think I'd ever be good enough," she said to him. "What are you going to have?"

"Isn't it all fish?" he asked. "I don't know. I don't really like fish. You choose for me."

Kathy ordered a steak pie for Jean-Guy and haddock and chips for herself. Piers requested the scampi with chips and mushy peas, and then all three sat at one of the tables in the attached restaurant and waited for their order to be brought to them.

"You are easily good enough," Jean-Guy told her.

Piers was looking out of the window. "Good enough for what?" he asked.

"To join the Strettos," Kathy told him.

"Oh? Have they asked you? Personally I wouldn't want anything to do with them."

"As musicians or as people?" Jean-Guy asked curiously.

"Musicians. Except I don't like Olga's attitude much. It's obvious she got her claws into Danny expecting to get British citizenship out of it but it seems the Home Office have got wise to her and although she's got a visa for this trip they're refusing to grant her any kind of residency."

The waitress plonked their food down in front of them, gave the drop-dead gorgeous one of them a definite come-on smile and then sashayed off to the counter again from where she watched him very carefully but, to her annoyance, he didn't even seem to have noticed.

"I got mine with no trouble," Jean-Guy pointed out. "I don't see why they would refuse her."

"Because you came here as a refugee with nothing, stayed here, kept your nose clean and paid your taxes. I got all this from Samuel as he got quite chatty in the end. It seems Olga keeps dashing back to Mother

Russia where her parents are and what she really wants is for Danny to move out there with her."

"What?" Kathy asked in disbelief. "But he's a driving teacher from Fulham. Why would he do anything like that?"

Piers set to work on his food with not quite his former speed but not far off it. "He wouldn't. That's why they've had to compromise on Sweden as a place to live. It's where Kristian is from anyway and he's still at music college in Stockholm so they all kind of live at his parents' place. So, Piglet, if you get the call to arms from them be very, very careful. OK?"

"They've got their gunsights on you too," she told him.

"Well, good luck with that. I've got to be bloody good at dodging bullets in my career. Except the one last year that sent me out to get your bloody sister," he finished wryly. "Ever hear anything of her?"

"Not a word. And I don't want to hear. When I think she came to us with the sole intention of betraying at least me if not all of us..." Jean-Guy stopped and ate his food almost angrily for a few moments. "The Strettos don't want me," he pointed out when he had recovered his good humour, and tried to sound as though he didn't mind too much.

"Yeah they will," Piers assured him. "We three come as a package." He gave Kathy a smile that made her blush. "Musically speaking, of course."

Kathy wasn't so sure doing a recital was the best thing for her confidence as she stood next to the piano the following evening and her violin persistently refused to tune. She had chosen to wear her dark green dress and wished she hadn't as it felt far too wintery for a summer evening but it was too late to change now. Her original plan had been to wear her red dress as that was her favourite but after Piers' comment about playing Schoenberg in the nude, she couldn't quite bring herself to wear the red. Piers was quiet as he sat at the piano, sounding the notes for her and not smiling as she had expected. This was the man who had accompanied Jean-Guy Dechaume and hadn't been happy doing that either. She was grateful he had agreed to this recital even though he had worked out it was to see if he would cope with Jean-Guy again, but right now she wished she'd never agreed with the Prof that it would be a good test run for the recovering Piers. She looked briefly across her audience and saw the Stretto Quartet had all turned up as promised and with them was a young woman with a lot of light brown hair plaited round her head. She had the brightest smile Kathy had ever seen and was sitting very cosily next to Samuel with her hand tucked through his arm.

Violin tuned, she looked across at Piers and gave him just a brief nod. It didn't help when he played a clashing wrong note in the second bar of the introduction to the Franck and from the look on his face it hadn't been the deliberate mistake he had once threatened. Then she picked up her part, the two of them settled down and it was as if they were back in the farmhouse sitting room with Audrey on the piano and only a handful of uninterested cats for an audience. She could sense a change in the audience mood during the slow movement and was only slightly distracted by Jean-Guy turning two pages of the piano score at once but fortunately Piers knew the piece well enough to play from memory until Jean-Guy realised his mistake and turned the music back again. She couldn't hear what the two said between movements but it didn't sound happy. But then the last movement was off and she deliberately set it slightly faster then she normally took it. To her relief, Piers stayed with her even during the trickier moments of the piano part and they got a very healthy round of applause at the end. A large part of it due to the five people at the back. It turned out the young woman with the plaits could whistle even louder than Emma could.

She stepped over to the piano between pieces. "What the hell are you two up to?" she hissed at them. "Just behave."

She could tell something had annoyed Piers so much he was having a struggle not to lose his temper on a concert platform. "Your bloody boyfriend here was getting very excited in the slow movement. And I couldn't help noticing when he turned the pages. Not what I want to see in the middle of a concert. I know the bloody Sibelius gets him all steamed up but now it seems the Franck does too. Is there any piece she can play without you having mucky thoughts?"

Jean-Guy wouldn't even look at her.

Kathy on stage didn't have the same sense of humour as Kathy off stage. "I'm changing the programme," she told Piers and glared at the page turner. "We'll do the Dvorak next. It's not quite so erotic and that'll give him a chance to calm down."

To her admiration, Piers somehow managed to turn a snort of disapproval into a small sneeze and neither of them had ever played better than they did that evening.

It was a short recital without an interval and when it was over, Kathy grabbed Piers by the sleeve and towed him along with her and Jean-Guy to the tiny backstage room where they had left their coats and her violin case.

"What the hell was all that about?" she almost shouted at them.

Piers discreetly closed the door. "Give the poor sod a break," he advised her calmly. "We all survived and it's not the end of the world."

"I can't believe you'd do that to me," she rounded on Jean-Guy. "This is the first solo recital I've done since I left college, you knew none of us was sure how Piers would cope with it and to be truthful I'm guessing he nearly didn't after that, that, behaviour from you."

"You're right there, I nearly quit on the spot," the pianist told them and they realised his temper hadn't quite cooled properly as he paused in pulling on his coat. "It was bad enough you had the balls to bloody set me up in the first place. What the hell did you think I was going to do? Run off the stage like a girl and go and cry in the bloody dressing room? Forget it. If that's all the pair of you think of me then you can just piss off and find yourselves another bloody accompanist. I don't have to take this shit from you and don't see why the hell I should."

"Please just calm down a bit," Kathy pleaded frantically before Piers carried out his threat. "Of course I'd never have asked you to do it if I thought you wouldn't cope. But you'd been so much better and you helped me so much with all the rehearsing. That didn't come out how I thought it would. Yes, we were worried about you. It was your first recital since you haven't been well but I wasn't going to jeopardise either your reputation or mine by expecting you to go on stage if you weren't in a fit state."

Piers took a sharp breath and spoke calmly, but clearly still annoyed. "I have been doing recitals since I was seven. I have done them with bombs and guns going off in the street outside, I have done them when I have been sick from food poisoning, I have done them cold, abused, terrified and in pain. I have never done them for pleasure before I started working with you two. So don't you ever, ever, tell me I won't cope with a recital."

The other two felt quite ashamed and mumbled apologies.

"No offence," he assured them and almost sounded as though he meant it. "Now get your coats and your party faces on as there are some Strettos out there who want to meet us and I bet the little sods will try to recruit us too. Good luck to them with that."

Suitably chastised, Kathy and Jean-Guy got their coats on and went back to the nearly-empty recital room. The three from the Dodman Trio met up with what were now five from the Stretto Quartet and they were introduced to Gisela who in spite of the German name was English and definitely lightened the dynamic of the group.

"Are you around tomorrow morning?" Olga asked Piers abruptly.

"Yes, we're taking Jean-Guy down to Manchester in the afternoon."

"Good, please come to church where we played yesterday, we have proposition for you. All of you."

Johannes Brahms – *Quintet in F minor, Op. 34*

The three duly reported to the church in the morning and there was no doubt that Olga was in charge of the entire operation which somehow didn't surprise any of them. Piers and Kathy were a bit wary expecting this to be some kind of recruitment drive but Jean-Guy was prepared to be amused.

Olga parked Piers at the piano which had clearly been put out ready for a recital that afternoon and he wasn't sure he should be using it but he was quite willing to blame the Russian if anyone said anything.

"We'd like to hear how you play with our group," Olga told him. "We have heard you with Kathy and you were OK but too many wrong notes for my liking. But the others have said you need another chance to prove yourself as otherwise you were quite good, but you also need to be able to play with larger group too."

Kathy could see that Piers was about to explode in a temper so she hastily cut in, "Hang on. One wrong note. Come on."

"That is one too many for me," Olga said crisply. "But I have been over-ruled."

Jean-Guy couldn't believe she was being so rude. "Excuse me," he interrupted, "but I had Piers as my accompanist at a very successful recital at the Festival Hall and I have booked him solid for the next three years. He is the best accompanist I have ever used, and I have used many over the years, and I wouldn't have another piano player now. My agent books my recitals according to Piers' availability. Do you want to criticise my musical judgment?"

"Got you there," Gisela told Olga triumphantly. "So for once in your life just be nice to the bloke who's doing us a favour after all."

Olga sniffed but did have the manners to apologise to Piers. He just gave her a filthy look and didn't say anything.

Before Olga could get going again, Danny took up the narrative. "OK, well, ignoring what Olga just said, the rest of us were impressed with how you two played last night and, if you're agreeable, we'd like you to consider maybe being part of the Strettos at some point in the future. I'm sure the two of you can rattle off the bog standard piano quintets in your sleep so what we are proposing, no, asking, is if you would think about playing another Orlov work."

There was a silence from those who didn't know what was going on.

Danny looked at the other four Strettos but none of them bailed him out. "Right. As you were told, I've stepped down from the viola chair and Gisela has taken over. It won't make for a balanced dynamic having two women do that part in the third movement, you all know the one I mean, but it's the *Lithuanian* that makes us different from all the other hundreds of string quartets out there. That and we always play from memory. Something else for you two to think about."

He stopped and the clearly impatient Gisela took over. "Quite honestly, Danny got so madly excited hearing you two play last night he spoke to Orlov at about midnight and I have no idea what was said as it was all in Russian but basically Orlov now wants to write for us all but, Kathy, he says you will need to play viola so then we have two of each plus piano."

"So does that mean Jean-Guy is in too?" Piers asked curiously. "You're not asking him to audition."

"Hey," Gisela told him. "Only one of us wanted you two to audition and I'm sure you can imagine the ructions that caused."

"Well," Piers told her, "quite frankly I couldn't give a tinker's cuss. I'm exclusive to Jean-Guy and the Dodman Trio these days but if I walk away now then I have a feeling it'll be at least twenty years before Piglet forgives me so what do you want us to do?"

"I don't play the viola as much as the violin these days," Kathy began hesitantly as the musician in her really wanted the challenge of playing with the Strettos and she silently blessed Piers for understanding that. Jean-Guy hadn't said a word which was a bit worrying.

"Leave her on violin," Danny advised. "Then you can have three on violin, I can always join Gisela on viola; he's not going to write the piece in five minutes, is he? Then that will leave Jean-Guy and Kristian on the cello part. You OK with that?" he checked with the other cellist.

He, like Kathy, wanted to try a work like the *Lithuanian* and couldn't understand why Piers didn't want to. "Yes," he agreed. "And I am happy to do your audition too as you have asked the other two. I have my cello in the car."

Olga resumed command but she was a bit more conciliatory this time. "No, we don't need your cello. We know you are good enough for us if we want you. So in total we will be eight. We have three women and five men. Equal balance would have been better. OK, Piers, can you just play your part to Brahms Quintet for us now, here is your music, and we'll try out bit of staging on you to see if you are able to concentrate well enough. Kathy, you can borrow my violin and take the first part. Jean-Guy, you can use Kristian's cello. He is youngest of us and most supple. Of course you will all have to memorise, even you, Piers as we may ask you to move too as this will be an Orlov work."

"How the hell do you move the piano?"

"Oh, not the piano. Just you."

Both Kathy and Jean-Guy had played the Brahms before although it was odd to play someone else's instrument and they both couldn't help remembering the question of the man in Hamburg and each privately decided they wouldn't like to have to play a different instrument as given to them by the venue.

Because they were in standard piano quintet formation, Kathy on the first violin had only a limited view of what Olga and Kristian were up to but she had to admire the way Piers managed to maintain his concentration no matter what those two did. And from the little she could see they were doing things to the piano player she wouldn't like to have done to her and she was glad her 'audition' wasn't going to be so challenging. Part of her did wonder if Danny had vouched for her as a willing performer but she didn't really want to follow that line of thought while concentrating on playing Brahms on someone else's violin. She guessed Olga played a Stradivarius and from the conversations she had had with Jean-Guy over the last year, she also guessed that the Russian violinist didn't own the instrument she played but it belonged to the State that granted her visas to travel knowing she would always return. Somehow she wasn't surprised the

British didn't trust her enough to allow her to stay. Danny, Samuel and Gisela had made sure they could see exactly what was going on and the Stretto musicians were satisfied by the end of the first movement.

"It will work," Olga declared. "Danny, you need to get tattoo."

"No I bloody don't," he told her and the others could tell he meant it. "It's bad enough you make me wear an earring."

"Do you think we should take his shirt off while he is playing or start with a torn one so tattoo shows?" Olga asked and dispassionately looked down the back of Piers' shirt while he was trying to pull it closed again.

Danny was amused for once as at least the comments this time weren't being aimed at him. "Torn one, or we'll need a new costume every night like we do for you. It was your idea to rip damn great holes in my trousers after all."

"Good," Olga decreed. "All is decided. We can tell Orlov to write work for eight of us and he can be as imaginative as he likes with staging."

The others were a bit surprised when Jean-Guy spoke rather sharply to Olga in Russian and what he said clearly annoyed her. Kathy hadn't expected to find out that Danny was pretty fluent in Russian too and for a while the three of them chattered about something.

Olga went from cross to thwarted then back to cross again. Then she laughed. "OK, as you choose," she said in English. She playfully landed a kiss on Piers' tattooed shoulder and finally let him pull his shirt back in place. "You'll do," she told him. "Just about."

June continued to bless the east coast of Suffolk with mild weather and light winds but Piers seemed to be there less and less as the airline stepped up his duties and on the day a kind of peace was brokered in the South Atlantic, they let him take a quick turnaround short-haul flight to Madrid. Euphoric to have been put in as full captain again, even if it wasn't supersonic across the Atlantic but a rather elderly Tristar now his type-rating had been reinstated, Piers arrived at the farmhouse in the evening of that day and the energy was fizzing and crackling off him as it had always done in the past and the others were genuinely delighted to learn why.

"Just Concorde to the USA to go then?" Kathy asked him as he rapidly polished off a second helping of the Prof's legendary bacon pudding.

"Yup," he agreed. "Just Concorde. It's been good to go back to the Tristar for a bit, they even let me loose on an old DC-10, not quite sure why as they didn't licence me for it in the end. But what the heck. It's been good to get back in the air other than training work, but, yes, still trans-Atlantic Concorde to go. Although it'll only be the short charter flights to begin with and I know they'll be monitoring me bloody closely. But if that all goes well, they said I've then got to let all my commercial type-ratings lapse except Concorde so I'll be pretty much back to where I was six months ago, having been taught a few bloody hard lessons on the way."

The Prof sympathetically offered him more pudding which was accepted. "And what have you learned from these lessons?"

Piers thoughtfully drank a glass of water. "That I don't have to fight alone." He paused and looked at them over the top of his glass. "That you three, and Sarah, won't hurt me in any way or form and I have to trust you. As I said, I'm being taught my lessons. I'm not saying I've learned them yet."

"You'll get there," the Prof reassured him. "You have perhaps more to unlearn than many of us do."

"True. Right, that's me done so I guess I'd better go and see what Sarah's up to and I'll meet you two in the café tomorrow morning for breakfast?"

The other two knew that breakfast after a night with Sarah meant a large soy latte and a bacon sandwich, then usually also some toast and marmalade or a slice of whatever dairy-free cake Alison had on offer that day.

"We'll be there about ten," Kathy assured him. "And we'll put your order in if we get there first. Ketchup with the bacon again?"

"Of course. Thanks, Piglet. See you all tomorrow."

Jean-Guy had been hoping for an evening working on the pieces for his recitals with Piers which were getting ever closer so he wasn't in the best mood as he and Kathy walked along the path on a warm, breezy morning, exchanging greetings with those they passed on the path. They didn't need to tell Alison what they wanted. She just saw them coming and got on with the white Americano and the mocha and cut two slices of lemon drizzle cake so it was ready for them by the time they got to the counter.

"Hasn't he got out of bed yet?" Kathy asked as she paid for the coffee and cakes. "He said he'd meet us here at ten and we're late."

Alison gave her some change. "Last I saw of him he'd gone to the shop to buy a paper so I'm guessing Sarah's mum has buttonholed him. I won't make his drink just yet."

"I'm sure he'll have his usual large soy latte and his bacon sandwich to begin with," Kathy requested.

"Hmm," was all Alison said. "I'll still wait until he gets here."

They could tell something had annoyed Piers from the way he banged down his cup of double espresso when he joined them at their table. They had learned over the last year or so that when he was in that mood the best thing was to let him get on with it.

"Bloody Prof," was the first thing he said.

"And good morning to you too," Kathy replied and smiled. "No soy latte this morning?"

"Not bloody likely. Do you know what Sarah called me this morning?"

"Not a clue," Kathy told him and for some reason wanted to laugh.

"Pudgy, that's what she called me. Bloody pudgy. No, don't you dare laugh at me, Piglet. Two bloody stone that Prof has got back on me and I'd swear it's all gone on my waistline."

Kathy managed to supress her mirth. "That's still three stone short, how bad can it be?" she tried to console him.

Piers stood up and showed them how the button of his trousers had failed to reach its buttonhole and the waistband was held shut by a safety pin. He sat down again and necked his espresso in one hit. "How the hell I never pointed out to her she's not exactly svelte herself I'll never know. Then the rotten bloody cow had the cheek to tell me I'm growing a set of boobs to rival hers. According to her, what else can I expect at my age and with the job I've got where I spend my working life sitting on my arse, or words to that effect."

The other two could only imagine how well that had gone down. "Oh dear," Kathy sympathised. "So I guess the two of you have now had a spectacular quarrel and you've flounced out, swearing never to eat another morsel ever again?" She looked into his eyes and saw his temper was passed and he was clearly amused now.

"Might have done except that bloody Alison was in earshot. So I told my less-than-slender wife that I didn't want to borrow any of her underwear and I was going to make bloody sure she never called me pudgy ever again. I've never been anything like pudgy in my life. That hurt."

"But you have such a strange diet now," Jean-Guy thought out loud. "Does that not get in the way?"

"No, not at all. I've never been able to eat some spices and the only thing that's changed is the medics advised me not to have too much dairy. I never did like milk or cream so that's no hardship. I do miss cheese though."

"Goat cheese?" Kathy suggested.

Piers pulled a face. "Christ, no. Can't stand the bloody stuff. OK, come on then. Let's be off."

"Off where?" Jean-Guy asked.

"Home," came the reply he was least expecting. "I understood from what you've been saying that we have a Mr Mendelssohn waiting for us."

Jean-Guy could have cheered. "We do indeed. How long have we got you for this time?"

Piers shrugged as he gathered their crockery onto a tray to return it to the counter. "No idea. Airline just said they'd page me but I can expect to be called back before the end of the week."

They set off back to the farmhouse with Piers ambling along at their speed, not striding off as he would have done once, and there was something oddly content about him. Kathy couldn't decide whether that was due to something Sarah had said, presumably before she insulted his waistline, or because he had done that flight to Madrid. It crossed Kathy's mind that perhaps the extension to the family had already started as it wasn't like him to stay at the shop house late enough to have breakfast so clearly something had happened. She thought maybe a little gentle fishing was called for.

"How's Sarah's plan to extend the family coming on?" Kathy asked. She looked back at the man trailing slightly behind. "And don't plead secrecy agreements on this one. That only covers what you got up to with Kerryanne. I'm sure Sarah will understand if you say you don't want any more."

He smiled then. "Doesn't bother me if she wants twenty. My part of the agreement was just to provide the kids. Sorry, just tired and really want a decent night's sleep alone tonight. Sparing your blushes, I've never met such an exhausting woman." He hid a yawn behind his hand. "And the rotten cow still kicks half my joints out of kilter. I've tried to explain but she just doesn't get it."

Neither Kathy nor Jean-Guy blushed in the slightest. "Had your joints put out by many have you?" Jean-Guy asked. He fell into step with the other man. "OK, I am curious. How many women have you 'met' as you put it?"

"Don't you think that's a bit childish?"

"Totally," Jean-Guy agreed. "So?"

"So I'm not telling you."

"I'll tell you my history first if it helps?"

"Up to you. But I still won't say."

To Kathy's secret delight as she was curious too, Jean-Guy seemed determined to find out. "More than fifty?"

"What?!"

"Oh, sorry. OK, maybe nearer, oh I don't know, you're quite old now, seventy?"

Piers looked a cross between amused and annoyed. "Why the hell does everyone think I'm such a slut?"

"Because you look like one," Jean-Guy laughed and finally let the matter drop.

Kathy had been doing some thinking and said to Piers, "I bet I can guess." She caught his hand and drew a number on the palm so Jean-Guy couldn't see. "Am I right?"

"Quite correct," he confirmed and gave her one of his lovely smiles.

"Tell me?" Jean-Guy asked as winningly as he could.

Kathy hooked a defensive hand through Piers' arm. "No chance. You can work it out too, just like I did."

Jean-Guy hooked a hand through Piers' other arm. "Just for that all day we will play Mendelssohn until your fingers hurt. You have had a long time to practise it now and it is no good you telling me you have left the music in London as the Prof has two copies so there is one here for you too."

"Give me a break?" Piers pleaded. "I captained a flight for the first time yesterday, then I had Sarah climbing all over me for most of the night and now you want me to play bloody Mendelssohn for hours on end?"

"Oh yes," Jean-Guy assured him perfectly seriously. "Because if we make you work hard between us all then you will not be, what was it? Pudgy, any more and you won't need to buy more trousers because your waists are too tight. So, you see, it is for your own good."

"Do you know what?" Piers said to him. "I think I preferred it when you didn't speak such bloody good English."

"Ha!" Jean-Guy exclaimed. "But now I know you also know French. So either way you will understand me. Do you prefer 'rondelet' or shall I call you 'le poupin'? Maybe I should teach you the words in Czech too."

Piers reclaimed his arms and shoved his hands in his jacket pockets. "Piss off the pair of you," was his reply, but he was smiling as he said it.

Jean-Guy had wanted to get straight on with some work on Mendelssohn's first piano trio in the morning when they got back from the café but Piers told him exactly what he thought of that idea and shut himself in his room. He looked a lot better when the Prof called him down for his lunch so they all knew he had been asleep.

"So," the Prof said to the one who joined them for the meal. "I gather Sarah thinks you're getting fat."

Piers looked faintly startled but worked out the other two must have grassed him up. "Well I am."

The older man let Kathy and Jean-Guy get on with sorting out the meal and he said very seriously to Piers: "I will acknowledge that perhaps your waist may be a few inches bigger than it was when you were in your twenties but do I need to remind you how sick you were in the New Year? Nothing to say? Well then, I won't say anything either except that I need you now to be more sensible than ever. If I so much as suspect you aren't eating properly then I will have you back here where I can watch you. No, don't give me that look. Do you want to be taken off flying again? Because that is what will happen."

Suddenly Piers grinned. "So I'm on diet watch now, am I? Oh well, been on worse watches in my life."

"Yes, you are," the Prof confirmed. "But lunch today is cold meats and salad so you can eat without a conscience." He returned the smile. "Of course, you will have to give up your penchant for custard creams and fruit and nut chocolate if you want to lose a few inches."

"The hell I will," Piers retorted and the others felt like cheering.

They settled to some hard work on the Mendelssohn that afternoon The two thirds of the trio who didn't spend their working lives flying aeroplanes were not surprised to find how much the pianist had struggled with the music at first, but he had stuck with it, spending hours working patiently on the passages he found the hardest and even Jean-Guy had to admit that by tea time that day the work was almost ready to play out. It was just a pity, he thought to himself, that the Dodman Trio didn't have any work scheduled at the moment. He half thought he might ring Jane and ask her if there was any chance she could find a slot for the Trio somewhere but before he could mention it to the other two, their peaceful tea break was interrupted by the phone ringing. The Prof was nearest so he answered it and handed the receiver to Piers.

"Airline for you, do you want to take it here in public, or go to the hall where it's quiet?"

Piers took the receiver from him. "Here will do, thanks. It'll save me having to repeat it all when they're done with me." The call didn't last long, the others couldn't hear what the other person on the line was saying and didn't glean much from Piers' monosyllabic comments. But he was smiling as he finished the call and gave the receiver back to the Prof. "Heathrow flight on Concorde on Wednesday," he told them. "They didn't say where to or even if there'll be any passengers on board but I'd better go up to London on the Tuesday as the buggers want me at some godforsaken hour of the morning."

"Will you be captain of the fight?" Kathy asked.

"Didn't say. I don't expect to be."

"Well even so that has to be good," Kathy told him. "Getting back in Concorde is in so many ways the last step of your recovery. I mean," she finished quickly, "not that we expect you ever to go back to where you were after what you've been through, but going back full time as Concorde crew is a pretty big step."

"Yes, it is," he agreed quietly. "When Chantal was in the early stages she told us that all she wanted was to be well enough to go back to work. I couldn't understand it at the time but having pretty much hit rock bottom myself I can appreciate now why it meant so much to her. She never made it. So I'm going to get back in that bloody aeroplane on Wednesday and, in a way, do it for her."

"Good for you," Jean-Guy approved.

Kathy didn't immediately speak but she hoped all went well on Wednesday. "Bring us back a souvenir of New York," was all she managed to say.

"It's almost certainly going to be a routine check flight," he protested. "I won't be going that far."

Kathy gently squeezed his hand and felt so proud of him. "Not this time," she agreed.

They spent the next few days working on the Mendelssohn but on the Tuesday afternoon Piers left them and travelled to Earl's Court to be ready for the tests and checks on the Wednesday morning and the house, missing his energy, again seemed quiet after he had gone. Neither Kathy nor Jean-Guy had any reason to travel with him so Kathy got him to promise to ring and tell them what the check pilot said then they all had to let him go and trust everything went well. Audrey wandered around looking in all the rooms, didn't want to snooze on the Aga and certainly didn't want to sit in the living room while Kathy and Jean-Guy had another go at the Ravel duet that they hadn't looked at for quite a while but tended to drift back to whenever Piers wasn't available.

"Audrey's restless," Kathy couldn't help commenting even though she knew Jean-Guy didn't like it when she used the cat as a kind of barometer.

"And so are you." He sighed. "Sometimes I think you and I just aren't meant to play this piece. Every time we try something distracts us. I don't know about you but I don't even like it very much any more."

Kathy happily tossed the violin part onto the floor. "Thank goodness you said that. I've been hating it for months. We're never going to play it in a recital anyway so I don't know why we're bothering. In which case, if you'll excuse me, I'm going to go to our room and do some work on the Shostakovich quartet I've got to play next week."

"Good for you," Jean-Guy approved. "I have my own pieces I can work on. But please take that cat with you, I can hear her singing from here."

Audrey had no objections to going upstairs with Kathy but wandered off to Piers' room, just to make sure he really wasn't there. She stayed in his room for the whole of Tuesday night which was what she usually did when Piers was away so Kathy felt a lot happier, and on

Wednesday morning the tortoiseshell was back on top of the Aga and purring her head off at the Prof in the hope he would make her some unseasonal porridge.

As Kathy had requested, Piers rang the farmhouse late on Wednesday evening and the Prof was able to report to the other two he had passed all the tests and checks and had been cleared to captain flights on Concorde again so he was staying on in London for a few days to get his next set of shifts worked out. He expected to be back sometime on Saturday and wanted to let them know he had picked up a second-hand set of parts for the Rachmaninov *Trio Elegiaque* and had already run through the piano part. The Prof assured the other two he had congratulated Piers on his reinstatement but couldn't help feeling their trio wasn't going anywhere any time soon. Jean-Guy was glad he hadn't got beyond thinking of ringing Jane and asking her to find the Dodman Trio some work.

The weather wasn't so good the next day, cool and a bit cloudy, but Kathy and Jean-Guy decided they would walk into the village anyway then maybe a bit further south towards Aldeburgh if they felt like it. They were about half way along the coast path when a noisier than usual plane going overhead made them look up expecting to see a low-flying aircraft in military colours, but instead there was a beautifully elegant delta wing plane passing high and fast heading out east across the sea with the sunlight sparkling on its white paint.

"Is that...?" Jean-Guy started to say.

"Yes," Kathy told him. "That's Concorde and isn't she beautiful? Do you have the same peculiar feeling I do that we know who's flying her?"

"Can't be," Jean-Guy told her firmly. "He only rang last night to say he's got his licence back and they can't have had time to work out the shifts for him. Besides which he flies to New York and back which means he goes out westwards from London and we are east so his route wouldn't take him this way."

"Well, Audrey and I say it is," Kathy replied, keeping her tone light even though she was certain of her conviction.

Jean-Guy wasn't sure she was being serious. "So you speak for his cat now?"

"Keep watching," Kathy told him without really knowing why and ignoring his comment on the cat.

Concorde had turned north, following the sea, and was still just about audible when there was a faint cracking boom from the sky.

"That's it," Kathy breathed. "She's gone supersonic."

Jean-Guy shook his head. "Bloody hell, he earns his living flying that?" He looked at the woman he loved who was still gazing skyward her face lit up with wonder like a child. "One day I will take you on Concorde even though I have no idea how we will ever afford it."

She reluctantly stopped trying to follow the aircraft which now couldn't be seen or heard and had crossed their lives like a dream. "No, neither have I, but I'd love to know what it's like." A ridiculous idea crossed her mind. "Maybe you should ask Jane to ask the New York Phil if they'll pay for our tickets? Anyway, let's stop dreaming about things that aren't going to happen. Are we having cake this morning or supporting Piers and just having coffee?"

"Just coffee," Jean-Guy decided. "I don't want to have you call me pudgy. It didn't sound a nice word to call someone."

They were not the only ones thankful there was a café on the beach and the place was crowded and queuing when they arrived.

"I'm takeaway only at the moment," Alison hollered at them when she saw them arrive. "Sorry, just really busy."

Kathy could see that Steph was up to her elbows in washing up in the kitchen while Amanda was buzzing between tables with the coffees and food as fast as Alison could turn them out.

"Chuck us a couple of pinnies," Kathy replied and saw the huge smile of relief on Alison's face. "What needs doing?"

With five people now working flat out, the queue was worked through with surprising speed and Alison began to relax a bit. By late morning Kathy and Jean-Guy were able to hand back their aprons and become customers again even though they had to accept it was now too close to lunchtime for a longer walk. The stream of customers had dwindled enough for Alison to send Steph off on her break and leave Amanda at the counter so she could join the other two to snatch a few minutes' rest.

Alison thankfully sat at one of the chairs at their table and plonked down her drink. "Well that was one of the most frantic mornings I can ever remember. Thanks for helping out like that. I assume you want your wages in takeaway cake?"

"Yes please," Kathy laughed and wondered why it was Piers couldn't get on with Alison. "How's the family?" she asked as it always put Alison in a good mood to have the triplets referred to as her family.

"Amazing," Alison smiled. "Sarah and I sometimes can't believe what a healthy set of triplets we've got. She's hoping this one will turn out as well." She stopped. "Oh, God. Sorry, she only told me last night and I wasn't supposed to say anything until after the twelve-week check. But the early signs are all there and I'm sure she won't mind you two knowing."

"Has she told Piers yet?" Kathy checked, finding it rather odd that Sarah would tell Alison of the impending arrival before she told the father.

"Oh, yes," Alison acknowledged grumpily. "She told him about a month ago when she had her first suspicions. Why the hell she had to tell him first when I'm the one who'll be bringing them up with her I have no idea."

"The sneaky beggar," Kathy said. "He never breathed a word to us." She remembered the smile on Piers' face when he had told her about the effects of starvation, and she was happy for him.

Alison looked a bit less huffy. "Oh well, I suppose at least she only told him. Probably so he wouldn't bother her so much in the bedroom. She told her parents and me last night. Anyway, if he sticks to his word then the surgeon will make sure he won't be any more use to her so perhaps that'll be the end of him." There was a bit of an awkward silence at the table and Alison hastened to reassure the others, "Sorry, that didn't sound like I meant it to. Of course he's always welcome to visit his children but I think it would be much less confusing for them if they accept Sarah and me as their parents. It would be like he and Sarah were divorced and he had visiting rights. I can't force her to divorce him but it's probably best all round if he steps back now."

Kathy focussed her mind on a more positive thought. "Does she know how many it is this time? I'm not sure she wants another set of triplets, does she?"

"I honestly think she won't care so long as it's fit and healthy. How's your friend's little boy? Has he had his first birthday yet?"

"Only just, he was born on the twelfth of June. And Emma's expecting again too, she said she's due sometime in the New Year. Her due date is actually Christmas Day but she hopes it doesn't come to that and baby Peter was nearly three weeks late as it was. Still, at least she and Derek are only popping them out one at a time."

"And what about you two?" Alison asked, feeling the conversation was leading naturally to this point.

Kathy looked at the man she still wasn't married to. "We've had a couple of conversations about it but right now I'm overloaded with work, Jean-Guy his up to his eyeballs in going all round the world and it's not a good time."

"There's never a perfect time," Alison pointed out kindly.

A brief thought flicked across Kathy's mind of how Piers and Chantal must have hoped for so long that their perfect time had arrived but it never had. "We've decided that maybe in a year or so would be better. But we can't tell. Nobody can." Kathy paused and was thinking aloud rather than speaking to either Alison or Jean-Guy. "But right now we're just waiting to see what happens. But you're right. If we wait for the 'perfect' time then it'll probably never happen and we're agreed we'd like a couple of kids at some point."

"I hope it all goes well for you," Alison told them. "I feel like yours will almost be cousins to ours. I'm sure Sarah and I will always be available for babysitting if you both want to go and play concerts somewhere."

Kathy had a cynical feeling that the offer came more from Sarah than from Alison but it was a lovely gesture. "Thank you," she said politely. "You'll both be among the first to know. But you don't need to start knitting baby clothes just yet."

Alison laughed as she got to her feet to go back to the counter. "You'll be lucky. I never could get on with knitting."

Sergei Rachmaninov – *Trio Elegiaque*

As he had promised, Piers was back at the farmhouse on the Saturday and he breezed into the house to find them all in the sitting room where he handed the Rachmaninov music to Jean-Guy then flopped down in an armchair rather than sitting at the piano.

"Sarah rang this morning," he told them bluntly. "I gather Alison has passed on her news even though she was specifically asked not to."

"She did," Kathy had to admit. "Are you pleased about it?"

"Not as much as she is," he admitted wryly. "What she hasn't told Alison yet is that it looks like another multiple pregnancy and the doctor's not happy about it because, basically, of her age. So he wants her to have an appointment with the community midwife before she's twelve weeks in case… well, in case they need to recommend she doesn't go ahead with it. But she's such a stroppy cow there's no way she'll ever agree to a termination. I said it's up to her and whatever she does I'll support her as best I can. We've got the three girls and it'll be a hell of a lot for her to deal with if she has a lot more in one go."

"Did you sort your shifts out with the airline?" Kathy asked him as the Prof declared it lunchtime and they all went out to the kitchen.

"Eventually. But at least I found out why they wanted me to go back. Some sod with more money than sense had chartered Concorde at the last minute to take his wife out to Singapore for her fiftieth birthday, and they'd run out of pilots as three had phoned in sick and the rest were either flying or on statutory rest. So they put me through the final tests and checks and sent me in as captain to replace one of the sick ones. Not my usual crew either which was a bit of a challenge but we did OK between us. And I took the incoming landing which, if I may say, was pretty near perfect, thank God. They seriously need to get more pilots to pass the training on that aircraft."

Kathy remembered what the blond pilot at Amsterdam had said and wondered how the other two crew members had felt when they had learned who their captain was going to be. "So it was you making your awful noises over the sea when we just wanted a quiet cup of coffee on Thursday morning," Kathy said delightedly. "Audrey and I knew it was. Congratulations, by the way. I blame having to concentrate so hard with Olga and Kristian climbing all over you for you coping with one silly aeroplane."

"Just for calling poor Concorde silly, I am so tempted to tell you that it wasn't and that I was going the other way to New York. But, you got me. That was my flight making all the noise again. They'd paid extra to go supersonic and we just about managed it over the North Sea then had to take a hell of a detour to make sure we didn't break any laws."

Jean-Guy plonked a plate down in front of him a bit miffed that Kathy's intuition had been right. "Talking of making noises, when does Sarah let you know how many she is having this time?"

"Monday. She said she'll come along here to tell me the news first. I offered to go with her but she said she'd rather do this one on her own." He looked at the others at the table and realised an explanation was due. "She needs to get her head round what's happening and her way of doing that is in her own time and space. Once she's clear in her own mind then she'll talk to me about what she wants to do. But right now she's not sure how Alison's going to react so she wants to make sure we're both solid in our agreement before she goes public."

Kathy was reminded yet again of how she had hidden things from her ex. All the things she hadn't told him. Had lied about. Just to save herself from what he might do. She hadn't realised at the time how scared she had been of his reactions. She had mistaken fear for excitement. She couldn't believe now she had ever been so stupidly naïve. "But she never comes here," Kathy couldn't help pointing out. "It's too haunted for her."

Piers smiled then and the others could see just how much he loved his wife. "True. But the daft cow is more concerned with the welfare of any impending babies than she is with any old ghosts who might be rattling round in this place. I'm guessing it's a hard session on the Rachmaninov after lunch?"

Jean-Guy caught the other man's ironic smile. "Of course. You have had time to practise it now so I expect no mistakes from you."

At just gone eleven o'clock on the Monday, Sarah got a lift to the farmhouse in the pig van and came in by the back door to find the other four waiting for her at the kitchen table.

"How did it go?" Piers asked her quite casually as Kathy rushed to make coffee for the visitor. He watched Sarah very carefully but her face gave nothing away which he had learned meant she was processing a lot of information and hadn't got her words in order yet. To his alarm, Sarah started to cry and he got to his feet to take her in a protective cuddle. "What? Just tell me. Is it triplets again?"

Sarah's turned her face into his neck. "Worse," she managed to tell him between half-stifled tears. "The midwife reckons anything from four to seven. She had a listen and said the babies are far enough along to have detectable heartbeats and there are so many hearts going in there she couldn't count them."

To her relief, her husband didn't let go of her but steered her gently into one of the chairs at the table and Kathy put a mug of coffee in front of her.

"How do you feel about it?" he asked. "It's going to be a lot of babies to cope with at once from the sound of it. You know I'll do what I can to help you."

"Right now I'm terrified," she had to admit and cuddled close against him as he pulled his chair next to hers. "The midwife worked out a due date of March the fourth and she said it's not going to be easy and they'll want me to go into hospital at about twenty nine weeks. It'll be a caesarean. No question of a natural birth with so many going on. I said I was OK with that but I'd like to keep them inside me for as long as it's safe. They can't make me have them early can they?"

"Well, no," he had to agree. "I don't suppose they can but you'll need to take their advice and if they say you or the babies are at risk then you'll need to do as they suggest."

Sarah hadn't expected him to be so calm and sensible about it all. She always thought of her husband as this mercurial bundle of energy who was in and out of the house like a whirlwind leaving her trailing in his wake, mentally and physically exhausted. "Yes, I know," she admitted. "And I will do as they say really but if I feel OK and they say the babies are OK then I may ask if we can all wait just a bit longer. They said we'll know exactly how many quite soon as they want to do an ultrasound in case there are lots of them." Sarah pushed herself away from him a bit. "And I'm really sorry, but I've been appointed a social worker."

"Why the hell would you want one of those?" he asked sounding not angry as she had expected but more bewildered.

"Oh, it wasn't my idea," she rushed to reassure him. "But the midwife doesn't believe I'm married as she's never met you. She's only met my parents and Alison. And she's never seen the birth certificates and I'd been discharged from her care by the time you turned up in the new year. I have to go and meet the social worker on the sixteenth of August and they'll book the ultrasound in for the same day as it's all being done at the hospital. The midwife said it's just so I can reassure them all that I can manage financially and emotionally with so many kids." She clutched the sleeves of his shirt like a woman in a nightmare. "Apparently this social worker has the power to say I can't keep the babies and put them up for adoption if they think I won't cope."

"Hang on, calm down a bit here," Piers advised her. "There is no way we're going to let that happen. I can come with you and that'll shut up the doubters." He did some calculations in his head. "Problem is that on the sixteenth next month I'll be coming back from Hong Kong with a stopover in Dubai. A regular crew asked me if I would add that one to my line as their captain will be in hospital and they're a good crew so I'd rather not back out now. Can you postpone the meeting say to the eighteenth? I'll even try not to look too much like a dosser."

"It was Alison who called you that, not me. But I've always promised you that you wouldn't need to be involved. I bullied you into marrying me in the first place, then it turns out I can't even have one child at the time and there's no way you signed up for all this when you agreed to my idea. You're a sweet man and I've come to love you dearly but I can't put you through this."

He gave her a gentle kiss on the lips. "Has it not occurred to you, you mother of my many children, that somewhere along the line I fell in love with you too? And there's no way I'm going to abandon you. Not now. Not ever."

There was such a look of love and tenderness exchanged between the married couple Kathy felt as though it was something too private for her to witness.

"OK," Sarah agreed, sounding quite practical now she knew she stood a chance against the unknown monster of the social worker. "I'll say you're not available until the eighteenth. Not that they believe I managed to catch myself an airline pilot anyway."

"Why wouldn't they believe you?" Piers asked and sounded quite puzzled by such an idea.

"Because I'm a fat, stupid Suffolk girl who works in a shop. I can just tell they think I've made it all up, especially as the last time they saw me I was with Alison. I think that's why they've got Social Services involved. They've labelled us as a gay couple but I'm bi enough to sleep with any thick yokel who'll have me just so we can have children."

"Whoa. Rewind a bit here," Piers asked her. "If they're that fussed you've got a bloody marriage certificate you can show them."

"They've never asked. They've just assumed. As people do."

"True," he agreed and suddenly smiled. "Want me to turn up in uniform on the eighteenth? Those two can tell you I don't always smell too good after fifteen hours in a cockpit."

The others knew that wasn't strictly true as the flight deck of Concorde was air conditioned, and he never spent that long in a cockpit anyway, but they decided to play along with the joke. "He doesn't," Jean-Guy verified without a smile on his face.

Sarah had totally lost the thread by this time. "Just look a bit tidier than you usually do," she told him. "But I don't think a smelly uniform would be a good idea."

Piers felt a bit mean because he knew Sarah couldn't always keep up with him and after the news she had just given him it seemed wrong somehow to get irritated with her as he tried so hard not to do. He awarded her a gentle kiss and one of his nicest smiles. "I shall turn up looking like the *Vogue* fashion plate you once thought I was."

That Sarah did grasp straight away. "I did, didn't I?" she giggled. "Oh well, maybe one day you will be."

Five people wept with laughter at the very idea of Piers as a fashion model.

Kathy and Jean-Guy were both thankful that their work schedules meant they could be back at the farmhouse by the fifteenth of August and they just hoped Piers wouldn't get any delays when he brought the Concorde charter flight back from Hong Kong via Dubai. He had been looking forward to Hong Kong, not having been there since his RAF days but he knew

Kathy would be worried, thinking he would get bogged down with memories of being there with Chantal and getting tattooed somewhere in the back streets, so he had taken the time to phone her from the other side of the world to reassure her that it was nothing like he remembered and the street where the tattoo parlour had been was now lost under a skyscraper.

He phoned again on the evening of the seventeenth to say he had only just got back to Earl's Court and would be driving up in the morning, going straight to the café where he was due to meet Sarah at ten o'clock.

By five past ten on the morning of the eighteenth, Kathy and Jean-Guy had walked into the village and having seen Piers was already sitting outside the café talking with Alison, were a bit reluctant to interrupt as the two were almost certainly discussing tactics for the day's meetings.

"Why are you hiding round the back of the café?" Sarah asked having sneaked up behind them, and both Kathy and Jean-Guy jumped.

"We're just admiring your hot date," Kathy told her.

"Oh, is he here? I didn't see his car. I thought he ought to be as I'm a bit late. I'm so fat round the middle already I can't find any clothes to fit. Took me ages to get dressed."

"His car's over there." Jean-Guy pointed towards the maroon Aston Martin looking so sleek and elegant and just a bit ferocious at the kerb.

"Where?"

"The red one."

"That's not his. He drives that beaten-up old Land Rover."

"He also drives an Aston Martin," Jean-Guy explained kindly, wondering why Sarah so persistently failed to understand the full implications of her husband's job. "He's an airline captain. Have you any idea what he earns? I thought I did quite well with my cello work, but his salary is just crazy. Especially now he's back on some longer charter flights. I have to do three concerts to get what he gets for one trip to Shanghai."

Sarah knew she still didn't fully understand how her husband earned his living, but she was slowly learning there was a lot more to it than just sitting in a plane and flying it. "That still doesn't explain why you're hiding."

"Just take a look before you go and say hi," Kathy advised.

So Sarah did what they had been doing and peeped round the corner of the building. "Did I really marry that?" she breathed. "I mean, I know he made that joke about looking like a fashion plate for *Vogue* but he really does."

Kathy tried not to laugh too loudly. "Even I have to admit he looks hot and I don't even fancy him."

"You think he looks hot?" Jean-Guy joined in, enjoying the absurdity of it all. "I'd date him myself if I thought he'd accept."

"You two are completely crazy," Sarah assured them. She had another look and sounded suddenly panic stricken. "I can't turn up at the hospital with him looking like that."

"Why on earth not?" Kathy asked. "You could turn up at Buckingham Palace with him looking like that."

"That's what I mean. They're all going to think I've hired him from an agency for the day."

Kathy and Jean-Guy turned away and tried to muffle their shouts of laughter but knew their cover would be blown now. The three all looked round the corner again to find the object of their scrutiny was looking straight at them.

"You know I can hear you, don't you?" he asked them with a laugh just starting in his cornflower blue eyes and the onlookers were reminded that fortunately this most beautiful of men also had a very well-developed sense of self-humour. "You ready to go?" he asked Sarah. "Or do you want to stop for a coffee?"

"We'd better go," she replied and tried not to gawp as her stunningly gorgeous husband got to his feet, and walked across to join them. No matter how hard she looked, there was no sign of his shadow that day and she slid her arms round him as he joined her and they exchanged a short kiss.

"And for the record," Piers told them. "Piglet, I'm flattered you think I'm hot but I really think you need to get your eyes tested. and I certainly don't want to date you, Jean-Guy."

Jean-Guy clutched his chest. "My heart is broken."

"Idiot," Piers told him and slapped a newspaper against him. "Here, read this."

Jean-Guy took the paper and looked at it. "Why the hell are you reading *Le Monde*?"

"I wasn't particularly, somebody left it on the table."

Jean-Guy switched to French. "You never told me you could read French."

Piers smiled and replied in the same language, "You never asked me. You were just rude about the way I speak it."

"Well you do speak silly French," Jean-Guy challenged without changing language which vastly amused Kathy who could still understand what they were saying.

"Of course I do, I learned it working in the Caribbean for best part of five years," Piers defended himself keeping up the French chat but in his own style. "You should hear me speak Creole."

"Makes sense," Jean-Guy admitted. "So you speak Creole which explains your crazy French. Anything else?"

"South American Spanish and some Chinese, mostly Cantonese."

Sarah didn't like it when people said things she couldn't understand. "I like your jacket," she interrupted. "Is it new?"

The men realised they were being rude speaking in French when one of them couldn't understand. Piers gave his slightly irritated wife one of his nicest smiles and went back to English. "Out in Hong Kong they do made-to-measure overnight for you. Whole outfit made for me for less than the cost of a jacket in Burton's. Glad you approve. How are you getting on?"

"Funnily enough, I feel better than I did with the triplets. I think I've got past the point of panic."

"Come on then. Where are we going and who are we meeting today?"

"Ipswich hospital. Social worker first then the obs and gynae consultant."

Kathy and Jean-Guy were working on the Rachmaninov together when Audrey set off the three-minute warning as Jean-Guy had named it and then they heard the alien sound of a grumbling Aston Martin making its cautious way down the bumpy track to the farmhouse.

"Wasn't expecting him this evening," Kathy remarked. "Hope the Prof has cooked for him."

"He always cooks too much. I'm sure I'm getting fat. No," he laughed. "I am getting pudgy."

They put down their instruments and went out to the kitchen having forgotten for the moment that their third was in smart clothes that day and it was a bit of a shock to realise he wasn't in tatty jeans and his old coat that had lost nearly all its shape.

"What news?" Kathy asked as his face gave nothing away.

To the relief of the other three, Piers suddenly smiled. "Social worker's not going to be a problem. Bossy cow who thought she'd walk all over Sarah."

"Did you bite her head off?" Kathy asked. "Or was it the frozen laser beam treatment you do so well?"

"The what?" Jean-Guy queried.

"You know the one. We've all seen it. He goes all Wing Commander on us and could freeze helium with one look. Anyway, what did the doctor say?"

Piers looked faintly amused at her description. "The doctor had a good listen and ran an ultrasound, and he said it's quins."

The other three knew there was more to come when Piers paused like that. He was getting his emotions under control so they didn't rush to congratulate.

"He says we'll be lucky if they all survive either the birth or their first year. Statistically we're likely to lose at least two of them. He also said that Sarah's not going to have an easy time of it and they may get her into hospital as early as twenty weeks in case she can't go full term. The babies will be born by C-section on February the fourteenth at the very latest as Sarah is adamant she wants to hang on to them as long as she can to give them the best chance, but any distress in mother or infants and they bring the date forward." There was another pause. "Piglet, can you come with me to the hospital and drive me back on Friday, please?"

"Yes, of course. Can I drive the Aston?"

"No you bloody can't. We'll use the Land Rover."

"Spoilsport. What's the occasion?"

"They told us Sarah mustn't risk another pregnancy after this one. Doesn't matter whether we keep all five or lose all five, her body just won't take it again. So on the doctor's very strong recommendation, while we were there I agreed he could book me in for my snip. I'd told her weeks ago I was going to get it done anyway and the consultant backed me up on it. Which is why I'm not with Sarah tonight. She has a crazy idea that she and I aren't going to last and I'm going to go off and want to have babies with a third wife. She's in quite a state about it and I'm not going to upset her so I've left her with Alison for now and told her that maybe I won't do it. But I will. And I won't be allowed to do much for a few days afterwards, including drive."

Jean-Guy resisted the urge to cross his legs but he was sure his eyes were watering. "You would do that? And you sound so casual about it."

Piers almost laughed. "Oh, trust me, nothing at all casual. But I can assure you the last thing I want in my life, ever again, is any more children. And now I'm going to get out of these city clothes, then I guess I'd better ring the airline and tell them my plans. I'll let you two choose the music for the evening."

Kathy thought how lovely it was for them all to be back together again, working on the Rachmaninov and with Audrey still determined to catch the pianist's fingers. Just for one evening, as Jean-Guy had said, they were breathing as one and the music had never been better.

Franz Schubert – *An die Nachtingall, Op. 98/1, D497*

The music for the Octet arrived at the farmhouse by post months before it was expected, on a blazing hot day at the end of August. Only Jean-Guy was in the house as the Prof had gone to the supermarket, Kathy had gone with him as she wanted to go to the nearby shops and Piers was in the village with his wife and children. He had had his 'little operation' as he called it, had hidden in the farmhouse until the bruises had gone down then told his wife what he had done before running away back to London and a supersonic flight out to New York. Sarah soon realised that he was still being the sensible one so she had phoned him in London to say she understood and she really was pleased he had done it for her as she now knew he loved her enough to go through with it. Piers just took the compliment, told her that of course he did, and never told her he had done it because he really, really didn't want any more children.

Jean-Guy took in the fat, buff envelope the postman handed to him as it was too big for the letter box, and looked at it curiously for a while. It was quite clearly addressed to him, with Piers' writing on it which confused him as Piers had been with them for a couple of days now and hadn't said anything about a parcel and why hadn't he brought it with him? Then he noticed the parcel had been franked in Earl's Court over a week ago and a more careful study of it revealed the original sender's name was given as Gisela von Aachen and it had started its journey in Stockholm. Suddenly filled with mad excitement, he forgave the Royal Mail for taking so long to deliver his parcel and he took it into the kitchen so he could tear it open.

Kathy and the Prof were back first with their bags of shopping and they found Jean-Guy at the kitchen table with music spread all over the place and, from what they could hear, swearing in four different languages.

"Problems?" Kathy asked quite innocently as she helped the Prof to put the food away.

"Just a few. This music from Orlov, it really should be banned. I don't care if they do call it music theatre. I mean I had been looking forward to a challenge and the music is difficult enough without what he is asking us to do as characters in the story. Here, you take a look. Someone with very bad handwriting has translated the original Russian directions into English for us."

Kathy thought that was so sweet of him to say 'us' as he was perfectly able to understand the Russian. She sat at the table and took the piano score from him while the Prof made some coffee for them. "That's Danny's writing," she told him. "He's very left-handed and never could write in a straight line. It's quite easy to read once you're used to it." She forgot about the handwriting as she read the text. "Oh my God," was all she said. "I'm only on page four."

"Cut to page thirty six."

Kathy did as she had been told. "They can't do that. Aren't there laws against it?"

Without looking at the score, the Prof said, "You may have to be careful where you stage it, or make amendments. What is so shocking?"

"I've just got to the bit where Green Violin, well, no other way to put it, pretty much sexually assaults the piano player." She wasn't sure whether she was relieved or not to have been given the part of White Violin and just hoped, for Piers' sake, that Green Violin wasn't Samuel.

"Hmm," was all the music critic offered. "Just remember stage directions can be interpreted many ways. I would suggest you concentrate on the music first and worry about the dramatics later. Are we expecting Piers for lunch?"

"Unlikely," Jean-Guy replied. "He was saying Alison was going to give them lunch at the café and Sarah's parents have offered to feed him this evening so don't expect him back much before midnight."

"He's taken the car so, yes, you're probably right and we won't see him until midnight. You two had better get on with looking at your parts."

They heard the Land Rover coming back to the farmhouse quite early for one of Piers' days out with his family. Kathy looked at the sitting room clock and realised it wasn't much after eight o'clock. Audrey leaped off the piano and went out to the kitchen in time to greet the man who had just come in through the door and then escort him into the sitting room. Kathy couldn't help but think how much better Piers looked than he had that bitterly cold day in January. The five stone he had lost hadn't been kind to him when they had started to go back on but now he was careful with his diet and was toning up with walks and she thought he looked better than she had ever known him look before. He still didn't have anything like a tan in spite of the late summer heat but his eyes had got their sparkle back and in a good light he looked closer to thirty than forty. In fact, Kathy thought, looking at the pair of them, if she hadn't known better, she would have said Jean-Guy was the older of the two.

"Octet's arrived," she told him before her train of thought got too interesting.

"Bloody hell, that took its time. I thought it had arrived days ago and it was so bloody awful you'd thrown it away. That's why I didn't say anything. What does it look like?"

"Um, interesting," Jean-Guy offered. "Come and tell us what you think." They went out to the kitchen where the pages were spread all over the table again and the Professor was studying them with his usual musicologist's interest. Jean-Guy made some coffee for them and Kathy unwrapped the leftover cakes Piers had left on the dresser.

Jean-Guy casually slid the piano part of the Octet across to Piers. "Here, look at that and pay particular attention to the stage directions at rehearsal mark K, second movement."

The other three watched very intently as he flicked through the score to the stage direction. "Oh for Christ's sake. What does he think I am? A bloody acrobat?"

"Now try page ten, first movement." Kathy told him.

Piers dutifully flipped back. "OK which one of the two is Blue Viola? Please tell me it's Gisela?"

"Sorry, no idea. I got the impression it doesn't matter," Kathy replied.

"Well, it matters to me."

"Remind me what is happening in the piano part on page ten?" the Prof asked curiously.

"The piano player appears to get soundly snogged by Blue Viola." He flicked through the pages and came to the section where even Jean-Guy's broadmindedness had faltered. "Oh, bloody hell. What the...not going to say it out loud... is that all about with Green Violin? If that doesn't breach decency laws it bloody well ought to." He looked at Kathy and tried not to get too hopeful. "Not sure whether I want that to be you or not."

"Sorry," she smiled although she could sympathise with his misgivings. "They've sent me White Violin."

"If it's bloody Samuel they can forget it. I'll be on the first bloody ferry home."

Jean-Guy could quite see his point and decided it might be time to soothe the ruffled pianist. "I'm sure we can negotiate if you're not happy about anything. Although I must admit I would have liked to have known who has which part. The only good thing for you is you don't have to memorise if you don't want to, but it would look better if you did. Up for a run-through tonight? And a letter came with it. We're all invited out to Stockholm for a joint rehearsal when we can co-ordinate diaries and find a flight."

"I'll take the ferry and the Land Rover. You going to risk it this time, Jean-Guy?"

"No bloody chance. You can pick me up from Stockholm airport."

The three of them ran through the parts for the Octet that evening as best they could, but Kathy was the only one who got any enjoyment out of it. Jean-Guy admitted he liked that the cello part was technically demanding but he wasn't impressed with the staging. Piers clearly hated every single note of it and wouldn't even discuss the stage directions. At ten o'clock he shut the score and announced that he was going to go and sit in the garden to get his thoughts in order then he was going to go to bed.

Sitting in the garden in the evening was something he had taken to doing when he had been ill and hadn't had the strength to go for a walk or the permission to fly aeroplanes and he had found he liked it so he carried on doing it. Kathy pulled a face at Jean-Guy and decided to risk it. She paused in the kitchen to make a couple of mugs of tea then took them with her to join Piers.

He was sitting at the old patio set with the garden lit only by the ambient light from the power station but his night vision was good and he gave Kathy a smile as she sat with him and handed across the tea.

"Thanks, Piglet. Sorry for being such a bloody drama queen. But I really don't want to play this piece and then I feel bad as if I pull out you've got to recruit another pianist and I don't think the others will be too happy about that. Then they could decide to get their own back and punish you by not letting you dep with them."

"Forget about me," she told him. "You have to do what's best for you. But isn't there just a tiny part of you that would like to go and visit Stockholm and see where they all live?"

"True," he had to admit. "They did make it sound like a nice place." He thoughtfully drank his tea and listened to the sounds of the sea hissing on the shingle for a while then tilted his head back so he could look at the stars in the sky. "Do you know how old I am?" he asked but clearly didn't expect an answer. "I'm so old I had to learn astronavigation as part of my pilot training. They don't need to bother with it now, but they made us learn our way about with no lights, no radios and just the stars to keep us on track. Last one back to base had to buy the beers for all the others."

Kathy looked up at the stars too and thought that sounded quite a nice thing to do. "So could you do it now? Find your way home by the stars?"

He smiled in the darkness and sounded oddly content. "Always. OK, just to keep you happy, I'll go to Stockholm and we'll try out this Octet with the others and we'll see where it goes from there. Not going to get performance ready in a week, is it?"

Kathy returned the smile and raised her mug to him. "Here's to Stockholm," she offered.

"Madwoman," he told her fondly. "Anyway, thank you for my tea but now it really is bed time for old farts like me."

Kathy stood up beside him. "Me too. It 's starting to get chilly out here in the evenings, isn't it?"

"Too much sea breeze," was his only comment as the two returned to the farmhouse.

It was all a bit of a mad rush in the end but with the musical engagements of six of the eight players still on the summer season, one of them due to go to Los Angeles in October and the eighth on a few days' leave from his day job, the Dodman Trio were on their way to Stockholm towards the end of September. Jean-Guy still refused to travel all that way by car and ferry and Piers still refused to fly as a passenger so they went their different ways with Kathy and Jean-Guy staying the night in Earl's Court then catching the Tube to Heathrow and flying across to Stockholm feeling fortunate that they didn't have to carry any heavy luggage. They told Piers he was an idiot but he chose to let them load the instruments and suitcases in the back of the Land Rover then set off quite cheerfully from Suffolk to Harwich to get the ferry to the Hook of Holland and then work his way north through West Germany and Denmark with roads and ferries taking well over a day to travel what the other two would manage in a matter of hours.

They had tried to make the timings connect but that had been not quite possible and even with the air passengers catching an afternoon flight, they still got to Stockholm two hours before Piers arrived with the Land Rover to collect them. He then had a minor spat with Kathy who told him he had been on the road for over sixteen hours and he ought to let her do the driving. Eventually he grudgingly gave in and let her take over for the last part of the journey out to the place where the Stretto Quartet had made their home. She hadn't even driven out of the airport car park before Piers was sound asleep, fallen sideways across the back seat. She was just glad she had Jean-Guy in the front with her and that he was a proficient map reader.

It was about an hour's drive north from the airport towards Uppsala but staying closer to the coast and heading into parts that were ever more remote. Jean-Guy reckoned they weren't far away when they passed what was obviously a small flying club rather like the one at Ipswich and he said laughingly:

"Now that is what we should have done. Hired ourselves a plane and got our tame pilot to fly us across from Ipswich to here and we could be door to door in what? Three hours?"

"About that," Kathy agreed. "Oh, look. There's Gisela dancing about in the middle of the road. Guessing they don't want us to drive straight past."

Gisela stepped back so Kathy could swing the Land Rover onto a well-maintained drive with white-painted gates next to the road and curving gently round out of sight between tall fir trees. She opened the rear door behind Kathy and let in the cold Swedish air which woke the man on the back seat.

"Budge up, lump," Gisela told him and climbed in beside him. "OK, just follow the drive and save me the walk."

The drive wasn't long and round the curve visible from the road they came into what had once been a farmyard and the three visitors thought they had seldom seen a more beautiful place and briefly envied the other musicians.

"OK," Gisela told them. "I'll just orientate you before we all get out. Much easier that way. The round building in front of you and slightly left is the apple store where Danny and Olga live, Samuel and I are in the old stables which is the building to your left and behind you is the main farmhouse where Kristian still hangs out with his parents and they've also got an adopted fifteen year old called Agnetha. She's a bit of a strange one and scared witless of strangers so please treat her gently. Big building straight ahead and slightly right is a purpose-built practice room converted from the old barn so we have group and individual practice facilities and we've also got recording equipment set up there as we find it can be useful to tape our practice sessions and play them back. What we didn't have was a piano in there as none of us really plays but we've borrowed a Steinway grand for you from the Conservatoire so hope that's OK."

"Amazing room," Jean-Guy complimented as he looked out of the windscreen and could see an elegant, empty space well lit by the huge windows and he couldn't help thinking of the cluttered sitting room back home in Suffolk where the sounds were muffled by curtains and carpet. and the lighting left a lot to be desired when playing on a winter's evening.

"Yes," Gisela agreed. "We even have a bit of a lighting rig set up so we can use it for video recordings or private recitals if we want to but mostly we just use it for practice. Out you hop and we'll go and find the others. At least Danny will be happy now you've brought him a new car to look at. He'll probably have stripped the engine down by tea time. Anyway, we'll park your instruments in the practice room and I'll take you across to the main house where you'll be sleeping and eating. We thought just a bit of light practice tonight, maybe some Mozart or Schubert if you like, as you've been travelling then we'll hit the Orlov tomorrow."

"Do you practice much?" Jean-Guy asked as the three travellers climbed a little stiffly from the Land Rover.

Gisela shrugged. "Depends. I suppose usually about six or eight hours a day. Longer if we've got something that needs extra work. Like this piece will," she finished wryly then smiled. "But don't worry, we're not going to do that to you on this trip. This is as much about getting to know each other as it is about the music and none of us honestly expects that Octet to be anywhere near performance level after just a week."

"All that practice explains your incredible stamina," Kathy complimented.

"We try. Danny's good, he goes to the gym a lot, Olga does yoga and Kristian does a lot of cycling and he's young enough, and mad enough, to go open water swimming all year round but Samuel and I are the lazy ones. I mean he does a bit of running and I go to tap dancing but we're not as committed as the other three."

Kathy and Jean-Guy just looked at each other and didn't dare say a word. Even though Jean-Guy could claim to put in the hours of practice, with Kathy not far behind, their exercise regime left a lot to be desired when compared with the Strettos.

"Do you think maybe we should join a gym?" Jean-Guy asked the other two as they walked across to the practice room for the evening session after a light meal in the kitchen of the main house.

Kathy was glad Piers said it first. "Nope. Waste of money. If you walk to the village it's a good mile each way which won't do you any harm." He opened the door for them to go in first and they could see the others were waiting for them. "Or you could just stop stuffing all Alison's left over cake."

To the astonishment of the five musicians already gathered in the practice room, the world-renowned cellist aimed a swipe at his talented accompanist and all three arrivals were laughing about something. It made the five realise that, just maybe, they had started to take themselves too seriously and were at risk of losing the fun from their music.

The proper Octet rehearsals started the next day straight after a healthy breakfast that was more to do with fruit than porridge and Kathy was afraid she would be hungry by the middle of the morning. She didn't have time to even think about getting hungry as the Dodman Trio found out just how hard it was to stage an Orlov music theatre work and that was without the distractions caused mostly by Olga. From the outset it was obvious she and Danny couldn't agree on half the things that were in the score and she accused him more than once of mistranslating them. He tried very hard not to lose his temper with her but pointed out that she had done half of the translating, he had just written it down. The two settled to work on the piece in a very frosty silence. The only thing Piers liked about it was that the stage directions quite clearly stated that none of the players was to wear anything on their feet, but he had struggled more than the other two with the piece as he still hated it and didn't want to do any of the staging. He hid his reluctance well for that first run-through even after two or three barbed comments from Olga which he drowned out by playing far too loudly each time she tried to shout at him. By the time they stopped for lunch, Kathy was surprised there hadn't been an all-out slanging match between Olga and either Danny or Piers. Gisela proved to be a very effective mediator but Jean-Guy, Kristian and Samuel kept quiet and didn't join in the altercations between the three more fiery musicians. Piers so nearly walked out of that rehearsal several times but for the sake of the two who had travelled there with him, he wouldn't lose his temper and shout back and consciously forced his mind to concentrate on the music no matter how much Olga needled him. He had the music spread across the piano as a prompt, but there wasn't much chance to look at it unless one of the other players queried a note or a stage direction. The top of the piano was down in compliance with the staging directions and he couldn't help but think that the closed piano with all the music spread on top would have been Audrey heaven which helped him to keep his temper even after Danny finally lost his and yelled something at his wife in what the others could only assume was very rude Russian as she shouted straight back and would probably have slapped him if she hadn't had a violin in her hands.

As this was just a quick run-through to sort out any major musical problems, they didn't do much of the staging before their break for lunch. Kathy felt quite drained as, apart from witnessing the slanging matches in two languages, she had been soundly kissed by Jean-Guy while she sat on his thigh playing her violin and he had somehow manged to play his cello round her, and she had had Danny's hand further up the front of her top than she had been expecting. Piers had been annoyed to learn he was going to get snogged by Danny but to the relief of the pianist, Blue Viola had laughingly said he'd save that pleasure for a later session. Olga made it quite clear she wasn't happy that she had to be the one to commit the act of minor indecency on the piano player and she hadn't strayed too far inside his trousers while he was trying to concentrate on madly cross-rhythmed music with his left hand playing in a different key and time signature from his right. He had been pleased in a spitefully juvenile way that although she had completed that move by trying to get the shirt off him she had instead got it tangled round her violin bow. Jean-Guy and Kristian had got in a muddle over the bow-swapping section of the work and the former had been quite grateful when the teenager had said there were too many shirts being taken off and as neither cellist had any tattoos he would rather they stayed fully clothed throughout. Samuel quietly agreed as he hadn't wanted to undress another man and Olga promptly staged her most dramatic tantrum about it, demanding to know if she was the only person willing to do the staging. She bad-temperedly gave up the argument when Danny told her she could take her top off if she liked and she could pick whichever player she wanted to go digging about in her knickers. They didn't get as far as the last movement with Kathy's dramatic moment with the pianist, but they all agreed that for a first rehearsal it had gone quite well although none of them had realised just how difficult it was going to be both musically and emotionally.

Kathy carefully put her violin on top of the piano after they had all agreed to stop for lunch and she waited for Piers to finish making some notes on his part. "Would you like me to swap with Olga?" she asked. "I mean, I don't particularly want to do that to you but at least you know me better."

He turned over a page and jotted down some fingering before he forgot it. "No, but thanks anyway. In some ways it's easier with a stranger."

Kathy could see what he meant but Olga had come across to put her violin on the piano too so Kathy changed the topic. "Well, I'm proud of you considering you're not a pro like the rest of us. And I'll tell you one thing, you'll find the Mendelssohn a walk in the park after all this."

"Oh, are you doing Mendelssohn One?" Olga asked as though she had never said a cross word all morning. "I think it is loveliest trio written. You must let me know when you are playing that one out and I will come and listen if I can."

"We don't have any bookings as a trio at the moment," Kathy explained to her and the two women set off for the main house as Danny had come across to check some notation from his part with what was written on the piano score. "For one thing Jean-Guy has got solo work coming out of his ears and for another Piers is working away a lot at the moment."

"What work?" Olga asked sceptically. "Isn't piano his work now? I don't like him but I have to admit he is good player when he isn't playing too loud."

"He's still a working airline pilot and still does some on-call shifts so it's all a bit of a mess as he could be sent anywhere in the world on a moment's notice."

Olga really couldn't see the problem. "But you are all good players, you must be good trio so he can earn money playing piano."

"Yes, but he doesn't want to stop flying and unless he breaks his exclusivity with Jean-Guy and the Dodman Trio he wouldn't earn enough to pay his mortgage."

Olga sounded even more impatient. "So he has private licence and does charter flights just to keep his licence if that's what he wants." She smiled coldly and her eyes never left Kathy's face. "You wonder how I know? Danny often takes charter flights for his modelling work."

"His what?!" Kathy queried, wondering if she was losing her hearing.

So Olga explained that Danny now had another job that was taking him more and more away from his music; one which had started out as a favour for friend but had escalated frighteningly quickly into something that had made him into a freelancer and able to command four-figure payments for a day's work.

"You should tell Piers to do same. Or I'm sure Danny could put in word. He earns millions at it. We have photo session here in couple of days. I think Annette will go crazy when she sees our handsome pianist, don't you?"

Kathy didn't often think about Piers' looks as she had got used to him now and Olga had given her something much harder to get her head round. "You mean Danny, the Danny who taught me to drive and lived in a crummy bedsit in Fulham and didn't have enough money to feed the gas meter, is now a millionaire?"

"Oh, yes," Olga replied as though it was the most natural thing in the world. "He's good at modelling now I have tidied him up. And his agent has now got him some acting contracts as well."

"No."

"All true. Ask him."

Kathy suddenly wanted to laugh. "Do you know what? We used to make jokes about Piers being a fashion model. Now you're telling me there's a very high risk he actually could be? He would absolutely hate it."

"Good," Olga said. "So we can parade him in front of Annette and see if she can catch him. That will be interesting to watch. He will agree to do it for money. They always do."

Kathy knew Piers had his mercenary side but she couldn't imagine even he would go that far. "Who's Annette?" she asked as they went into the house.

"Annette Delaney," Olga explained, wondering how on earth anyone didn't know. "She is head of fashion house coming here. You'll see."

They sat round the large table in the farmhouse kitchen and the shy Agnetha joined them. She sat between Kristian's mother and Gisela and looked worriedly at Jean-Guy and Piers who were down the other end of the table. Kathy couldn't hear what she said but she muttered something to Kristian's mother, Berit, who then spoke down the table to Piers.

"Agnetha says she is sure she knows you from somewhere. Have you played in Stockholm?"

He looked faintly startled. "Not since I was about fourteen which I'm guessing is long before she was born."

This much was passed back to Agnetha who got a bit more animated but still spoke only in Swedish. "No, she is sure she has seen you somewhere. She says you look very familiar."

So everyone at the table tried to work out how a fifteen-year-old girl who had never left Stockholm could possibly recognise a man who hadn't been there for over thirty years.

It was Jean-Guy who worked it out first. "Do you know the mezzo Roisin Thompson?" he asked Agnetha in English but she understood the name.

There was a mad babble of Swedish from the girl and Berit said, "She is very sorry but this is who you remind her of. Mrs Thompson has been teaching masterclasses where Agnetha is studying her singing."

Piers sighed inwardly and realised that now he was back on the classical music scene this was going to start happening a lot. "We're related, it's too complicated to explain. I have been her accompanist in the past and a lot of people say there is a strong family resemblance."

This was translated into Swedish for Agnetha who went bright scarlet and whispered something in Berit's ear.

Berit smiled ruefully at their guest. "I am sorry, but she wants to know if it's at all possible you could accompany her while you are here? None of us plays the piano well enough and it would be good for her if you could. I understand if you don't want to."

Piers had been hoping for a bit of a rest as his wrists and hands were threatening to ache after the exertions of the morning and he had begun to wish he had done more work on his technique after the Prof's intensive coaching. He also had a mild headache coming on after playing split music for a lot of the morning, and didn't even want to think about going back to accompanying a singer. But then he looked at Agnetha who couldn't look back and heard himself say, "No problem. When would she like a run through?"

Berit translated again. "She says after the evening meal if you wouldn't mind. She has the music for you and would you please just take her through a few Schubert songs as they are what she has to study for her next class."

"Can we come and listen?" Kathy asked, looking at the sweet face of the child trying so hard to be brave among the strangers.

Berit asked Agnetha and smiled apologetically. "I'm sorry but she says you can come, I will be the translator and Danny will be page turner but nobody else."

Agnetha caught Kathy's eye and suddenly each knew the other understood.

"Who raped her?" Kathy asked quietly.

"Her father, many times since she was about nine. She came to us when she was twelve as a friend of mine runs a refuge and didn't want to keep a child there. She, for some reason, trusts Danny but no other man is allowed anywhere near her although she has got used to Samuel as he is such a quiet man and she has learned Kristian and his father won't hurt her. But Danny is now her guardian angel. She has been so brave asking Piers to play the piano when she doesn't know him."

Kathy looked along the table but only Gisela was paying any attention to them now. She knew why

Agnetha had trusted Piers; it was the same reason she had. But rather than get mystic about it she offered a more rational explanation. "Piers has been through a very bad time in his life. He recently lost someone close to him to cancer and, oh, it's all too complicated. But it has put something, I don't know, a kind of sympathy in him that wasn't there before."

"It is the same with Danny. He never speaks of it but there is something very bad in his past. Like his hand. He never says how it was injured but I had to translate for him in the early days and the surgeon who first examined it said it was old injuries, would have happened when he was a child and was the result of repeated and deliberate injuries that we can't understand."

Kathy hadn't even realised but it did make some kind of sense. "He always said it was an accident. But I think maybe there's more to his past than we know."

Berit smiled in agreement. "He is a man of secrets. So is your Piers. They need to be careful of each other."

Kathy felt quite honoured to be part of the little group that went across to the practice room after the evening meal. It had been a hard afternoon of playing difficult music and they still hadn't done much work on the staging. They had also found out there were several differences between the full score which Piers was playing from and the individual parts so there had been a lot of discussion and rewriting to do for all of them.

Agnetha shyly handed her music to the man who sat quietly at the piano really hoping this page turner wouldn't behave like the one he had had at the recital in Yorkshire. He consciously wouldn't let himself think he was about to accompany a singer again, and it didn't help that the score Agnetha gave him was a direct reprint of the one that had been beaten into his memory all those years ago. He didn't really need a page turner for this but it somehow helped to feel the solidity of someone next to him to help drive away the demons that were circling. He wouldn't look across at Kathy as he could see she was chatting with Berit. So he thought of Sarah, his extraordinary wife who saw shadows and always knew when he needed her help the most. He had felt her trying to get through the protection he had put round himself when Chantal was so ill but she hadn't managed to breach it. Many times since he had wished he had let her through. Just that one time she had caught him on the bridge and he had felt her next to him, silently taking his hand and leading him away from the veil towards a new life with her and their children.

"You OK?" came the sharp query from the man sitting next to him. "Your face matches the piano keys and I don't mean the black ones."

"Yes, fine. Sorry, been a long day."

Danny just laughed and said, "You'll never make a Stretto. Where's your stamina?" There was a rattle of Swedish between him and Agnetha now she was in position in front of the piano. "She says please can you start with the one about the nightingale and why do you take your shoes off to play?"

"Helps me feel the pedals. I've always done it," was all he said as he went straight to the right page for the song and silently thanked Sarah for her help. "What speed?"

Agnetha nodded a beat for him after his reply had been translated by Danny and a smile spread over her face as Piers so lightly and expertly played the introduction. Kathy and Berit were sitting side by side on the cellists' chairs and Kathy wondered for a moment why the older woman seemed to be holding her breath. Then Agnetha started to sing and Kathy, who had never allowed herself to believe in such things, seriously began to wonder if there was some kind of enchantment in the room. The musician in her noticed how Piers adapted his playing to the pure, soft tones of the young singer and knew then what the Prof had meant about him being such a perfect accompanist. She wasn't surprised to see that Berit was trying very hard not to cry.

The last notes of the song died away and Agnetha looked at the man who had played so beautifully for her. She didn't say a word but walked over to him, gave him a hug and then went back to where she had been standing, saying something to the two men when she was back there.

"Next one in the book, please," Danny translated.

Altogether Piers helped Agnetha to work on the Schubert for an hour with Danny as a very well-behaved page turner and translator, and with Berit helping when he got stuck. It wasn't long before the others realised that when it came to Schubert Lieder, Piers knew what he was talking about. At the end of the hour there was such a feeling of calm and serenity in the room nobody really wanted to say anything for a few moments after Agnetha had closed her book of songs and quietly said thank you in English to her accompanist. She said a lot more in Swedish to Danny but he just smiled and didn't immediately translate it.

Danny firmly closed the lid of the piano. "OK, I'm for a cigarette. Want one?" he asked Piers.

"Sure. Why not. Thanks."

"Come on then, we have to go outside or we set the smoke alarms off."

Agnetha watched the two men leave the practice room and go out into the yard where it was already dark as evenings were early in a Swedish autumn. She suddenly smiled the happiest smile Kathy had ever seen on her face and laughed as she said something to Berit. Berit clearly agreed with her then said to Kathy,

"Agnetha says she will tell Mrs Thompson tomorrow that she has played with her relative who looks so much like her and that he is the best accompanist ever. She actually asked Danny if he would ask Piers if he would go to tomorrow's masterclass with her as she is due to sing in front of Mrs Thompson and she can bring her own accompanist."

Kathy knew this was something she really, really wanted to see. "Are the masterclasses open to the public?"

"Of course."

"Then if he goes I will ask if I may go too. Do you suppose Danny is asking him now? Away from Agnetha so she wouldn't see if he said no?"

"I would guess so."

"That reminds me," Kathy said politely. "Excuse me, but I must just ask Piers something before I forget."

She went out into the yard where the two men were in the middle of their cigarettes and were engrossed in a conversation she thought maybe she shouldn't interrupt but then she picked up some of their words and realised they were chatting about the discrepancies in the Orlov work, so she went across to join them.

"Was it odd playing with a singer again?" she asked as an opening gambit to see what he would say.

"Not as much as I thought it would be," he replied.

"Leave you two to it," Danny commented and stubbed out his cigarette. "Thanks for that. I'll go and pass the news on to Agnetha. Means a lot."

Kathy waited until she was alone in the yard with Piers. "You agreed to play at the Conservatoire then? You know it means you'll meet up with Roisin again?"

Piers took one final long drag on his cigarette and put it out in the same sand bucket Danny had used. "Yes, and yes. Thirty years ago I swore blind I'd never play the piano again and now look at me. Gone right back on everything I promised myself."

Kathy was intrigued. "What changed your mind?"

He gave her one of his lovely smiles. "That bloody Prof set me up. He took me into the living room so you could phone Emma and sat me at the piano and I just wanted to, I don't know, not play anyway. But I'd watched you and Jean-Guy and you'd both shown me that music isn't all about … well, what my family made me think it was about. So I guessed it wouldn't kill me to play his game. Didn't expect to see him again after we'd all got away so just thought 'why not?'. He would have rumbled me as soon as he knew I was being sent to stay. Think about it. The first thing he did was call me Ciaran Maloney. He'd been told my past by the security services, although not the musical side of it. He's a musicologist and he'd read Roisin's autobiography. And above all he's not an idiot. He put some Mozart in front of me and said could I run through that for him. So I had two choices. Try to kid him it was a coincidence of name and I wasn't the Ciaran Maloney whose sister believed he was dead or let him know he was right and play the bloody thing. I have no idea why the security services didn't tell him about my musical childhood when they sent me there but just about the nastier side of what my family taught me. I'd guess they didn't care. It didn't matter to them as it made no difference to their plans for me. Anyway, I looked at that Mozart which I'd first played when I was about five and that was it really. Few wrong notes as I was thirty years out of practice and he got so happy when he realised his hunch was correct and I wasn't sure if he was going to give me a bear-hug or cry on my shoulder. Fortunately you came in and saved him from anything so emotional."

Kathy remembered the scene all too well. "But it obviously upset you to go back to the piano. Why didn't you just walk away and refuse to play ever again? You were playing a hell of a dangerous game anyway by showing your hand as Roisin's supposedly-dead brother."

Piers looked away from her for a few moments and shook his head. "I know. But, I don't know if I can explain so you'd understand. First there was the cat on my doorstep. A cat is my guide and finding Audrey like that just spooked me. Then the next day you turned up in the pet food aisle of Sainsbury's and I knew the fates, or whatever you want to call them, were lining up. I have told you lots of times that I walk the old ways and I just started walking that path. Couldn't stop it. And I still don't know where it's going to end."

Her extraordinary experience listening to Agnetha had opened something in Kathy's mind but she didn't know how to express it. She could sense some kind of feeling, like she had known just over five years ago when the bird on the balcony rail had persuaded her to run and she looked at the man with the raven-black hair who spoke so knowingly of guides and the old ways. It was a frightening concept and she knew she wasn't yet ready to walk that path with him even though what he had said made perfect sense to her. She stood in silence for a few moments, trying to think of the words she wanted to say.

He looked at her hard in the half-light of the dark yard, lit only by the lights from the buildings. "Don't fight it. You told me months ago of how you get images in your head. You just need to learn not to be afraid of what you can see."

She opened her mouth to protest but his touch on her lips was cold and silenced her.

"And don't deny it. The raven is your guide as the cat is mine. It told you to run all those years ago and you let it guide you. Now, let's go back in the farmhouse where it's warm and see if we can find a cup of tea." He put a comforting arm round her and murmured in her ear, "Is your mate Danny not as straight as he pretends to be?"

Kathy was grateful to him for getting her off the mystic route but hadn't expected anything like that. "What? Of course he is."

"Ah-ha!" came the triumphant response. "Told Jean-Guy about the pair of you yet?"

"And you complained about the Prof rumbling you. No I haven't, but if we're going to be working together on this Octet then I think he needs to know. Don't you?"

"Definitely."

She sighed. "He's going to think I'm a right slapper."

"And I bet he doesn't know the half of it."

"Oh, shut up. Why would you think Danny fancies you anyway?"

"I never said that. He just paid me a rather unexpected compliment."

"Oh? About your piano playing?"

Piers opened the back door for her so she could go into the farmhouse first. "Something like that."

Nobody found out exactly what Danny had said to Piers, but they both went with Agnetha into Stockholm the next day and she agreed Kathy could come too. Danny drove them there in a bright red, Swedish-registered Saab and he discreetly made sure the two women were in the back so Agnetha didn't feel threatened by the man she didn't know.

"It's good of you to agree," he said to Piers on the way into town. "She's been too nervous to sing in front of Mrs Thompson before now and today is the last day she's here."

Kathy wanted to keep the conversation away from exactly how Piers and Roisin were related so she leaned forward and poked Danny on the shoulder. "So what's all this about modelling, huh?"

He looked slightly annoyed. "Oh, that. It started out as a favour for a friend."

"Earning millions, Olga said."

"She wishes." He glanced at the man in the passenger seat. "I meant it, you should try it. I told you've got the looks for it and it's money for old rope. Annette will look you over when she's here tomorrow and once she gets her claws into you then you've had it. So you might as well go voluntarily. Why should I be the only one making a fool of myself anyway?"

Piers almost smiled at the sheer ridiculousness of the idea. "Think I'll stick with flying aeroplanes. But thanks again for the compliment."

Kathy was satisfied that whatever Danny had complimented Piers on had been more in self-interest than in any kind of unwelcome intent.

Danny and Agnetha clearly knew their way round the Conservatoire and led the other two to a recital room on the first floor. Students and audience were already gathering and Roisin Thompson was standing next to the piano, talking to a young woman who was leafing through the music on top of the instrument. She wasn't paying much attention to the audience building up so had no clue her brother had quietly slipped in with three other people and they had been directed to some seats at the side so Agnetha would be able to get out when it was her turn. Agnetha wasn't saying much, just the occasional remark to Danny, and she fell totally silent when the class began, concentrating on the tips and techniques Mrs Thompson was giving to her pupils, her comments translated by one of the Conservatoire lecturers.

Agnetha was called fifth and the lecturer asked her a question in Swedish to which she replied in an obvious affirmative and the lady at the piano obligingly vacated the piano stool so those who spoke no Swedish gathered the student had confirmed she had brought her own accompanist. Roisin Thompson didn't pay attention to accompanists as her job was to teach the singers so her smile was just for the very young blonde girl who took up her place in front of the piano while the lecturer explained something to the audience.

Danny obligingly translated for Kathy. "He's just explaining that she's only fifteen but she's so talented that she's here as a special pupil as well as attending the local high school."

At the first light touch of the introduction to *An die Nachtingall* Roisin visibly jumped and looked at who was playing the piano. She shrieked loudly with delight which startled everybody in the room, most of all the young singer who hadn't managed a note yet.

"Good reaction," Danny approved and Kathy nudged him in the ribs as a reprimand even though she wanted to laugh herself.

There was a bit of a babble on the stage and then the lecturer informed the baffled audience that the accompanist was actually a relative of Mrs Thompson and she hadn't seen him for years. Roisin apologised profusely to Agnetha and gave her a bit of a hug then encouraged her to start the song again.

There was a profound silence in the room while Agnetha performed the song so simply and so beautifully, the teacher had no comments to make except to praise her interpretation and musicality. Kathy did wonder if the teacher had worked out that the student had maybe had a bit of extra coaching from her accompanist. After Agnetha's performance, Roisin called the lecturer over and they all had a huddle round the piano. Kathy was again grateful for Danny's translation.

"She's just said that she hasn't sung with him for many years but if we'll all excuse her she'd like to indulge herself just once before he goes."

"Better than we could have hoped," Kathy said delightedly and clutched Danny's arm without realising she was doing it.

For the first time in over thirty years, Roisin Thompson sang Schubert's arrangement of *Ave Maria* while her brother accompanied her at the piano and everyone in the room was aware of just how special a moment it was as soon as the music started, even though only one member of the audience knew why. Just for a fleeting moment Kathy remembered how Roisin had said in her autobiography that was the one song she wanted to sing again with her brother and she was happy that dream had come true for her. Kathy hadn't thought of herself as being spiritual in any way for a long time but her experience listening to Agnetha last night and then talking to Piers in the yard had started to open up her mind. She was too scared to go there so she made herself watch the way Piers was using the pedals and knew what Jean-Guy had meant about an unusual technique. All the other pianists she had ever met just stamped on the things, but he was using hands and feet to coax a sound out of that piano which, along with Roisin's superb voice, wove an enchantment into the music that was finding its way into her bones. She leaned against Danny's arm just to give herself something solid to anchor her body and keep her soul and spirit safe from the music's magnetism.

The song ended and for several seconds nobody made a sound. Then Piers stood up, rather noisily scraping the piano stool on the stage, and the audience came out of its trance and started applauding. Singer and pianist quietly embraced then he put his shoes on and left the recital room.

"Just how closely are they related?" Danny muttered to Kathy as Roisin took a few moments to gather her thoughts and then called the next student forward. "I've never heard anything like it before."

"Not very," she replied, sticking to the story they had worked out last year and hoping it would still hold good after that performance. "Not sure exactly. Don't think they are either. Sorry. I must go and find him."

For a brief second Danny searched her face for clues but found none. "Take him to the cafeteria, ground floor. I'll sit with the kid and we'll join you there when the class is over. Probably be about an hour or so."

Piers hadn't gone very far and Kathy found him in the corridor just outside the recital room door, sitting on the floor with his back against the wall, head bowed and eyes closed.

"You OK?" she asked, not sure she wanted to hear the reply.

He got up and his smile reassured her. "Do you know what? I think I am. It's surprising how many thoughts you can have while playing a couple of pieces of Schubert."

"Want to share any of your thoughts?"

"No, because I'm not sure you'd understand."

She stood on tiptoe, took his face in her hands and gently kissed his cheek. "I think I'm starting to," she said softly.

He put his hands over hers for a few seconds and didn't speak, but she felt as though he had let her touch his soul.

They found the cafeteria and bought themselves some coffees and a cake for Kathy and settled at a table by the window.

"I think Danny may have rumbled you," Kathy began, not sure how to deal with this.

"What do you mean?" Piers asked absently, totally absorbed in watching a large dog taking a small owner for a walk.

"About you and Roisin."

"Can't have. If he's read the book he'll think the same as everyone else."

"Not if he's heard any of her early recordings. You do have quite a distinctive style of playing."

"And so do hundreds of other accompanists."

"Should we tell him?"

Piers thought about that as the dog triumphantly led its owner away from a well-sniffed lamp-post. "Can we trust him?"

"I would say yes."

"Then you can tell him the absolute truth. But only if you trust him completely to keep his trap shut. At least it should stop him pushing the point when the wrong people may be listening in. Shouldn't be surprised with his musical upbringing. He may well have heard some of Roisin's early recordings or maybe even gone to some of our later recitals if he's old enough as his uncle tried to recruit me not long before he died."

"But you're not happy about him knowing?"

"No, I'm bloody not. So get him to peddle the distant relative story too, huh?"

"And if anybody else asks in the future? Like that bloke in Hamburg?"

Piers did look at her then. "Tell them the agreed lie. And pray."

"And that's your best solution?"

"Got a better one?"

"No. Sorry."

They carried on with their coffees but without speaking again, and in less than the estimated hour they were joined at their table by Danny, a very animated Agnetha and a rather hesitant Roisin.

"OK if I join you?" she asked.

Her brother just got to his feet and gave her a hug. "Grab a seat and tell us what you've been up to."

"Oh, you know," she smiled as she sat next to him. "Singing. You?"

"I wouldn't know where to start. Tell me about your family? And please give me your address and phone number before you go. I'd like to stay in touch this time."

Roisin's smile was so warm and thankful, Kathy wondered how on earth Piers could have ever walked away from his sister as he had done all those years ago. Roisin took a card out of her bag and wrote on the back of it. "That is my London address and number on the front, and on the back I've put my Moscow details. Probably better to write to London as the Russian postal service can be a bit hit and miss, but you can always ring me there."

He looked at the card, smiled, and showed the London address to Kathy. "That's the posh bit of Wimbledon," she explained. "I'm from the other side of the railway."

Danny had never seen the shy Agnetha as vivacious as she was while they all had coffee and the women indulged in pastries. He had to work hard translating but Kathy could tell he was pleased to see Agnetha so relaxed considering she was sitting in a group with two men, one of whom she hadn't even met until a few days ago and a teacher she idolised so much she had been too awestruck to sing in front of her. He sounded quite regretful when he checked his watch and said they had to go as the others would be expecting them back.

To Agnetha's joy, Mrs Thompson gave her a card too and said she was to keep in touch and if ever she came to England then she would be delighted to offer some singing lessons without charge.

Danny and Kathy walked behind the other three and both had to smile to realise Agnetha could actually speak more English than she had ever let on.

"Amazing kid," he praised her.

"She's very talented."

"For a fifteen-year-old she's bloody incredible. So go on, tell me. I can keep secrets. What are those two? You don't play music together like that if you're fourth cousins twice removed who only ever see each other for the occasional family Christmas booze up."

Kathy looked into his eyes and knew she could trust him. "Have you read her autobiography?"

"Yes, a few years ago."

"She had a brother?"

"Ciaran. Yes, she said he died." Danny stopped and shot her a hard look. "Ciaran Maloney didn't die, did he?"

"That one didn't. He changed his name and ran away to join the Air Force. But you must never, ever tell anyone. Promise. His life could depend on it."

He smiled that lovely, gentle smile that had convinced the traumatised Kathy to let him so intimately into her life all those years ago. "Promise. I have a special part of my memory where I keep all the secrets locked away and I shall add that one to it."

Johannes Brahms – *Trio in A minor for piano, viola and cello, Op. 114*

The weather was noticeably cooler the next morning when Kathy went downstairs for her breakfast. She was getting used to the generous bowls of fruit but still rather treacherously missed her porridge and was in a way glad they only had another couple of days left in Sweden before heading back to the cosy Suffolk farmhouse with its bowls of porridge and leftover cakes from Alison.

Only Gisela was at the table and wasn't eating anything. "Day off today," she greeted Kathy. "As we've got a fashion shoot taking place. Unfortunate timing with this being the only week you could all be here but they're always great fun. You'll get to see Danny doing his other job. And if we get too bored I'm sure we can find somewhere to put in some extra practice."

Kathy spooned some fruit and yoghurt into a bowl. "How did that even start?"

"Have you heard of the fashion house Viola?"

"Oh, yes. I saw a dress or something in the paper once and it cost about three months' wages."

"That's them. Well, the founder of it is Annette Delaney who used to live in the upstairs flat from Danny when he was in Fulham and she's the one he did the favour for that got all this going. He still doesn't like it as she keeps dyeing his hair and putting make up on him. But he just kind of sighs a bit and smokes a lot and lets her get on with it. And the fees she pays are enough to make your eyes water, so I can understand why he lets her do it to him. So you, me and Olga can have a girlie day laughing at it all as she's doing her menswear range today."

"What about Kristian and Samuel?"

"Kristian is at college for the day and Samuel takes himself into Stockholm or Uppsala whenever Annette is anywhere near the place as he's always terrified she'll try and recruit him."

"Is that likely? I mean no offence to Samuel but he doesn't seem model material to me."

"That's how she works. She won't use professionals. Danny put her up to it right at the beginning and now it's a bit of a trademark for her. She finds people from all over the place to model her clothes and she does pay them often more than the going rate so it's not a money thing."

Olga came to join them, grinning hugely as though at a private joke. "Well, that's Danny in really bad mood now. He doesn't want to do this today as we are getting on so well with Octet. But I have had best idea ever that will put Piers in front of Annette and we can watch her pull him in like fish. Where is Jean-Guy?"

"Jean-Guy isn't out of bed yet and I have no idea where Piers is."

"Oh, he is in practice room with Danny," Olga told her. "They are talking about Octet and Piers doesn't like choreography so they are looking for compromise. Anyway, to my idea. I want Piers and Jean-Guy to be in practice room with Danny when Annette gets here. They can play Brahms trio and it will be so funny to watch her try to recruit them. Because she will go for Jean-Guy as well. He has sweet face and looks as though he is confused half of time."

Kathy wanted to smile at that description of Jean-Guy which had summed him up so well but she wasn't sure her Moly would ever agree to be a fashion model either. For one thing he wasn't that tall and although she thought he had the dearest face and could blissfully ignore the fact the Prof's cooking was starting to stick to his waistline, he was very conscious of it and was also convinced that his hair was thinning. Two traditional traits of men as they got older and she knew he was a bit miffed that neither Danny nor Piers had succumbed to either although they were both older than him. She didn't think he was vain enough to be coerced by flattery but it would be interesting to watch.

"That is mean," Gisela giggled. "But, you're right, it will be fun. She'll get both of them."

"I don't know," Olga replied. "I say she will get Piers because no man can look like that and not want to wear designer clothes and be photographed. But I think maybe Jean-Guy will have too much self-respect to let her do that to him."

"Nah," Gisela disagreed. "Have you seen the way Piers is dressed? Awful old things, it's a miracle he's not still in flares, if he ever went into them in the first place. He'll bite her arm off for the money not for vanity. I think Jean-Guy may do it for a laugh as he must be on a good whack as a cellist." She laughed and looked at the petite blonde woman next to her. "And I also bet she'll want you on her books. I usually run away with the others but I want to see her go into action on those two. She'll be so besotted with Piers she won't be the slightest bit interested in me today." She guessed what Kathy was thinking. "And she can't have this lovely Russian beauty either as she hasn't got a permit to work for a British fashion house."

"Do you mind?" Kathy asked.

"Not really," Olga admitted with a surprising honesty. "All my concert gowns are Viola design so I get to wear them anyway."

Kathy thought of her three dresses made from commercial patterns by Sarah's mother and, just for a moment, wished she could wear designer dresses too. Even at her height.

Two innocent men and one complicit one couldn't see any reason why they shouldn't have a go at the Brahms trio if it helped Danny to kill some time while waiting for the Viola fashion shoot to descend. Samuel, Kristian and Agnetha had all fled well before Annette and her entourage were due which left Kathy, Olga and Gisela to get very silly and giggly over cups of coffee in the apple store.

"How are you finding Orlov work?" Olga asked Kathy after a ludicrous conversation on what Annette's latest wardrobe would look like,

"I'm really enjoying it. Not sure how I'll cope with the choreography with the piano in the last movement. I haven't had the courage to try it yet."

"Yes, Jean-Guy warned us you may have problems with that."

"So that's what the Russian chat was all about?"

"Yes. He didn't say much. Just that you have trust issues with men. But I have watched you and Piers together, and you trust him. No, reason I ask is how would you feel about learning quartet we did in Yorkshire?"

Kathy couldn't help feeling a little bit excited that this might be the invitation to dep with the Strettos after all. "Well, I'm flattered you think I could cope with it."

Olga waved a dismissive hand. "You can play notes I am sure. Will you be alright having Danny on top of you on floor? I'm sure he will behave much better with you as you're not married to him."

"I won't know until I try," Kathy managed, still not quite sure where this was going, and realising Olga probably didn't know that she and Danny had once been lovers. A fleeting thought crossed her mind and she wondered if Olga even knew Danny had had a brief marriage during his Army days. She had only found out because he had received a birthday card during their dating days and it had been signed by Tom and Sue, posted in Llandudno. So he had explained that he had married the sister of one of his Army buddies; it had lasted just over two years, produced two children, then his wife Pauline had dumped him for a childhood sweetheart in her native Wales and Kathy got the distinct impression he was grateful to be living the free and single life again.

"OK, we'll try you on staging tomorrow. You see, I am now four months pregnant with my second and I won't do *Lithuanian* for a while. And Gisela doesn't want to climb on another woman so it would be Danny. And although we would be happy to welcome you into Stretto, we don't want too many others on our lists so no back-up viola player."

Now it had happened, Kathy couldn't quite believe it. "What?" she breathed. "You would seriously put me in a performance of the *Lithuanian*? I really don't think I'm good enough."

"Yes you are," Olga told her sternly. "We do not extend invitations to anyone. So we'll give our dates to your agent and she can block-book you with us. I'm taking six months off completely after birth which is due in early March, so we will need you for maybe eight months. Your agent will have to cancel any bookings you already have on our dates. You'll need to come here more times to get you used to our way of playing."

"But," Kathy started, feeling as though she had just won the Pools. "But what about Jean-Guy?"

"What about him?" Olga demanded. "You have said yourself he has plenty of work and I presume two of you aren't joined at hip?" She was thoughtful for a few moments then turned to Gisela. "We need to book Piers as pilot too. It'll be much easier with private plane."

Kathy was scarcely able to believe how Olga made decisions to suit herself without thinking about anyone else and she looked at Gisela who just shrugged.

"She's a one-woman bulldozer," Gisela remarked. "I keep telling her. I even learned the Russian word for a bulldozer so she couldn't claim she didn't understand. And if I'm not mistaken that's the sound of a fashion shoot invading our yard."

Kathy had thought Olga was quite bossy enough. Then she met Annette Delaney, head of Viola fashion house. A volatile redhead who blasted into the apple store and dashed round greeting Olga and Gisela like old friends then stopped short when she was introduced to Kathy.

"You're just what I need," was Annette's rather abrupt greeting. "I need to work on a petite range. How tall are you?"

"Um, five foot two."

"Turn round, let me have a look at you. Hold your hair up on top of your head. Yup, you're in next summer's collection. I'll need you for a fitting session at some point."

Kathy realised she had just been recruited and hadn't managed to get a word in. She smiled to herself and thought it might be quite fun to get all dressed up in designer clothes. Especially if she was going to be paid to do it.

"OK, where is he?" Annette wanted to know. "He dropped some rather interesting hints when I spoke to him yesterday evening."

"Practice room," Gisela giggled. "What hints?"

"Very obscure ones, but he told me to make sure I brought a full load of stuff as there should be at least one other potential model for me to dress today. You got any ideas what he meant? I know what he's like and he's probably brought a bloody dog along."

"Oh, no. No dog," Olga assured her.

Gisela was almost snorting with laughter now. "Quite the opposite of a dog," she managed to say. "We left them in the practice room."

The four women crossed the yard and Kathy was surprised just how much accompanied a fashion shoot. There were two cars and a medium-sized van and already an efficient crew were getting lighting set up and pulling garden furniture and tubs of flowers all over the place to make sets up for the photos.

Annette knew her way round the yard and went happily crashing into the practice room then stopped short in the doorway. "Oh my God. Where the hell did you find that one?"

"Which one?" Olga asked. "We give you two."

"The cellist. That is just the face I need for my preppy look. Little boy lost in chunky knits and corduroy with tweeds. I'll have all the mothers buying the look for their sons."

The three who had been playing Brahms looked a bit astonished at being so rudely interrupted.

"Come on, Danny, time to get you made beautiful," Annette greeted him. "And you with the cello. I'm going to need you too. What's your name?"

"Jean-Guy Dechaume. And you are?"

"How delightfully French. You look it too. Me? I'm Danny's worst nightmare, aren't I?"

Danny gave an audible sigh of resignation and put his viola away in its case. "You are indeed," he agreed. "Come on, Jean-Guy. This is Annette Delaney, head of House of Viola and you can't say no. She does pay remarkably well."

"How well?" Jean-Guy asked suspiciously. Danny whispered something in his ear and his dark eyes opened like saucers. "For a day's work?"

"Yup."

"But I'm too short to be a model. I am even shorter than you."

There was a touch of triumph in Danny's snort of laughter. "This is House of Viola. They don't play by the rules."

Jean-Guy was satisfied. And it was a hell of a fee for a day's work. "OK, I'll do it."

Kathy realised they had misjudged Jean-Guy earlier and he was clearly going to do it for the money. That just left Piers to be drawn in too, either for the fee or for the glory. Or both.

"Good," Piers commented. "You still haven't paid me back yet, and the year is long up."

Jean-Guy had genuinely forgotten he had pledged his cello. But he knew when Piers wasn't being totally serious. He just laughed and put his cello on its side on the floor. "Hey, if what Danny says is true, I'll pay you it all back tomorrow and buy you your own cello as well."

Piers smiled in that way he had. "Just don't buy me a ruby ring."

Jean-Guy waved a dismissive hand. "You bloody Concorde pilots are way out of my price range."

Kathy was curious and so were Gisela and Olga. Having secured two models for her shoot and sent them off to get showered and handed over to the stylists, Annette didn't seem the slightest bit interested in acquiring a third although she was looking at him very intently especially when he got up from the piano and closed the top.

"Don't you want pianist too?" Olga asked, saying out loud the disappointment the others were feeling inside.

"You must be joking," Annette snorted. "Wouldn't touch him with a bargepole."

"Oh, I thought you would have been all over him," Olga admitted. "He is very beautiful."

"I know Danny told me to expect to get my socks knocked off, but, wow, that is the most heart-stoppingly, breath-takingly gorgeous face and figure I think I have ever seen in my life. But there is no way I am going to risk being sued by his agency for poaching by booking him right now and cutting out their commission."

Kathy had to try so hard not to laugh as she knew quite well that those rabbit-ears would be tuned in to all this.

"Why would his agent sue you? We're going to use him in our octet," Olga persisted.

"Yes, as a musician. I can't use him as a model."

"Oh my God!" Olga shrieked, knowing better than the other two how Annette's mind worked. "You think he's already professional."

"Well he must be. I'm dribbling just looking at him. And Christ knows what his fees are. I'd kill to have someone like that on my books, even if just for one session before all the other hyenas bite him into chunks for their share."

Kathy thought that was a singularly bloodthirsty image but the other two didn't seem bothered by it so she guessed they were used to Annette's rather outspoken style. She couldn't help wondering what Piers was making of all of this as he was just standing by the piano and watching them, looking faintly amused.

"That is Piers and he has never been model in his life." Olga told her. "So make it good session, because as soon as you put him out there, hyenas will be circling."

Annette looked as though all her dreams had come true at once. "Piers," she instructed, "come here a minute." She watched every movement of his body as he walked across the barn to join them and couldn't believe such raw talent had arrived in her life. He was even more stunning when she got a good look at him, with those unusually dark blue eyes and those incredible cheekbones. With looks like that he was going to earn her millions every time she used him. "I'm going to recruit you today as well."

He looked at her squarely and wasn't smiling. "No you're not."

Annette was skilled at working the vain, pretty ones. They always held out for the highest prices. "Has Danny warned you not to argue with me?"

"Yes."

Annette had a bad feeling that if she wasn't careful she was going to lose this one after all. "And has he told you how I recruited him all those years ago?"

"Yes, But he was broke and I'm not."

It was when he smiled at her that Annette knew she wasn't going give in without a fight. "Name your fee," she offered.

He seemed to be genuinely thinking about that. "Well, I heard what Danny told Jean-Guy so if that's your daily rate then that's maybe a week's salary for me. Without overtime. What's your offer?"

"Christ, if that's the case you're on a bloody good salary. I'm paying them my standard rate for a one-day shoot. I've used Danny many times before and I know what sales he will generate. I reckon Jean-Guy will net me about the same. But you are in another league altogether. So, OK, stick a zero on the end. I'll be putting you on the runway too. And that pays even more."

Piers suddenly forgot he didn't want to be a model and just looked at her as though she had started speaking in a language he couldn't understand. "Excuse me?"

"Runway. You. Viola designs."

"You're mad." Piers picked up his coat from where he had left it. "Thought I'd go souvenir shopping in Stockholm while we're not playing music for the day. Guessing you don't want to come, Piglet?"

Annette forcibly stopped him with a hand on his arm. "I am offering you what you asked for a day's work and you want to go shopping in Stockholm?"

"Yes, because who in their right mind pays that sort of fee to an ordinary bloke like me who doesn't know the first thing about modelling?"

Annette snatched the tatty waxed cotton coat from him, and knew this was her last chance. "Right, first of all, I don't know what kind of mirrors you're looking in, but believe me, there is nothing 'ordinary' about you. Second, I may use amateurs but I don't think I have ever had one with your potential. And, lastly, I don't offer any fees to anyone if I don't think they'll earn me even more in sales, and if that means I'm out of my mind then I'll live with it."

Piers shoved his hands into the pockets of his jeans. "You will pay me that much for a day's work? Seriously?"

Annette hoped that the smell of the money was making this unpretentious beauty waver after all. "Deadly seriously. I have a coat that is the main highlight of my menswear this season and I want you in it. I pay you as promised and on top of that you can keep the coat as my publicity stunt just so long as you chuck this rag in the bin which is where it should have gone years ago. I publish the photos in my autumn collection and I'll be paying in taxes twenty times what I pay you as a piddling little fee, so do the maths and calculate my profit margin." Piers' hesitation was his downfall. "Just let me put the coat on you and see what it looks like. And if these three ladies don't approve all deals are off."

He cast a look of despair at Kathy but seemed to know his fate was sealed. "What do you pay for runway work?" he asked curiously.

Annette smiled, finally convinced she had won, and whispered something to him.

"Jesus wept! Just to walk up and down a bit?"

"For you, yes. And a ten percent bonus if you can persuade Danny to join you."

Piers looked at her as though he still didn't believe it. "And you really were serious about the fee if I do the work for you today?"

Kathy somehow wasn't surprised to learn that he was, after all, prepared to sell himself like that. But then he did still have a heck of a mortgage eating into his salary, to say nothing of helping with the costs of raising what would soon be eight children, as she couldn't imagine for one minute he would leave Sarah to cope totally on her own.

Annette's smile was triumphant. "Yes."

"Jesus! If I hire myself out to you for the day and do the runway job that's one hell of a chunk of my mortgage cleared even after the tax man's finished with me." He offered his hand. "Done."

Annette took his hand and then gave him a hug. "Thank you," she said briskly, her designer mind already going into overload. "I won't be able to keep you long so I'm going to make the best of you. Go and take a shower, no hair products, if you've even heard of such things, and nothing under the robe as from the look of you there'll be holes in your pants where I don't need them. Then I'll turn the stylists loose on you as we'll have to do something about your godawful hair. Danny did warn me about that but I know just the look I want for you now I've seen you. You're not in the Army by any chance are you? There's no excuse otherwise."

Piers wasn't quite sure which of her remarks insulted him the most but he only got the chance to voice one of them. "You mean that bloody Danny set me up?"

"Of course. You and the cellist. And you have no idea how glad I am he did. You and I are going to be working with each other for just as long as I can keep you and I hope that'll be for a long time to come."

The absurdity of it all made him laugh. "Holey pants and all?"

Annette could see the overflowing order books in her mind already. "Holey pants and all."

Kathy had never thought she could enjoy a day so much as she did in the company of Olga and Gisela watching a fashion shoot, even if the excitable Annette's shouting did give her a headache. Danny grumbled a bit, smoked a lot and swore like a trooper but Kathy had to admit he looked casually stunning in Annette's designs with coppery highlights in his hair and, Kathy was convinced, just a touch of make-up on his eyes making their cool greyness look a bit more smoky somehow. Annette's stylists had given Jean-Guy some soft curls in his rather untidy hair but there wasn't any obvious make-up on his face, and he looked scholarly but still very desirable in what she called 'preppy' clothes with a nod to 1950s American college fashions which hid the fact he wasn't as slim as he had been. But Piers, everyone involved in or just watching the shoot had to agree, made the other two look like a couple of donkeys no matter what Annette put him in. The look Annette wanted started with a wig which gave him a very unfamiliar tousled mane of raven-black hair with a long fringe that was clearly irritating him as it kept getting in his eyes. Subtle make-up had brought out his cheekbones and taken away the crow's feet so he looked younger than the other two. Annette made him work hard for the fee she was paying him and Danny was definitely thankful someone else was taking all the flak for once while Jean-Guy just looked beautifully bewildered which suited the image he was portraying that day.

The coat Annette was putting out as key to her collection was as long as the tatty waxed cotton coat but it was in a thick woollen cloth dyed such a dark shade of indigo it looked almost black. It had Annette's trademark asymmetrical buttons, military-style epaulettes, and its turned back cuffs and stand up collar were a steel grey velvet. The top was semi-fitted and the lower half had steel grey inserts that gave it a dramatic swirl as Piers walked up and down the yard for the photographer. Kathy could tell Jean-Guy was starting to get a bit bored now as he had the least work to do of any of them and she guessed he was wishing he could be back in his habitual comfortable clothes and in a quiet corner somewhere practising his cello.

There was a pause in the shoot at about midday and the three by now rather fed up models were idly chatting at the round metal garden table which had been moved to just outside the back door of the farmhouse. Jean-Guy and Danny were sitting at the table, one looking homely and scholarly in Annette's 'preppy' designs and with his Moly glasses on, and the other sophisticated in a slate grey suit with a matching fedora and with a cigarette in his hand. Piers, still in the coat but with it now undone as were the top buttons of his shirt, was standing leaning on the open doorway with the kitchen behind him, looking as though he had just crawled home from one heck of a party to join his friends for breakfast at a pavement café.

"Don't any of you dare move!" Annette screamed at them. "I need some props! Now!"

Her assistant knew exactly what was needed, shot into the kitchen and came out with cups, saucers, a cafetiere of coffee and a plate of pastries. Danny was given a newspaper to pretend to have been reading, Jean-

Guy had a stack of books at his elbow and the half-smoked cigarette was passed across to Piers. The stylists tidied up hair and make-up and the photographer got the shot that was to give House of Viola the most profitable season it had ever known.

Annette took pity on her models and crew and finally declared a break but held Piers back for a few minutes while most of the others swarmed off to the apple store where a very generous buffet lunch had been laid out for them.

"Well?" she asked and felt as though she was holding her breath. "Are you walking down the runway alone?"

"I earned my ten percent."

"Good. I had a feeling you would. But I think a stunner like you will walk down there alone anyway. Maximum dramatic impact. Go and join the others for lunch."

He looked towards the apple store. "I'm really not that hungry. I don't usually eat lunch so I'll eat tonight."

A concerned Kathy had been loitering close enough to hear and she arrived promptly at his side. "Oh, you're going to eat. Come on, there's loads of stuff that won't upset you."

"And I don't do models with eating disorders," Annette told him sharply. "I can cope with Danny's vegetarianism, I've met another man who won't eat any vegetables at all and at least two gluten intolerant women. Them I will forgive. What's your excuse?"

"I get fat too easily. That and I'm dairy intolerant."

"For the fees I'm paying you, you will maintain the weight you are now, give or take the odd pound or two. If you lose or gain too much weight then I will sue you for every penny you lose me in revenue plus compensation which will wipe out everything you may have earned and leave you destitute and homeless. Or rather my husband will sue you on behalf of Viola and he is a fully-practising QC who likes nothing more than a good court case. Want to risk it? You can blossom to thirty stone or starve yourself to death after I've done with you. I'm just protecting my investment for as long as I need it. I've now got several million quid tied up in you and don't want to lose it."

Kathy and Piers realised just how ruthless the head of Viola could be.

"So that's it? I'm just an overpaid body in your clothes?"

"Got it in one. And I don't need models with brains either. So stop arguing and go and find something to eat. And don't throw your dinner down that coat, it doesn't wash."

Kristian, Agnetha and Samuel timed it to perfection so they got back to the farmhouse about twenty minutes after the photoshoot had packed up and left. The remains of the catering feast were still in the old apple store and the nine people spent the evening draped over the furniture laughing about the day's events and generally polishing off the food.

Kathy felt as though she had spent a glorious day in the company of good friends as she and Jean-Guy wandered back to the farmhouse to go to bed leaving Piers to follow along behind when he and Danny had finished their cigarettes.

"We'll have to stop him smoking all over again now," Jean-Guy remarked.

"I don't think that'll be a problem once the Prof gets hold of him. That's only the second one I've seen him smoke since we've been here and I guess he's had a bit of a busy day."

"And I haven't?"

Kathy snuggled against him as they went into the kitchen. "Well, maybe just a bit. Which of Annette's designs did you keep?"

"I only asked for the grey striped shirt so she said I could keep the trousers as well. I think Danny has said he's keeping the hat and nothing else which made Olga laugh. It's been a funny sort of a day."

"And tomorrow I have to climb all over Piers at the piano and have Danny wipe the floor with me."

Jean-Guy didn't answer her until they were alone in their room and then he took her gently in his arms. "They have agreed to rewrite if you're not comfortable doing it. And Danny doesn't do anything to you except what he has done already in our first rehearsal. Which you said just tickled a bit."

Kathy took a deep breath and told him, "He does in the *Lithuanian*. But I promise I will be wearing very substantial underwear, if not a T shirt."

Jean-Guy listened while she told him what Olga had said to her, including the plan for the charter flights for the concerts abroad. He had started kissing her when she was only about halfway through and barely let her finish before he took her to bed.

"Now tell me all that again," he whispered to her as they lay together between the sheets. "You have no idea what a turn-on that was."

"Oh I think I have," she smiled back at him. "Are you sure we can't change the choreography so I get to throw myself at you tomorrow?"

"Want to practise now?" he asked her.

Kathy and Jean-Guy thought Piers was very quiet at breakfast and hoped their 'nocturnal noises' as he called them hadn't kept him awake.

"You OK?" Kathy asked, deciding to risk the comments on her night-time behaviour.

To her surprise he didn't even smile. "No, not really. I'm still not sure I can do this piece and today it's just you and me. Not looking forward to it. Sorry." He gave up any attempt to finish the rather small bowl of fresh fruit he had taken to eat.

"I'm sure you'll be fine," Kathy tried to console and hoped he wasn't about to slide into one of his scary depressions again. "We've known each other a long time. Ever since I was in your way when all you wanted was a tin of beans to put on your toast for your tea."

That memory seemed to cheer him a little. "True. Sod it, I used to have dreams about you climbing all over me so all you're doing today is making one of my dreams come true."

"Cheeky sod," she said to him, not daring to look at Jean-Guy. "Eat your breakfast or I'm telling the others I want to swap that part with Olga."

Piers finished off his meal in two mouthfuls. "Personally I blame the cat. If she hadn't made me go into Sainsbury's to buy cat food, none of this would have happened. I guess I may have wondered where the mysterious blonde had gone when I didn't see her in the grocery store at midnight, nicking the last of the custard creams from under my nose, but that would have been it."

"Was I mysterious?" Kathy asked curiously. "I should have thought I was about the least mysterious person on the planet."

"You were to me. But I didn't know what you did for a living and I couldn't work out why you would do your shopping at that hour of night. You nearly always seemed to be in evening dress and that Paddington Bear coat which was a puzzle in itself and you had that strange oblong case with you. I mean I know it's a violin case now but in those days all I could think was that you had some kind of weapon in there." He had to laugh at himself. "Never occurred to me you were a musician. And the fact you had a hunted look about you in those days made you totally fascinating. Used to look forward to seeing you there."

Kathy looked at Jean-Guy then, but he just seemed mildly amused by this conversation as he had been the one the 'mysterious blonde' had chosen in the end. She knew a delaying tactic when she saw one and, if she let him, Piers would probably spin this one out for half the morning. "And then Audrey stuck her paw in the pie and now look at us," she finished the train of thought smartly. "I finally got myself the big brother I'd always wanted rather than the annoying little sister my parents gave me. Gayle and I never did have anything in common even when we were kids." She fondly patted his hand. "I'll try not to kick you in the head."

"It's not my head I'm worried about," he told her and realised he was now out of excuses and they had better get across to the practice room where the others had probably been waiting for ages.

Kathy could quite see his point as she stood on top of the piano and realised she was somehow expected to fall off it, miss the keyboard and land facing him with her legs straddling his right thigh. There didn't seem to be a lot of room between him and the piano. The choreography involved her starting to fall, he had to catch her before she hit the floor and help her get into position. It didn't make it any easier that she had her violin and bow in her hands and he was expected to be playing some crashing chords with his left hand at the same time. It was that old falling backwards trick again. She had to trust him to catch her and he had to trust her not to put her foot somewhere delicate. Then she was trapped in front of him for ten chords while his right hand joined his left on the keys, he had to duck so she could kick her right leg over his head and then she walked away free to resume her own playing. But first she had to let herself fall.

"Try it without the fiddle first," Gisela suggested kindly after Kathy had stood there for a while and hadn't moved, and gently took her violin and bow from her. "It's OK, take your time. I'm just bloody glad it's not me having to do it. It doesn't matter if you chicken out. Feel free to chicken and practise it at home in your own time. We've only been rehearsing it for a couple of days after all."

"And without piano chords as well," Olga commanded, sounding much less tolerant and understanding.

Jean-Guy looked at the woman he loved and couldn't believe how brave she was being even just getting up on top of the piano and standing there. No way he would ever consider throwing himself off a piano.

Piers felt so sorry for Kathy as she stood there looking at him and trusting him, her blue eyes huge and terrified but he sat quietly on the piano stool, as far back from the keyboard as he could get and still reach the pedals and waited for her. He knew the worst thing he could do was tell her he wouldn't hurt her as that was what her ex had said to her just before he held the knife to her throat and forced himself on her. There had been many times over the last couple of years, and this was one of them, when he wished he could hunt that man down and put some of his childhood lessons into practice on him.

Absolutely terrified, Kathy kept her eyes on the man calmly waiting for her to throw herself at him and remembered him quiet and broken in the new year. He had found the courage to pick himself up, accept he had been given another chance at life and get on with it. Somehow it made falling off a piano seem like nothing. "Ready?" she whispered.

"Go for it, Piglet."

In a blind moment of faith, Kathy let herself fall from the piano. She had closed her eyes as she went but she felt Piers catch her perfectly round the waist and then she was somehow whirled into position and found herself sitting on his thigh with his arms either side of her. He mouthed a silent 'well done' at her and gave her one of his nicest smiles while all around them the others breathed a collective sigh of relief that she had landed on her feet and nobody had got hurt.

"Ten piano chords," Olga instructed, impatient now to get on as they were so near the end of the piece.

Piers played his chords, saw Kathy's right leg move and ducked sideways but there wasn't enough space and she caught him a hefty wallop on the side of the head. The two of them ended up in a rather inelegant tangle with her leg on his back but she somehow managed to slide off only to find the others were all weeping with laughter.

"Oh God," Danny wheezed. "You looked like you were getting off a camel."

Olga stopped laughing first. "I thought it was strange piece of choreography. Let me have try." She handed her violin to Samuel then put herself as Kathy had been with her legs either side of Piers' thigh but didn't sit on him. "This way is easy," she announced and with a suppleness that Kathy envied, kicked her left leg over Piers' head without him having to duck. "But from here there is no way out." She thought about that for a while. "OK, so we've had ten chords then you are just playing left hand only, yes?"

"Correct," he agreed, looking rather wary and clearly not liking having this cold, Russian beauty getting so familiar with him, especially with her husband watching them.

"Keep your left hand on keyboard," she instructed and then got her left leg out and stopped, tucked hard against him and straddling his right hip. "It's no good. Whichever way we do it, it's going to look like getting off horse. You can't do kick from here or you will dislocate his hip. See."

"Ow!" said the pianist and wondered if she had done it deliberately. "Mind what you're doing with your knees."

"Maybe this way," Olga mused and tried something else but kicked him so hard he knew he was going to have a bruise on his thigh.

"Do that one more time," he told her, "and I am out of here and you can find another piano player to kick to pieces, you vicious cow. And don't do that either, you tart. Your husband is standing just over there. Just piss off and leave me alone. Piglet and I can work something out later when we're back home."

"Always!" Olga exploded and nearly showered his face with spit. "Always you refuse to do as we ask. Maybe you are good piano player but you won't join in. You won't become one of us and show no attempt to try. Do you want to be part of this octet or not?"

"Not," he told her firmly. "I haven't wanted anything to do with this bloody thing since I first saw it. But I'll tell you one thing and if you refuse to understand I'll get Jean-Guy to put it into Russian for you. I've had enough of you, your attitude and this bloody piece of music."

"Can you two just calm down a bit?" Danny interrupted sharply. "Olga stop being such a bloody bitch and, Piers, get out of diva mode. Come on, there are eight of us here and it can't be that hard to work this out. Jean-Guy, how the hell do you ever keep control of your trio?"

Jean-Guy flinched as he saw what Olga did to Piers before she disgustedly stomped away from him and threw herself into one of the chairs at the side of the room.

"We talk about anything we may disagree on," he said cautiously.

"And," Piers pointed out viciously, "we're not in the habit of inflicting bodily injury on each other."

Gisela, used to being the peacemaker, had been watching and thinking and had come up with an idea. "Think I've got it. Kathy, back you come, I'm way too heavy to demonstrate this."

Kathy climbed back and Gisela looked at the two of them while she had another think. "Right, pay attention the pair of you, this is quite a tricky move but I've done something similar in my tap dancing."

She showed them how Piers could roll Kathy round his hip and although it involved some very close body contact between them, she didn't kick him too often after the first few times they tried it. It was more dancing than donkey-riding and everyone approved.

Olga got up from the chair where she had been sitting and glowering at the choreography that was being worked out. "Good. Now we start again. Kathy, back up on top of piano and don't stand there so long this time. Audience will get bored."

They had spent so long working on the exit from the move, they had all forgotten how it started.

Kathy was euphoric by the time the musicians decided they had had enough for one day and all went across to the stables for an evening meal. She and Jean-Guy walked across the yard with their arms round each other and he murmured in her ear,

"Any chance you might want to practise your dance moves with me tonight?"

"Ask me again when my legs have stopped shaking. I think I got more personal with Piers today than I've ever been with you with your clothes on. Poor Piers, he didn't like this piece in the first place and now he's had two of us kicking him to bits for most of the day. I actually wouldn't blame him if he did walk out. I mean, did you see what Olga was doing to him?"

Jean-Guy had seen exactly and had been full of admiration that the other man had coped with it as well as he had. He was about to say he was glad it hadn't been him, but he heard someone behind them and remained silent.

"You OK?" Olga asked Kathy in that abrupt way she had as she fell into step with them.

"Yes, I think so. Not what I'm used to but I'm enjoying the challenge."

Olga smiled with her mouth only. "Have you slept with Piers?"

"No I haven't!" Kathy declared indignantly. "Nor am I going to."

"You should. You need to seduce him more as I do to Danny in *Lithuanian*."

"No way!" Kathy retorted, her temper rising. "He and I don't have that kind of relationship."

Olga carried on as though Kathy hadn't spoken. "I think next time you have no bra and you open your blouse for him. Yes?"

"Definitely not 'yes'," Jean-Guy said hotly while Kathy was still trying to think of a polite way to tell Olga what she thought of that idea. "And it's that attitude that has got you banned in half the cities of the world."

An unrepentant Olga looked across to the man who was in a corner of the yard having a quiet smoke with Danny. "Hey, Piers, how do you fancy having sex with Kathy?"

He wasn't so easily shocked. "Not on stage, thank you."

Olga just laughed but there was no warmth in it. "And off stage?"

"You must be joking. We don't have that kind of relationship."

"You really are sweetly inhibited Englishman, aren't you?" Olga told him with a sneer in her tone.

"If you're going to insult me, at least get it right. I'm a sweetly inhibited Irishman." He looked across at

Kathy and Jean-Guy and had a good idea what had happened so he walked across, caught hold of Olga and held her hard against him. "I'll have sex with you though if you like. It's what you want, isn't it? Why else would you have done that to me at the piano?"

It made Kathy smile to remember how he had once almost made her believe he was a conman with such behaviour but now she knew it was just his sense of humour. And she guessed Olga could be about to find out she had messed with the wrong man this time.

Olga looked at him as though she couldn't decide whether he meant it or not. She realised he wasn't as slight as he appeared but there was a frightening strength to him and he wasn't smiling.

"Right now, over there among the flowers," he offered. "Or, no, even better. We'll work it into the choreography and do it on stage in front of your husband and the audience. How about on top of the piano?"

Danny saw the way the other man had got hold of his wife and knew this was someone trained in unarmed combat. Besides which, it had taken him quite a while earlier on to calm a very angry Piers with some cigarettes and reassurances and now he found it rather amusing to see Olga not have the upper hand for once. He hoped she would learn something from this, but he doubted it.

Olga was feeling the first stages of panic as she realised Piers had actually got her in quite a professional restraining hold and there was no way she could get away from him. "But I'm married," she told him and tried a bit of useless struggling.

Piers let go of her as abruptly as he had grabbed her as though she physically repulsed him. "So am I.

And I'll thank you not to impose your double standards on me. Or Piglet."

"Kathy isn't married," Olga pointed out viciously and cuddled unsubtly against her husband who didn't quite move away but certainly didn't put his arm round her either.

Piers looked at the couple quietly holding hands and looking at him as though not sure whether he was the bravest man they knew, or the most foolish. "Trust me, those two jumped the broomstick a long time ago."

"Did what?" the non-native English speakers chorused.

"For pity's sake," Piers exclaimed. "Gisela, have you got a broom I can borrow, please? You know what I'm going on about, don't you?"

"Certainly do," she agreed and went quickly into her house. She brought out an old-fashioned besom broom and offered it to Piers. "I mean, this is a bit spontaneous and we at least need to invite the elements to attend or it won't count."

"True. Do you know any Swedish spirits? I can call up a few Irish ones."

"There's always Freya, she started out round here somewhere."

"I walk the old ways and follow the Goddess and the God. But I'm sure Freya will be happy to provide the blessing."

"I'll ask her," Gisela offered and closed her eyes. "You can call on the elements."

"What are they doing?" Jean-Guy whispered to Kathy.

"I have no idea," she whispered back and felt a strange sensation as though they had been joined by other presences. Gentle, calm presences who were watching and waiting for them.

Gisela put the broom down on the ground and she and Piers stood at each end of it while the others gathered round to see what was going to happen next. Gisela held out her hand to Jean-Guy and Kathy and said to them, "Right, our guests are here to bless your union. Now hold hands the pair of you and stand the other side of the broom from me and Piers."

Kathy and Jean-Guy obediently shuffled across, both feeling a little foolish now.

"Good," Gisela encouraged. "Now you need to make your vows to each other. Just something simple like you'll stick together and love each other."

To Kathy's surprise, Jean-Guy got the idea first. He took her right hand and gently pulled the ruby ring from her finger then kissed it and said to her: "Kathy, I gave you this ring once in friendship. Now I give it to you again in love and I want to spend the rest of my life with you." He slid the ring back onto her finger and she wanted to cry.

"I don't have a ring for you," she realised and her voice sounded all croaky. "But even without a physical symbol of our union, yes, I want to spend the rest of my life loving you as I do now."

"Perfect," Gisela told them. "Now jump over the broom."

"What are we doing?" Jean-Guy wanted to know.

Kathy could feel a deep happiness inside her as though she had been blessed at last in her life. "Let's do this," she said and took his hand.

Jean-Guy dutifully hopped over the broom with Kathy while they held hands and didn't understand why she was laughing all of a sudden.

Kathy could feel the lightness and joy in the yard. She was vaguely aware that Gisela and Piers were saying soft thanks to someone who wasn't there, but she ignored them and gave Jean-Guy a kiss on the lips. "That's it," she told him. "Now we're married."

"We are?" he asked finding the whole thing very eccentric but rather fun.

"Married enough for me."

Olga looked slightly puzzled by the crazy round of hugs the others gave the couple who had jumped the broomstick, but she shrugged, and smiled, and joined in.

"I always knew Gisela is a bit of an oddball, but you three really are completely screwy," Danny told them. "No wonder you're such a bloody good trio."

Kathy felt a lot more relaxed than she had expected when she and Jean-Guy joined Danny in the apple store the next morning. The other five had gone off to the practice room to play some standard quintets while they had a pianist available and it was Kathy's time to see how she would cope with the *Lithuanian* choreography. She had asked Jean-Guy to come with her as he wasn't needed for the quintet work while Kristian was available for the cello part. It hadn't been easy, but she had finally told Jean-Guy last night about her relationship with Danny when he had had long hair and taught people to drive. It had been a short-lived, meaningless, but extremely physical relationship which had suited both of them at the time as it had given her some kind of revenge for what her ex had done to her, but she knew it wasn't something she wanted to rekindle. Jean-Guy had been thankful for her honesty. He knew the woman he loved was no innocent. He had worked that out the first time they had ever slept together and guessed she had probably discovered the same about him.

"Hi," Danny greeted them vaguely as he answered Kathy's discreet knock on the door. He was clearly relieved to see she wasn't alone so she guessed he didn't want to relight their fire either. "Got over yesterday yet?"

"Fine. Piers said he's got bruises in places he's not going to show anyone though."

"Not surprised. I think I got bruises just watching it. Come on then. Come and get hurled on the floor."

Kathy had to admit that after the brutality of the kicking and hip-rolling routine with Piers yesterday, it was quite fun to be on the floor with Danny on top of her and politely trying very hard not to squash her. Jean-Guy was just thankful neither Kathy nor Danny appeared to have any inclination to resume their relationship. But at least it meant there wasn't any awkwardness between them as they sorted out what to do with instruments and legs with a lot of giggling and squirming.

They didn't need to do much of a run-through for them both to realise that the quartet wasn't going to be nearly as problematic as the octet looked like being. By eleven o'clock they were sitting at the table in the apple store drinking coffee and Jean-Guy was asking Danny about the operations on his hand and how that would affect his long-term playing.

Although he knew Olga didn't like it, Danny lit a cigarette to accompany his coffee. "I can't see I'll be playing much," he admitted and didn't sound particularly regretful. "We've got Gisela now for the quartet work and until Orlov gives us this quintet he keeps promising or we decide we're ready to have another go at the Octet, I can concentrate more on the other work I've been given."

"Going into acting I believe," Kathy offered.

Danny smiled wryly. "Yeah. I'm flying out to Los Angeles next month and look like being away for about three months. Want to see the script?"

"Sure, why not," Kathy agreed. She and Jean-Guy were a little surprised to be presented with what looked like quite a large book. "Which part are you?"

"Alan McKenna. Some kind of psychotic gunman who uses vagrants for target practice."

"Sounds a nice light piece to go to bed on," Kathy remarked as she saw the character's lines had all been highlighted in the script.

"It's not what you might call Shakespeare, is it? Then I just about get back from that in time for Annette to put me on the runway at some event or another in London, walking down it next to some bloke who's so bloody hot I want to screw him. How the hell do I let myself get talked into these things?"

Kathy was genuinely shocked to hear Danny admit to such feelings for another man as, unlike Jean-Guy would have done, he sounded as though he meant it. She remembered Piers' comment about Danny not being as straight as he seemed to be and a tiny part of her mind started to wonder. "Would you rather be teaching people to drive?" she asked, deliberately turning away from such thoughts.

The brief moment of intimacy was gone. "Not if they're all like you," he laughed. "Anyway, time you two got your packing done if you're being dropped off at the airport for the afternoon flight. I can't imagine that heap of a Land Rover goes very fast. Why the hell doesn't he get a better car?"

Jean-Guy had to smile. "He sold a Ferrari to buy it."

"Bloody idiot. What did he want to do that for?"

"As you may have heard, he and his wife have triplets. Not the easiest thing to fit in the back of a Ferrari. But he does also have an Aston Martin which is almost practical for us."

"Good. Got some sense then." Danny had a very unwelcome thought. "I hope Olga doesn't have triplets. She really didn't even want this second one."

Hoping it wasn't going to open what would be some fairly new wounds, Kathy finally asked, "Where is the first one? I haven't seen any signs of it."

"No, you won't," was the bitter reply. "Sally Natalya is currently in the depths of Soviet Russia with her grandparents. Olga takes her out there and leaves her behind for weeks, sometimes months at the time. I tell her I'll look after the kid but she just tells me that I need to be at work and earning money and she's too busy to look after her. I expect she'll do the same with this one. But Piers manages a working life and kids so I don't see why Olga and I can't."

Kathy felt rather sorry for him. "It's not the same. Sarah lives with her family and her friend Alison and they all help out with the childcare so it doesn't matter if Piers isn't there most of the time."

Danny was thoughtful for a few moments then something occurred to him. "Did Olga ever ask him if he'd be the pilot for the group on their travels?"

"Don't think so," Kathy said. "At least not while I've been in earshot."

"Oh, Christ. Better go and ask diplomatically before she sets off World War Three by telling him after she's booked everything. Let's go and interrupt them now. I've seen his temper once and I sure as hell don't want to see it again."

They got to the practice room to witness a disjointed performance of Bartok's quintet which wasn't a piece Kathy had ever played but had heard several times and knew it wasn't supposed to sound like that.

"Time to hand over your piano player," Danny greeted them.

Piers thankfully closed the score. "Thank Christ for that. That has to be the worst bloody quintet ever written."

"Well, I like it," Olga snapped straight back at him.

Danny looked from one to the other then at Gisela for an explanation.

"What you might call a clash of temperaments," she said briefly. "It's been daggers drawn for most of the morning between those two. Again."

Danny sighed but knew this had to be done. "So guessing this isn't a good time to ask if you could be the pilot for the Strettos when they go travelling."

"No, I bloody can't," came the flat reply.

"Now you're just being spiteful," Olga said waspishly.

The others weren't surprised to hear a note of irritation in Piers' reply. "No, I'm not. Just let me explain a few things to you all. First of all, what with Jean-Guy's bookings, Trio bookings and a full-time job, I just don't have any spare time. But more than that, if you're going any distance you'll need a jet aircraft which will come with at least two pilots, who will almost certainly be employed by the same company who will hire you the aeroplane. So unless you want to stump up the fee to hire Concorde, which can be done, you can leave me out of your plans."

Kathy looked at Olga's pretty face and saw an expression like a thwarted child, but she didn't say anything.

Piers got to his feet and picked up the Octet score which was still on top of the piano. "I'll go and put my stuff in the car," was all he said. "I'll need your baggage too, you pair and we can't leave too much later or you'll miss your flight. And I certainly don't want to miss the ferry."

"What the hell's been going on?" Danny wanted to know when the piano player had left the practice room.

"He is impossible to work with," Olga declared and did one of her spectacular flounces out.

Gisela she shook her head. "She had one of her wobblies and he just told her to stop being such a bloody infant. I don't think anyone's ever spoken to her like that before in her life. He's bloody scary in that mood and I wouldn't want to get on the wrong side of him."

"As Kathy puts it so well," Jean-Guy consoled, "he goes all Wing Commander on us and could freeze helium with one look."

"That's the one," Gisela exclaimed delightedly. "Couldn't have put it better myself. What do you do to defrost him?"

"Nothing," Kathy advised. "He gets over it."

"Will they be able to carry on with the Octet?" Jean-Guy asked, thinking it was very unprofessional of both players.

Gisela shrugged, but she was the optimist of the group. "They're both pros. They'll do what they have to do. But we'll need to fasten our seat belts as it'll be one hell of a bumpy ride."

Sergei Rachmaninov – *Cello Sonata in G minor*

Petr Mihaly laughed so hard on hearing about the 'marriage' that the other three at the table with him wondered if he was ever going to stop. The Prof eventually regained his dignity, solemnly congratulated them and told Kathy that Emma would never understand.

"She probably won't," Kathy agreed. "But it's good enough for me for now." She had to smile. "Never thought I'd have a pagan wedding in Sweden."

Piers gave her one of his lovely smiles. "It was either that or sleep with me."

"What a choice!" she laughed.

"Are you three playing this evening?" the Prof asked before the conversation got a bit too risqué for his liking. He felt he understood the young less and less with each year and he had to keep reminding himself that one of those three was only seven years younger than he was in spite of his looks and his attitude.

"I'm not," Piers announced. "I've had that long crossing on not the calmest of seas, so if you'll excuse me, I'll get a load in the washing machine ready to put on the line tomorrow and then I'm having an early night."

Kathy and Jean-Guy had been planning on doing some practice that evening but in the end settled for looking through the Prof's collection of cello sonatas so Jean-Guy could put together a programme for his concert at the Wigmore Hall in December. He had done his first and only recital with Piers at the Festival Hall just about a year ago, and had originally hoped to push the repertoire for this gig but Piers had told him months ago, when Jean-Guy had accepted the booking and even before he had been so ill, that he wouldn't be available as he always worked over Christmas and the New Year period. A lot of pilots wanted the time off to be with their families so those who didn't have families tended to work extra lines as much as they could to cover. It also improved their pay packets so wasn't totally selfless on their part. But Jean-Guy still had hopes that one day they would get beyond the Grieg, Fauré and the others that Piers could rattle off so easily and, above all, he wanted to make sure that this laziest of pianists didn't have such an easy ride any more.

In the meantime, he now had to put together a programme but he had surprisingly little enthusiasm for it. It was at such times he missed the huge library of music he had left behind in Prague and felt himself cast adrift in an alien land again with nothing left of his past to anchor him to his present.

He looked at the few pieces the two had managed to find by going through the Prof's entire collection, but Petr Mihaly's daughter was a violinist and he was a pianist so although those two instruments were well catered for there wasn't much for the cello unless the Prof had been reviewing a recording and had bought the score for reference.

"Maybe next time we're in London we could go shopping?" Kathy suggested. "I mean you've already run out some of these, which you say you don't want to repeat, and we've now found the Rachmaninov and Brahms' two. How many do you need?"

"It is for a whole programme. So if we say each is about half an hour then I will need at the most four."

Kathy looked at him as he sat next to her on the floor of the living room with piles of music surrounding them and thought he looked a bit sad somehow as though he regretted having left so much behind. "Do you ever wish you hadn't run?" she asked. "And think about it before you reply. Don't just say 'no' to make me feel better."

Jean-Guy flicked through the Rachmaninov, thinking how well Kathy understood the slightest change in his mood. "Just sometimes. Like now. I must have had fifty pieces in my library back home and here I have maybe a half dozen. I have drunk all the tea my mother sent me last year and each time I put a teabag in my mug I wish I had some more. Then I am in the bathroom and I see my back in the mirror, or I think of some of the, let's call them conversations, that took place and I have no regrets whatsoever. I can live without tea and I can buy or borrow more music. And, anyway you know I am going to say that if I hadn't run I would never have met you and fallen in love more than I had ever thought possible. So if I am being honest, yes I do have regrets but they are just little things when I look at the bigger picture." He passed the Brahms across to her. "Have a look at the last few pages of the first one and then tell me you can't hear Piers playing the piano part. It will suit him but it will also challenge him and test his playing probably to its limits. I wish I could use him for my Wigmore Hall recital."

Kathy had to give him a smile and a hug, consoled he had told her the truth. "Why can't you? I know Jane booked you this, what was her name? Felicity? But I'm sure you can pay her a cancellation fee and use Piers instead."

Jean-Guy sighed. "You are always the one for the bright side," he told her fondly. "Jane has had to tell me that Felicity has cancelled on me. She is trying to find someone else but I asked Piers in case maybe he could. Not pushing it, I hope, but he stayed nice to me and said he has his Christmas rota sorted now and he cannot do that date. And I don't like to ask him if he will change a shift so he can do it as I think he needs to have some stability in his work for a while now."

"I'll ask him, I don't care."

Jean-Guy smiled at her. "That will just make it harder for him to say 'no'. He hates to be unkind to you but to me he doesn't mind so much." He showed her the piece he had in his hand. "It's the Chopin. I think perhaps this is my favourite of all sonatas. But the piano part is so hard."

"Don't underestimate our pianist. He's got the ability. And I'm not sure he isn't as stroppy with me as he is with you. He just uses different words."

"Yes, he uses his words well. But I have no problems with his ability. What he doesn't have is time. I could not ask him to prepare this programme in such a short time. I will definitely use the Chopin. It's not as cliché as the Grieg which I have played so often now. So I think I will have Brahms' first to open which will make the audience sit up and take notice, then the Chopin as he is dramatic to close the first half. After the interval I will open with the Rachmaninov and finish with the Saint-Saëns Two. Which means I can then add the Fauré *Élégie* as an encore. So I hope Jane has a very good accompanist on her books who is available. Last time I spoke she has approached two who are both experienced in the cello repertoire and happy to discuss the booking with me."

Kathy wondered why he hadn't mentioned this before. Then worked out it was probably to stop her rushing off in her usual impetuous manner to tell Piers he was going to have to do it and he must change his shifts. "But it's going to be hard for your accompanist to pick up that programme so quickly, unless you pay a lot of money for a very good one. Assuming all the very good ones aren't already booked on that date. It's now only three months away. What happened to Felicity?"

Jean-Guy looked at the music he was holding. "Jane said she is a very experienced accompanist and should have been perfect for me. She has been booked for over a year but she cancelled last week. Just said family reasons. I never even got to speak to her and we should be thinking about having a first run-through about now."

Kathy wondered if maybe Felicity had got to hear of Jean-Guy's reputation with accompanists and had chickened out.

"It does leave me in an awkward position," Jean-Guy continued. "I hope nothing bad has happened in her family."

Kathy thought that was so sweet and gave him a kiss on the cheek. "Well, I have faith in Jane. She's pulled rabbits out of hats so often in the past."

"Kathy, do you know a lot of your crazy English sayings?"

"Oh, yes, quite a few."

"Please write them down for me so I know to expect them."

Kathy smiled. "Maybe. Anyway, do I get a ticket for this gig, assuming it's going ahead?"

He kissed her gently. "Best in the house. Now, I shall go and find a pen and paper and I will draw up a list of all the music I can remember I left behind and I will add anything else I want to put in my repertoire to it and then, as I am getting paid quite well now, I will start my own library. I know now there is a shop in London who can get me music quite quickly by post if I phone them or I can pick it up when I am down there."

"Good idea. Are you using Piers for your other recitals?"

"Yes. They have been booked well ahead but this one he told me a long time ago he would rather not do as it interrupted his day job too much so I told Jane to find me someone else. Now it seems I have missed the chance to book Piers as he is so much better and is back to full flying again."

"Better, yes. Over it? Nowhere near. And the date is very close to the anniversary."

"I know. Which is why I didn't like to push it with him. I think he is going to find it very hard all over again for the anniversary and we must make sure we look after him this time even if he doesn't do Christmas."

Kathy thought she would have one try. "Tell you what, tomorrow I will ask Piers on your behalf with no great hopes he'll ever agree but you never know, and we can watch him get out of it so charmingly as he always does."

"For you, yes. For me it would be black looks and bad words."

Piers was deeply suspicious the next morning as Kathy rushed to make him a cup of coffee when he came in to the kitchen after pegging his laundry on the line. She had only eaten half her breakfast and something had amused the Prof no end.

"What do you want?" he asked cautiously.

Kathy very pointedly gave him the coffee without milk in it. "Me? I don't want anything."

"Don't pull the innocent face, Piglet. I know you too well for you to get away with that one."

Kathy went back to her bowl of cereal. "I've finished Jean-Guy's sweater so now it's your turn on my list. There's still some stuff left from Sarah's old stock or I can always get more. What colour would you like?"

He took the spoon out of her hand and batted her on the nose with it. "Stop babbling, Piglet. Just tell me what it is you want."

With a huge grin, she recovered her spoon. "Well, you know you take the JFK flight most Tuesdays?"

"You want to cadge a lift and go shopping in New York?"

"On Concorde? In my dreams, unless you can either get me a free ticket or smuggle me in as baggage. As Jean-Guy's accompanist has pulled out at short notice is there any chance you could kind of reschedule one of them and do his Wigmore Hall recital with him? Please. I'll knit you a sweater and make you a cake. Cake every week until the recital date."

"I've given up cake."

"Not completely. Lemon drizzle?"

"Shut up, Piglet. When is the recital anyway?"

"Twenty first of December."

"Can't. Sorry," was the short reply and the coldness of his voice invited no discussion.

Kathy wasn't going to be put off. She was getting used to him in full Wing Commander mode. "At least do me the courtesy of telling me why," she replied equally frostily.

He had been about to get up to add some cold water to the coffee as Kathy had forgotten this once, but instead banged his mug down and some of the hot coffee slopped onto the table. "Oh, I'll tell you why," he replied and there was a vicious edge to his voice. "Because three days later will be exactly one year since I lost Chantal. Nine days after that I will probably be cursing Dacre for not leaving me to die on the floor of the crew area. So I've booked myself annual leave which has pissed off those who rely on me covering their bloody cosy family gatherings and on the twenty first I will be in Tokyo where they don't really do Christmas or New Year. And when I am there I intend to shut myself up in a hotel room and do nothing but drink so much bloody frozen vodka I won't be able to remember a bloody thing about it. And that is why. Sorry for all the swearing but I could do a lot worse."

She was furious with him for speaking to her like that, apart from what he had said, and didn't trust herself to reply for a few moments. The only thing that made her decide to push the matter was his apology for his language. And she knew he could do a lot worse. He had a very colourful vocabulary which, for some reason, he chose not to let rip with in front of the Professor.

"So you're going to run away from us? Do just what you did a year ago and push us away? We have walked on eggshells beside you for a year, and now you're just swanning off to Tokyo to get smashed out of your skull as your only way of coping? Are you going to do this every year? Every time something happens that rocks your world you're going to run?"

"You ran when your world rocked," he said sulkily and she knew she was getting through.

"Yes, I ran. I ran before that man put a knife to my throat and raped me again. I ran to save my life. And then I met Jean-Guy, and you, and you both gave me the strength to stand my ground and to turn and face what I was running from."

"Then you are stronger than I am." He got up and added the cold water to his drink and it was as though all the energy suddenly left him and he somehow appeared physically smaller. "I don't know how to fight as part of an army," he confessed sadly. "And I'm so tired of trying to fight alone."

Kathy joined him at the sink, put her arms round him and leaned her head on his chest but the raven had lost its strength, she was now the comforter and supporter. "Then don't think of us as an army. Think of us as part of you. Take some of my strength, some of Jean-Guy's mad impetuousness and some of the Prof's wisdom and in exchange we'll take on some of your sadness and loneliness and the four of us can sort this whole thing out together." She gently touched his back in what she hoped was about the right place. "You're the moth, remember? The one that survived."

Just for a brief second he held her close but didn't speak and she heard him catch his breath above her head.

"Have you booked Tokyo yet?" she asked softly.

He sniffed rather inelegantly but didn't let her go. "Not definitely but I'm on the lists for a free standby flight and the airline has all sorts of arrangements with various hotels."

"You're on the lists to fly as a passenger?" she checked.

"Yes, as a passenger," he agreed and seemed to know where this was going.

"But you hate being a passenger. And Tokyo is a very long flight."

Piers looked down at her upturned face and knew she had won. "Do you know what? I give up. I just bloody give up." He crossed the kitchen and flung open the door to find Jean-Guy loitering outside in the hall. "Thought I heard you. OK, you win. I'll do your bloody recital. Just promise me you will never, ever turn that she-devil loose on me again. She could persuade the Pope to turn Jewish."

"She is pretty incredible, isn't she?" Jean-Guy said admiringly. "Music's on top of the piano if your cat hasn't sent it all over the floor. You'll need to start work on them now to get ready in time and I still need to buy two of them but should have the whole programme by the end of the week."

Piers picked up his mug of coffee without another word and went into the sitting room leaving Jean-Guy to give Kathy a kiss and a cuddle.

"Well done, you," he said softly to her. "I think I heard most of it."

"Impressive piece of negotiating," the Prof agreed, having watched the altercation in a respectful silence, waiting to see who would win. He was profoundly relieved it had been Kathy and was certain neither he nor Jean-Guy could have handled the unpredictable Piers so well. "But you have made him a promise and now we must all honour it. Whatever plans we have for Christmas and New Year we must make sure Piers is never alone with his thoughts. If he wants to go to London to visit the grave then at least one of us must go with him and take some flowers. If he wants someone to sit and drink with him or just listen to him in the middle of the night then one of us must do that too."

"And you have promised him a sweater," Jean-Guy reminded her. "Good luck with that. I think you will find he's not as small as he looks." He looked across at the Prof. "I don't suppose there's any chance you could give him some coaching? I wasn't expecting to be able to use him and it's a hell of a programme."

The Prof sighed but smiled. "I will try but I don't think he will find my interference welcome. I tell him time and again he is the laziest pianist I have come across for a long time. He pretends he finds it harder than he does and then misses bits out because he can't be bothered to play it. But I'll see if maybe your programme has frightened him so much he will allow me to give him some coaching."

The Prof headed straight off to the sitting room and Jean-Guy felt rather guilty. "I think our pianist is going to hate me."

"No he won't. He'll grumble a lot and swear even more when the Prof can't hear him, and then he'll knuckle down to some hard work which will make you raise your standards too. It's going to be a brilliant partnership between you two."

"It could be. Sadly I have to share him with the love of his life."

"Sarah? Why is she a problem?"

Jean-Guy lovingly kissed her nose. "No, Sarah has never been a problem for our music. I mean the other love of his life. The one that is very noisy and flies crazy fast."

"Ah," Kathy agreed. "That one."

After breakfast, Jean-Guy went into the sitting room where Piers had had a strict if short tutorial on the

Brahms and was at the piano, making a few pencil marks on the score.

"I'd just like to thank you for giving in to Kathy," Jean-Guy said feeling a bit awkward.

"It was what I needed. I've just had the Prof being very nice to me and pointing out that I'm going to find it hard to avoid Christmas altogether but he's going to see if you can go more Yule instead this year. So, thank you. That's something that hasn't happened since my father brought us all back from Donegal in 1945. Go on then, get your cello out while the Prof's lesson is still fresh in my mind."

"I was going to open with the Brahms. It is going to be a lot of work for you. I am sorry. I didn't expect you to be available as you told us you always like to work over Christmas."

Piers half laughed. "Hmm. I've just had the Prof calling me lazy again too. Cheeky sod."

Jean-Guy picked up on the other man's restored humour. "You are like the children we all knew at school who did as little as they could and still came out top of the class."

"What do you mean 'knew'? I was that kid."

Jean-Guy settled himself with his cello and looked into Piers' twinkling eyes. "Do you know? I think I believe you."

Another half laugh and Piers rescued the other music he was going to need from underneath his cat. "One day you will learn not to believe everything I tell you."

Kathy came into the sitting room as the two started work on the Brahms as only they could. Bothered by a small tortoiseshell cat, they brought their own incredible interpretation to the music and Kathy could have listened for ever but she was a woman on a mission.

The two musicians stopped briefly at the end of the second movement and Kathy interrupted before they got going on one of their debates again.

"I haven't got much wool left from the stuff from Sarah's shop to make something in your size," she told Piers and held up two balls. "I've only got brown or grey until I get round to buying some more."

Privately Piers thought both colours were rather unpleasant but didn't want to be mean to her as he guiltily knew he had been less than polite to her earlier. "Can't I have stripes?" he asked lightly.

"They are a bit naff aren't they?" she agreed and Jean-Guy wondered how she knew what he had meant. But that was just them.

"Yes."

"Wide stripes or narrow ones?"

"Surprise me."

"Or I could go and buy some wool next time we're in Ipswich or somewhere and you can choose the colour."

"You haven't got time to go shopping."

"Why not?"

"Because I have agreed to play at Jean-Guy's recital so I will need a page turner. And since the incident in Yorkshire I feel a lot safer with a female one."

Kathy could feel a huge smile spreading across her face and from the look of him this was the first Jean-Guy knew about it too. "You want me to go on stage at the Wigmore Hall and be your page turner?"

"Yup. You know you won't get a better seat in the house. And I still want stripes. Not too wide but not really narrow either. Something tasteful. Can you even do tasteful?"

"Are you going all Wing Commander on me again?" she laughed and crossed the room to sit with him on the piano stool so she could give him a brief hug round the waist before settling down to the serious business of page turning.

Sometimes he wished she wouldn't sit that close to him and put her arms round him like that. He tended to like it just a bit more than he should. "You be thankful I didn't accept the promotion to Group Captain. Ready? Just try to keep up this time."

Jean-Guy looked at the two of them sitting so cosily on the piano stool but something told him that Kathy would always come back to him. He saw the way Piers shifted a little away from the woman who had chosen another man and wondered, just for a second, if Piers had any regrets he had chosen Sarah. But for now the Dodman Trio was finding a way forward. Two musicians and one pilot breathing as one.

Kathy kept her mind strictly on the notes in front of her so she wouldn't miss a page turn. Her gaze flicked between the printed music and the pianist's hands as they moved across the keyboard and she only had to fend off Audrey's swiping paws twice in the first movement. She had learned a lot about being a page turner since she had first sat with Piers and he and Jean-Guy had gone through the Grieg Sonata so impressively it had made her feel totally inadequate. But these two men had helped her so much. More than she could ever say. And even when he had been so close to the Samhain veil, Piers had come back to them. Broken mentally and physically, but the fractures were mending, slowly but surely, and the Dodman Trio was going to be around for a long time to come. She reached for the third page in the second movement but Audrey beat her to it and fingers and paw collided, causing the music to fall off the stand and onto the keyboard in a dissonant crash of notes.

Jean-Guy sighed in exasperation as the two at the piano collapsed into fits of the giggles while Audrey frantically washed her front. "That cat…" he started to say.

"That cat," Kathy finished for him as she mopped her eyes, "is as much a part of this Trio as you are. I wonder if she'll ever learn to sit on the piano for a concert?"

"Wouldn't put it past her," Jean-Guy remarked.

Kathy looked at Audrey and could have sworn the cat was laughing at her. "Who knows?" she mused. "This is the Dodman Trio and anything could happen."

"Yes," Jean-Guy agreed. "And it probably will."

The three were still in good spirits when the Prof called them in for coffee at his strict time of 10:30, seemingly unaware that they were reluctant to break their concentration and stop just at that moment.

"Sorry," he apologised briefly as they dutifully arrived in the kitchen. "I know you are in the middle of your rehearsing and it is sounding very good from out here. I wasn't going to interrupt you but I have now officially caught up with all my deadlines for the year and can start my Christmas break. So, quick coffee for now then I promise to leave you in peace."

Part of Kathy wished that she had finished for Christmas too and could take the whole of December off but it was traditionally a busy month for musicians and she knew that in a few weeks she would be heartily sick of Christmas music. But the concerts always paid well and her last gig of the year would be the best one of all even if she was the page turner and not one of the musicians. She sat in her usual seat at the table and saw the envelope next to her mug.

"What's this?"

The Prof seemed faintly amused that she should have asked. "I don't know. I don't open your post and that is clearly addressed to you."

For a brief, horrible moment Kathy remembered when getting a plain white envelope like that meant Richard had found out her address again. But the Prof had put the letter down with the address upwards so she could see that it had a second class stamp, Richard always used first class, and had been franked in Wimbledon. "Well, if I didn't know better I'd say that's Gayle's writing on the envelope. How very odd. It's too early for the family Christmas card and Mum always sends them anyway."

Piers was watching her with undisguised amusement. "Is she always like this?" he asked Jean-Guy.

"Like what?"

"Sits there looking at the bloody envelope and wondering about it when any normal person would just have opened it to find out."

"Oh, yes. She's even worse with Christmas presents as you'll find out."

"She does know Christmas Day is only twenty four hours long, right?"

"Oh, shut up the pair of you," Kathy said fondly and opened her envelope. "Oh. Now, I would never have expected that." She laughed and read out loud, "*Mr and Mrs John Fairbanks request the pleasure of Miss*

Kathy Fairbanks and guest at the wedding of their daughter, Gayle Constance Olive, to Colin Bernard Gardner on Saturday 19th May 1984 at St Anne's church, Wimbledon. Sit-down reception meal and evening dance included. Dress formal. RSVP requested."

"Well," Piers deduced, "she's planned her wedding better than you two seem capable of putting a recital programme together. I hope I'll get to see all the music at least one day before the actual gig."

"Cheek," Kathy laughed, suddenly cheered at some happy news for her baby sister. "That's probably the first date they could get as St Anne's is incredibly popular. I never even knew she had a boyfriend. At least I don't think I did. I haven't seen her for over a year."

"Going to go?" Piers asked and Kathy knew he understood.

"I don't know," was her honest admission. "Part of me is a bit indignant that she didn't ask me to be bridesmaid but then why the hell would she as I spent nearly all our childhood being really horrible to her. My parents both adored my ex so if I go to Gayle's do I just know they'll have a go about how it should have been me first but I ran away from it."

"Did you ever tell them the whole reason you bolted?" Piers wanted to know, not failing to notice that Kathy hadn't been able to say the word 'wedding' but had just about managed to refer to her own experience as 'it'.

Kathy paused. "Not the whole reason, no. Only Emma and the Prof ever knew all of it." She looked at her adorable Moly and knew there was one truth she had to speak now. "I also know they won't greet me with open arms when I turn up with a Czech boyfriend in tow." She caught Jean-Guy's hand. "I'm sorry. I don't know if it's because of their ages or what it is but they both have this thing about 'foreigners'. I used to be quite ashamed of them and never told them that one of my best friends at school was born in Ethiopia."

"So you haven't told them of me?" he asked and his voice was colder than she had been expecting. "I thought you would have done. Or are you ashamed of me?"

Kathy gave him a soft kiss and was relieved to feel his instinctive response. "I could never be ashamed of you. I've told my parents about both of you but, well, I maybe kept it more musical than personal. I mean they know we're both living with the Prof and they're happy with that as he's kind of my second Dad so I won't get up to anything while he's keeping an eye. Will I?" she finished with an amused glance at the Prof.

He gave her a delighted smile. "Of course not. But I think your parents at least deserve the honesty of the truth. Or you and Jean-Guy will be living your whole future life with a secret and what happens if one day you two decide to marry?" There was a silence at the table. "I'm sorry, have I spoken out of turn?"

"No, not at all," Kathy said a bit too quickly. "We, um, haven't really talked about things like marriage. I'm still not sure I want to go through all that again," she said and took Jean-Guy's hand. "Sorry. But I like things the way they are at the moment."

Jean-Guy's gaze flicked briefly to the platinum ring Piers always wore and he wondered if he would ever wear a wedding band. "For now we are happy," he agreed. "But one day I may ask you again," he finished lightly and kissed her on the nose.

Piers had been watching the two of them intensely and suddenly smiled. "I'd watch it if I were you. Piglet is just the kind of woman to ask you instead. Anyway, you young lovebirds, are you wanting to play any more today?"

Kathy knew what she had to say. "In a bit. First I am going to do what I know I need to do and ring my mum to let her know I won't be coming for Christmas again and to ask her to tell Gayle that I'll be happy to go to the wedding. I can always conveniently go down with something contagious nearer the time if I can't face it."

"Ah, the get-out clause," Piers agreed. "Going to tell them who your 'plus one' is going to be?"

"Not in the first phone call."

"Chicken."

"No, I'm not. I know it'll take them a while to get their heads round the idea that I'm going out with a foreigner." She saw the way Piers was looking at her. "Yes, I know we haven't actually gone out anywhere but there's no way I'm telling them we're sleeping together. No, stop laughing at me. Ratty, shut up. Just stop it. I know exactly what's going on in that mucky little head of yours."

Piers mopped his eyes on the cuff of his sweater. "Oh, you have no idea. Right, you do your dutiful daughter bit. Jean-Guy, please can we have another run through the last movement of the Chopin? I know the bloke was pretty bloody sadistic with his piano works but that cello piece is even more of a stinker."

"Yes, we need to," Jean-Guy agreed and the two left the kitchen.

Kathy looked at the Prof. "Piers is right, isn't he? As he annoyingly so often is."

"Yes," the Prof agreed and collected up the mugs to put on the draining board ready to be washed. "I am so glad we didn't lose him in the new year. It came so close to us."

"Will he be alright do you think?"

"I wish I could answer that. But we all have much to look forward to now. You have New York in March, and didn't you say Piers is going to be a model again before you go out there?"

"Yes," Kathy smiled. "I get the impression he's really not looking forward to it but it appeals to his sense of the ridiculous." She paused on her way to the door as she had been planning on making a start on the sweater for Piers. "I bet that when he was lying on the floor of the crew area he never thought for one second he'd finish up on the runways of London. And I don't mean the kind of runway he's used to either." The Prof didn't answer her straight away and she looked across to see he had his serious, fatherly face on. "What?"

"Remember my warning to you," he told her softly. "Keep him as a friend, yes, but don't get involved."

"I wasn't…"

"Kathy, I listen to the two of you, I watch the two of you. I hate to tell you but I have even had to send in reports on the two of you. When he was barely conscious in Intensive Care, he asked for you."

"I…"

"Yes, I know. You would have gone to him. That's why I never told you. I can't tell you much but those I work for have plans for him and, as I did for Emma for many years, I will fight as hard as I can to keep you away from them. So will Piers. So don't get involved with him because in the end, for the sake of both of you, he will break your heart. Do you understand?"

Kathy sat back at the table and put her head in her hands. "Everything's all broken, isn't it?"

"Not at all. We all have much to look forward to. Just be careful, that's all. Now, are you going to go and play trios?"

Raised voices were heard in the sitting room and Audrey came trotting out to the kitchen. Glad of the distraction, Kathy rubbed the cat's head. "I think you're needed," she said to the Prof.

He gave her a fond smile. "We are both needed," he told her. "That is going to be one hell of a musical relationship between those two and that is one thing we mustn't allow to break." The two went off to see what the argument was about this time and a small tortoiseshell cat raced after them.

The story continues in *Beautiful Sonata*

Printed in Great Britain
by Amazon